I0552029

The Last Trip

ALSO BY ROWEN CHAMBERS

The Surprise Party
Behind Closed Doors
The Last Trip

THE
LAST
TRIP

ROWEN CHAMBERS

JOFFE BOOKS

Revised edition 2025
Joffe Books, London
www.joffebooks.com

First published by Waltham Publishing LLC in USA in 2023

This paperback edition was first published in Great Britain in 2025

© Rowen Chambers 2023, 2025

This book is a work of fiction. Names, characters, businesses, organizations, places and events are either the product of the author's imagination or are used fictitiously. Any resemblance to actual persons, living or dead, events or locales is entirely coincidental. The spelling used is American English except where fidelity to the author's rendering of accent or dialect supersedes this. The right of Rowen Chambers to be identified as author of this work has been asserted in accordance with the Copyright, Designs and Patents Act 1988.

No part of this book may be used or reproduced in any manner for the purpose of training artificial intelligence technologies or systems. In accordance with Article 4(3) of the Digital Single Market Directive 2019/790, Joffe Books expressly reserves this work from the text and data mining exception.

Cover art by Nebojša Zorić

ISBN: 978-1-80573-298-3

CHAPTER 1

"Are you sure this is the right way?" I ask Derek as we drive along a narrow road surrounded by dense rows of snow-covered pine trees. We turned off the main road about a mile back, and since then, I haven't seen a single house.

"That's what the nav system says." He points to the screen on the dashboard. "According to the map, it's just up ahead."

"You know, sometimes those things are wrong. I've heard stories about people following the directions their car gives them and driving straight into a lake."

"Honey, we are not going to drive into a lake. For one, any lakes we encounter will be frozen solid, and two, I'd like to believe I'm smart enough to not blindly follow directions that lead me to drive into a body of water."

"I'm just saying, this doesn't seem right." The road is taking us deeper into the woods. "There's nothing out here but trees."

"James told us the place was remote. I figured it'd be out in the woods like this."

"I guess." I notice a chill go through me as the trees fully shadow the road, hiding what little light was peeking through the clouds. "I just thought it'd be closer to the main road. What if a storm comes? We'll never get out of here."

"I'm sure the snowplow comes through this way."

It doesn't look like it. We're driving on a layer of snow. We were on dry pavement when we were on the main road. "What if we get a storm this week and can't get home?"

"Honey, relax. That's the whole point of this trip. To relax and spend time with our friends."

"I won't be able to relax if we get stuck here. I start a new job in a week. I can't not show up on the first day."

"Your boss would understand. You've known her forever."

The job is at an outpatient clinic attached to the hospital where I've worked for the past five years as a surgical nurse. I liked working at the hospital, but the clinic will allow me to have normal hours instead of the twelve-hour shifts I've been doing. The woman who runs the clinic is a friend of my mother's and offered me the job as soon as it became available.

"I know she'd understand, but I'd still feel bad if I wasn't there on my first day." I look at Derek. "Maybe we should leave on Friday instead of Saturday, just to be safe."

"I'm open to it, but let's see how it goes. This might be our last chance to be together like this. James and Olivia will probably have a kid by this time next year." He glances at me and smiles. "Maybe we will too."

My heart warms at the thought of that. Derek and I could be parents in a year. Our lives could be totally different. We haven't started trying yet, but we plan to when we get back from this trip.

"I can't see James being a father," I say. "He's still like a kid himself."

Derek glances at the navigation screen. "It should be just up ahead." He drives around a tight curve and I feel the back wheels of the car slip on the snow.

"Honey, slow down," I say, bracing my hand against the dashboard.

"We're fine." He turns onto an even narrower road that goes up a steep hill.

"This doesn't look right," I say, noticing there's not enough room for two lanes.

"It's right." He points straight ahead. "That's it."

My eyes rise to the two-story house. James called it a cabin so I was expecting something much smaller than this, and not nearly as nice. Stacked fieldstone lines the base of the house and meets up with dark gray siding. There are several tall peaks to the roofline and there's a large stone-covered chimney poking out. The house is nestled among the trees and the only house out here, as far as I can tell. It's a gorgeous location, but too isolated for me. I like having neighbors nearby.

"The house is stunning," I say, gazing at it.

"I wonder how much it cost to renovate," Derek says, parking the car in the circular driveway. "It couldn't have been cheap to get construction equipment and supplies up here. I bet it cost them close to a million."

"And this isn't even their main home. Can you imagine having this just for when you want to get away for the weekend?"

The house was originally built by Olivia's parents nearly fifty years ago as a vacation home. They planned to renovate it when they retired but died before they could, in a tragic car accident. It was a terrible loss for Olivia, who was very close to her parents, and their only child. Knowing how much her parents loved this area of New Hampshire and the memories they created here, Olivia decided to go forward with their plans to renovate the house. She certainly had the money after inheriting her parents' fortune. Her father had a very successful company and made millions when he sold it a few years ago.

It was nice of Olivia to invite us here, especially since she really doesn't know us that well. But she loves James and knows how important this week is to him, given that it'll probably be the last time we do this. As Derek said, James and Olivia will likely have a child by next year and no longer have time for these reunions. I'm actually surprised we're still doing them. It's been ten years since we graduated from college, and even though we made a pact to get together every year, I didn't think it would actually happen, especially for this long.

Every summer, we've been meeting up with James, Tyler, and Shelby. We find a house to rent and just hang out for a week. This year, we decided to skip the summer and meet up in the winter instead, after James insisted we all come stay at his newly renovated house in the mountains. Being someone who doesn't like the cold, I wasn't looking forward to a winter getaway, but seeing this house, I'm glad we decided to do it. It's a beautiful location and the house is stunning.

Derek was right. I need to stop worrying about the weather and my new job and just relax and enjoy the week. Like he said, this may be the last time we get to spend with our friends.

CHAPTER 2

"I can't wait to see the inside," I say to Derek as we walk up to the house.

Before we can ring the bell, the door opens. James is standing there, dressed in light-colored pants and a dark wool sweater, his thick blond hair cut much shorter than I'm used to. He's always worn it longer and swooped to one side with a few strands hanging over his forehead.

"You made it!" He smiles and steps aside. "Come on in and warm up."

We walk into the house and my gaze rises to the high ceilings, then to the massive windows that look out at the snow-covered trees and the mountains in the distance. Glancing around the large open-concept room, I take in the rustic plaid throw pillows on the brown leather couch and the animal-hide rug covering the knotty pine floors. There's a massive stone fireplace, and along the walls are large lantern-like light fixtures. The decor gives the place a cozy cabin vibe, but the renovations make it feel new — more like a luxury lodge than a cabin. I'm a little surprised Olivia chose to keep this house. My initial impression of her was that she was more of a city girl than someone who'd want to spend time in the mountains, enjoying the great outdoors. But maybe I was wrong about her.

5

I only met Olivia one time, at her wedding to James, which was the summer before last. It was a very upscale wedding at an elegant hotel in Boston, which is where James and Olivia live when they're not here. Olivia wore a sleek, silky designer dress that looked absolutely gorgeous on her tall, thin frame. I remember thinking what a contrast she was to James, with his thick, stocky build. She seemed very poised and sophisticated while James has always been rather crude and immature. Derek and I were shocked when he told us he was getting married. We assumed he'd remain a bachelor for at least another ten years. But people change, and seeing James now, it's clear he's grown up. From his appearance to the way he speaks, he's definitely changed since getting married. The old James would've made at least one crude joke by now and would have greeted us wearing one of his faded and stained college sweatshirts.

"It's good to see you guys," James says, giving both Derek and me a quick hug. "Seems like it's been forever."

"Almost two years," Derek says. "We haven't seen you since the wedding."

"Has it really been that long?" James pauses to think. "I guess you're right. You weren't able to make it to New York last summer."

Last August, James invited us to meet him in the city for a weekend, but Derek and I couldn't go because my cousin was getting married and I was in the wedding.

"You spent that weekend with Tyler?" I ask James. "Or was Shelby there too?"

"I hung out with both of them. I stayed with Tyler. He let me crash at his place."

"Is Tyler here?" Derek asks.

"Not yet. He's bringing a girl. Hope that's okay. I probably should've told you guys."

"It's fine." I smile at him. "We couldn't expect it to always be just the five of us. You have Olivia, and now Tyler has someone. So who is she? Did he tell you anything?"

"Just that she was his makeup artist on a commercial he shot a few months ago. That's all he said."

Tyler was a theater major in college. By now, he thought he'd be starring in movies, but he's been auditioning for ten years and has only been able to get work doing commercials along with a few appearances on TV shows.

"Can I get you something to drink?" James asks. "Or I could give you a tour of the house."

"I'd love a tour," I say. "I'm impressed with what I've seen so far. The decor is so warm and inviting, and yet the place also feels really upscale."

"That's all Olivia's doing." He smiles at Derek. "You know how bad I am with decorating."

"Yeah, you'd throw a poster on the wall and call it done."

Derek and James were roommates their first two years of college. Derek's side of the room was always kept tidy while James' side was a mess. His only decorative item was a poster of a band he tacked up behind his bed, while Derek's side of the room had a rug, chair, bookcase, and some framed prints on the wall. It wasn't anything great, but for a teenage boy, he did an okay job decorating.

James laughs. "I wasn't that bad. I bought a lamp that one time."

"Only because you broke the one my mom gave me," Derek says. "And she didn't appreciate you replacing it with a lamp shaped like a naked woman."

"Hey, that was artistic," James says. "It was more like a sculpture than a lamp."

"That thing was so tacky," I say. "I don't know where you found something like that."

"The flea market," James says. "Remember how Shelby was always dragging us to those?"

Shelby was an art major. On weekends, she'd scour antique stores and flea markets in and around Syracuse for things to inspire her artwork. She does the same thing now, but in and around Manhattan. She lives in Brooklyn and is working as a waitress until she can make a living as an artist. But it's been ten years, and as far as I know, she's only sold two pieces of art.

"I was somehow able to avoid those trips," Derek says.

"Because you always told her I'd go," I say. "But I didn't like them either."

"You liked them better than I did." Derek puts his arm around me and gives me a kiss.

When I look back at James, I see him smiling at us. "You two were meant for each other. I always knew you guys would end up together." He turns and walks off. "Follow me. I'll give you the tour."

He walks us farther into the room, which includes a sitting area with a long leather couch and two club chairs that face the fireplace. Along the windows, which show off a spectacular mountain view, is a large dining table that seats ten. The room is open to the kitchen, which is huge and has a commercial-sized refrigerator and professional-grade ovens. Just off the kitchen is a wine room, filled with what I'm sure is very expensive wine.

"The place looks brand new," Derek says as James takes us up the open staircase to the second level. "I can't imagine what it must've cost to renovate."

"Honey, that's none of our business," I say to Derek, although I am curious. I'm guessing whoever did the work charged extra to deal with the hassle and challenges of getting equipment up here.

"It was nothing," James says with a smirk. "I mean, if you consider how much Olivia got from her parents, what we paid to renovate this place was practically nothing."

"Are you serious?" Derek blows out a breath. "I can't imagine having that much money."

James stops at the door to one of the bedrooms. "Just invent some new kind of software. You're in IT, Derek. You know how to do that stuff."

"I know how to program, but I don't have the next great idea. If I did, I would've done it by now."

James shows us into the bedroom. "This one is yours."

"Wow," I mutter as I take in the spacious guest room. It has a king-sized bed, two nightstands, a tall dresser, and two leather chairs flanking a gas fireplace. Our room has its very own fireplace! And the incredible view out the windows looks like a painting of snow-capped trees against a backdrop of mountains.

"What do you think?" James asks. "Will this be okay for the week?"

"Yeah, definitely." Derek smiles as he looks around the room. "This is better than the place Beth and I went for our honeymoon."

"It's absolutely gorgeous." I look back at James. "And the views are stunning."

"I know, right?" James glances out the window. "I never thought I'd have something like this. Sometimes I can't even believe it's real."

James grew up poor. His dad took off when he was five and left his mom to raise him and his two brothers. If it weren't for his football scholarship, James never would've gone to college. He really didn't need to. He ended up going into sales, which didn't require a degree. He's done well for himself, mainly because he can talk people into buying almost anything. He started out at an auto parts company and quickly worked his way up to the sales manager position. If he'd stayed there, he'd probably be head of sales by now, but James can't stay in one place for too long. He changes jobs every couple years. He's currently not working at all, and if he's being truthful about how much money Olivia has, it sounds like he doesn't need to work.

"You deserve it, buddy," Derek says, patting James on the back. "It's nice to see you doing so well."

"Bathroom is through there." James points to an adjoining door. "Olivia loaded it up with products, but if you need anything, just let her know."

I go into the bathroom and let out a dreamy sigh when I see the large soaking tub and the shower with its multiple shower heads. Thick, white towels are stacked on a metal shelf. Next to it is a rack filled with bath and shower products, all from brands that far exceed what I can afford. It's like I'm staying at an upscale spa where everything's included.

"Beth," I hear Derek call. "You coming?"

"I love the bathroom," I say, returning to the bedroom. Both James and Derek are waiting for me at the door. "I can't wait to try out that tub."

"I should get our stuff from the car," Derek says.

"I can help you," James says. "Let me just finish showing you around."

The remaining two guest rooms are just as luxurious, making me wonder how they plan to use them. James said this would be a house where they'd someday bring their kids, but none of the rooms look like something a child would stay in.

"Where's Olivia?" I ask as we go back downstairs.

"She went to the store," James says. "She forgot something she needed for dinner."

"I hope she'll let us help out. I don't want her thinking she has to do all the cooking for us."

"We could go out," Derek says. "Though I think the last restaurant we passed was like ten miles away."

"More like twenty," James says. "The nearest town is twenty miles away. We're in the middle of nowhere out here."

"How will we get out?" I ask. "I mean, if a storm comes. The weather said we might get a blizzard later this week."

"I wouldn't worry about it," James says, going to the kitchen. "They're always predicting a storm and then it never happens. You guys want a beer? Cocktail? Glass of wine?"

"Just water for me," I say.

"I'll have a beer," Derek says, joining James in the kitchen.

I gaze out the window and notice the clouds moving in, the sky turning darker. "But if we *did* get a storm, could we make it back to the main road?"

"We could eventually," James says as he grabs a beer from the fridge. "There's a guy in town that'll come out and plow the road that comes out here. We just have to call him."

"See, honey?" Derek says to me. "We'll make it back. Everything will be fine."

But I have this strange feeling that it isn't true. That we won't make it back. And that things definitely won't be fine.

CHAPTER 3

I hear someone coming down the short hallway from the garage. Olivia appears, holding two canvas bags overflowing with groceries.

"Welcome," she says, noticing Derek and me in the kitchen. "Did you just arrive?"

"They got here about a half hour ago," James says.

"Let me help." I rush over to Olivia and take one of the bags from her, surprised that James didn't help.

"Thank you," she says, setting the other bag on the counter. She's bundled up in a long, black puffer coat. "It's freezing out there." She shivers as she removes her coat. Underneath it she's wearing jeans and a fitted black sweater. She looks like she's lost weight, and she's not someone who had any to lose. I wonder if it's due to her parents dying. James said she's struggled to move on after losing them. He was hoping renovating the house in their memory would help her.

"It's good to see you again," Derek says, going over to Olivia to give her a hug. My husband's a hugger, which can make some people uncomfortable. Olivia seems to be one of those people, as she weakly wraps her arms around Derek and looks at James to save her.

"Hey, that's enough." He laughs as he pulls Derek away. "Get your hands off my wife."

"Sorry about that," I say to Olivia. "Derek's a hugger."

"Unfortunately, there's no cure for it," Derek jokes. "But I promise not to do it again."

"It's fine," she says, smiling as she unloads the groceries. "I just wasn't expecting it. So how was your trip?"

"Great!" I say, helping her take the groceries from the bags. "It was a beautiful drive."

"Did James help you get settled?"

"Yeah, I showed them around." James nudges Derek. "Why don't we go get your stuff from the car?"

"Good idea."

They take off, leaving me alone with Olivia.

"This house is beautiful," I say, watching as she puts the vegetables away in the fridge.

"Thank you. For a while, it seemed like the renovations would never be finished so it's nice to finally see it done."

"I'm sure your parents would've loved it," I say, then realize I probably shouldn't have brought them up.

"They would've hated it." She shuts the door to the fridge and goes to the sink to wash her hands.

"Did you say they would've hated it?" I ask, thinking I must've misheard her.

She shuts off the faucet and dries her hands. "My parents' style was more elegant." She gazes out at the expansive room. "This would've been too rustic for them."

"Oh. Then, um, I assume this is more what you and James wanted."

"Yes." She turns to me and smiles. "I suppose it is." She continues putting away groceries. "So you and Derek are still living in Syracuse?"

"Yes," I say, surprised she doesn't know this. I'm sure James has told her at least a little about us. "We both got jobs there after college. I'm a nurse and Derek is an IT manager for a small company."

"A nurse." She pauses, her eyes darting over to me. "What kind?"

"Surgical. Up until last week, I was working in a hospital, but starting a week from Monday, I'll be working at an outpatient clinic."

She goes back to putting away groceries. "I don't know how you do it. I couldn't handle all that blood."

"You get used to it, although personally, I've never really had a problem with blood." I walk up to her. "Can I help? I feel like I should be doing something."

"It's actually easier if I do it myself."

The front door opens and James and Derek walk in with our suitcases.

"It's getting colder out there," Derek says. "I should've put on my coat."

"I'll add more wood to the fire after we put these away," James says, heading upstairs with Derek following behind.

"It was so nice of you to invite us," I say to Olivia as she moves quickly around the large, open kitchen.

"I was happy to." She takes a platter out from one of the cabinets. "We have all this space. We might as well use it."

"I assume you know the rest of our group? Tyler? Shelby?"

"We've met, but I can't say I know them. We only spoke briefly at the wedding."

"James said Tyler is bringing a girl." I sigh. "I hope she's not like the last one he brought."

"What do you mean?"

"A few years ago, when we all met up, Tyler brought a girl who was barely out of her teen years and spent all week fawning over him. She kept whining that he wasn't doing enough with her, even

14

though he told her he was there to spend time with his friends. We all wished he'd never invited her. She's not part of our group, and having her there changed the dynamic."

"Yes, I suppose outsiders ruin things for you," Olivia says.

"Oh, no, I didn't mean you. Sorry. That's not at all what I meant. You and James are married. That makes you part of our group. This girl I was talking about was just a fling. Tyler wasn't serious about her. If you knew Tyler, you'd know he's a bit of a player. I can't see him ever settling down. He's always with a different girl."

She turns to me. "You used to say the same thing about James. That you couldn't imagine him settling down. Isn't that right?"

"That was years ago, and obviously he's changed. He was very immature in college, but look at him now. He's grown up, married, and it sounds like you two are hoping to start a family soon."

"He told you that?" she asks, in a way that sounds like he wasn't supposed to.

"Um, not me, but he mentioned it to Derek."

"I suppose that makes sense." She rolls her eyes. "Those two and their little secrets."

"Secrets?" I laugh a little. "I don't think they have any secrets."

Her perfectly trimmed brows rise. "Is that what he told you?"

"I'm not sure what you mean."

Before she can explain, Derek and James come down the stairs.

"Honey, your stuff is in the room," Derek says, "if you want to go rest or take a bath."

"Maybe later," I tell him, wondering if he's hiding something. What secrets was Olivia talking about? My husband isn't keeping any secrets.

"I'm going to get more wood for the fire," James says, going past us to the room just off from the kitchen. I follow him and see it's a laundry room — a large one, big enough to have a bench to sit on, hooks on the wall for coats, wire baskets for scarves and gloves, and an area by the door for boots and shoes.

"This is nice," I say. "Very organized."

James turns around, smiling when he sees me. "Hey. You want to come out and help?"

"Sure. I just need to grab my coat."

He laughs as he pulls on his boots. "Beth, I was kidding. Stay inside where it's warm."

I lean against the door frame, watching as James puts on his coat. "Where do you have the wood?"

"In the shed. We keep some tools in there too. Come over here. I'll show you."

I walk over to where he's standing and peer through the window. There's a small shed about fifty feet from the house, nestled among the trees.

"Olivia didn't want the firewood anywhere near the house, since it attracts mice," James says.

"Mice?" I shudder. "Yeah, I'll be staying here."

James laughs. "I don't get you, Beth. You look at disgusting stuff all day as a nurse, but can't handle seeing a mouse?"

"I don't like how they scamper around and leave droppings everywhere." I look at James. "You don't ever get mice in the house, do you?"

He leans down to me and whispers, "We had one when we got here a few days ago, but I got rid of it. Don't tell Olivia. She'll freak out."

"Where was it?"

"Here. In this room. It must've snuck through a crack, or maybe it got in when I opened the door."

I jump back, searching around my feet for mice.

"Relax," James says, laughing. "It's gone. I promise. Go have Olivia pour you some wine. You'll forget all about the mice."

He goes out the back door and I watch as he tromps through the snow. There must be at least a foot out there and the gusty wind is blowing it off the trees, sending snow swirling in the air. Just seeing it makes me shiver.

I'm about to go get that glass of wine James mentioned when I notice him stop a few feet from the shed. He looks back at the house and sees me watching him. I give him a wave, but he doesn't wave back. And he's not smiling. He's just staring at me, like he's waiting for me to go. Like he doesn't want me watching him.

Backing up from the window, I turn away, my pulse going faster. The way James looked at me was strange, almost threatening. Was he angry I was watching him? Why would that upset him? He's just out there getting firewood. Or is he doing something else? Something he doesn't want me seeing?

CHAPTER 4

"Beth," I hear Derek say. "Where'd you go?"

I leave the laundry room and return to the kitchen. "I was just talking to James." I watch as Derek cuts slices of salami while Olivia arranges an assortment of cheeses on a wood platter. "Can I help?"

"I think we've got it." Olivia glances at me. "But maybe you could pick out some wine to go with the cheese platter?"

"Sure. Red or white?"

"A few of each, please."

Going into the wine room, I'm overwhelmed by all the choices. I like wine, but I know nothing about it. Derek and I just buy whatever's on sale. I'm sure everything in here is good, but I'm not certain which varieties go best with cheese. I'll look it up. Getting out my phone, I open the internet browser, but notice I don't have service. Maybe it's this room. It's climate controlled and probably has extra insulation to keep the temperature from fluctuating.

Walking out to the hall, I run into James, holding a pile of wood.

"Did you get some wine?" he asks.

"I was trying to, but . . ." I lower my voice to a whisper. "I know nothing about wine. I don't want to embarrass myself and pick out the wrong kind."

He nods, smiling. "Give me a minute. I'll put this wood away and meet you in there."

James knows Derek and I don't have money to buy expensive wine and understands that picking the wrong one could be embarrassing for me, especially when I know his wealthy, sophisticated wife is a wine expert who can probably rattle off details like flavor notes and origin for every bottle they own.

"So what are we looking for?" James asks, joining me a few moments later in the wine room.

"Something to go with the cheese platter Olivia is making."

"Got it." James scans the rows of bottles, grabs two reds, and hands them to me. Then he opens the glass door of a wine-chilling cabinet I hadn't even noticed was there and takes out two bottles of white. "This should be enough to start."

"How do you know so much about wine?"

"Working in sales, I was always taking clients out for dinner. I didn't want to look stupid ordering the wrong wine, so I taught myself. I even took a class."

"Really? I didn't know that."

He winks at me and smiles. "There's a lot you don't know about me." He holds up the bottles. "Let's take these out there."

As I follow him back to the kitchen, I wonder what he meant. What don't I know about him? We've been friends since college. I think I know him pretty well. And Derek lived with him, so he knows him even better than me.

"Great choices," Olivia says as she takes the bottles from me.

"Thanks," I say, noticing Derek giving me a smile. He must know that James helped me. But did he know James was a wine expert? Is that one of those secrets he and James have that Olivia alluded to earlier?

The doorbell rings and Olivia's eyes dart in that direction.

"I'll get it," James says, going to the door. He opens it. "Hey, man, how's it going?"

"It must be Tyler," Derek says, heading over to join them.

I head that way too and see James step aside as Tyler comes into the house, followed by a woman with short black hair, a nose ring, and piercings along both eyebrows. This must be Tyler's girlfriend, or girl of the week is more like it. He never stays with a girl long enough to call her a girlfriend. This woman looks nothing like the ones I've seen him with before. He usually goes for tall, blonde women who are much younger than him. This woman appears to be close to our age.

"Hey," Derek says, giving Tyler a hug. "It's been a while."

"Only because you bailed on us last summer."

"We wanted to be there," I say, walking over to them. "The timing just didn't work out."

"Hey, Beth." Tyler gives me a hug, talking in my ear but loud enough for everyone to hear. "What are you still doing with Derek? Aren't you sick of him by now?"

"Not at all," I say, laughing as he lets me go.

"I'm Amber," the woman behind Tyler says, giving us a wave.

"Shit, sorry," Tyler says. "I should've introduced you. Everyone, this is Amber." He motions to Derek and me. "Amber, that's Beth and her husband Derek. And that's James." He looks at him, then says, "Is Olivia around?"

"Right here." She's drying her hands on a towel as she walks over to us. "It's nice to meet you," she says to Amber. "I hear you're a makeup artist."

"I also do hair, but yeah, mostly makeup."

Olivia glances at me. "Maybe you can give us girls a few tips while you're here."

"I don't really have any," Amber says. "Makeup for the screen is totally different than what you'd wear in real life."

"Hey, Olivia," Tyler says, smiling at her. "Sorry you couldn't make it last summer."

"I don't think James minded." She looks at James, a tight smile on her face.

"She's kidding," he says with an uncomfortable laugh. "I wanted her to go, but she had things to do."

I'm sensing tension between James and Olivia. Maybe they had an argument before we got here. I hope it's not anything more than that. I don't know Olivia that well, but I think she's been good for James. He's definitely matured and mellowed since marrying her.

"Can I get you two a drink?" Olivia asks Tyler and Amber.

Tyler looks at James. "You got any whiskey?"

"You really need to ask?" James says with a smile. Whiskey was James' drink of choice back in college. He drank it every day. I always thought he had a drinking problem, but Derek insisted he didn't. "I'll show you what we got."

James takes off for the kitchen with Tyler and Derek following behind.

"This house is huge," Amber says, not sounding impressed as her gaze darts around the open room. "Why do you need all this space?"

It's a bold and rather rude question, but maybe that's just her personality. Maybe she's just someone who's very direct and says whatever pops into her head.

"The house belonged to my parents," Olivia says. "They wanted it to be large so they could invite friends here. They designed the first level to be open like this for entertaining."

Amber shrugs. "It seems like a waste to have all this and only use it a few times a year."

"Yes, well, James and I feel it will suit our needs going forward," Olivia says, straightening her shoulders. "I don't believe you mentioned what you'd like to drink."

"I don't want anything." Amber looks up at the stairs. "Is that where our room is?"

"Yes, I can take you there if you'd like."

"I can do it," I tell Olivia. "So you can finish what you were doing in the kitchen."

"Thank you, Beth." She gives me a polite smile. "It's the room right next to yours."

"Right this way," I say, motioning Amber to follow me up the stairs. I take her to her room, noticing it's smaller than the one Derek and I have and doesn't have a fireplace.

"Small world, huh?" Amber says, walking around the room, her gaze going to all the upscale furnishings.

"What do you mean?"

"You don't remember me?" She huffs. "Guess I shouldn't be surprised."

I stare at her, noticing there's something familiar about her, but not sure what.

She stops and turns to me. "You seriously don't remember?"

"I'm sorry, but I don't. Are you saying we've met?"

She sits down on the bed, leaning back, her palms resting on the mattress. "You came into the bar with some girl. You were already drunk when you got there. You spotted Miles behind the bar and couldn't stop smiling at him. Then you—"

"Stop!" I race up to her, my heart pounding as I realize how I know her. "Just stop talking!"

"Why?" She gives me a smug smile. "Because you never told anyone? You just went on with your life? Got married? Is that him? The guy I met downstairs? Is that the guy you married? The guy you—"

"Yes." I look closely at her face. It's her, but she looks different than I remember. She didn't have piercings back then, or the tattoo I just noticed on her neck. And her hair was bright red — almost orange — not the black it is now. "You were the waitress."

"Yeah." She stands up. "And Miles was my boyfriend at the time."

"I . . . I'm sorry," I say, backing away from her. "I didn't know. He never told me. It all happened so fast. And I was really drunk that night. I promise you, I had no idea you two were—"

"Forget it. It's ancient history. And it's not like it was the only time it happened. The asshole never could keep it in his pants. He was always taking girls to the back room." She walks over to the dresser and picks up a decorative item — a cream-colored rope tied in a knot. "What the hell is this thing? And why would you spend money on it?"

I go up to her and grip her arm. "You can't tell Derek about that night. Promise me you won't!"

She yanks her arm from my grasp. "I don't make promises." She sets the knotted rope down. "So you never told him." She laughs a little as she walks over to the window. "I don't get married people. They claim they're in love, but all they do is lie to each other."

I go over to the door and shut it, not wanting anyone to hear us. I can't believe this is happening. Of all the girls Tyler could've brought here, he brings the one girl who knows a secret that could destroy my marriage? The odds of that are nearly impossible, and yet somehow it happened.

"I *do* love Derek," I say, coming up beside Amber. "What I did that night was a mistake. I was young and careless. And I'd had too much to drink. That girl you saw me with was my cousin. She talked me into going to the city. Spending the night there. Derek didn't want me to go." I look down. "I should've listened to him. If I had, that night never would've happened."

Even my cousin doesn't know what I did that night. She drank too much and didn't feel well so she went back to the hotel. It was only a block from the bar so I decided to stay and finish my drink. After my cousin took off, I left the table we were at and sat at the bar so I could talk to Miles. He'd been flirting with me all night. I'd never had a man that good-looking flirt with me. I flirted back, and before I knew it, we were in a room behind the bar, doing something I never should've done.

The next day, I felt terrible. I've tried to forget it ever happened, and now this woman shows up, reminding me what I did. I honestly didn't know Miles was her boyfriend. She didn't act like it that night. I don't remember the two of them even talking.

"Stop making excuses," Amber says. "You were with Miles because you wanted to be. You were testing the waters, making sure Derek was the guy. And hey, I get it. Chaining yourself to one person for the rest of your life is a big decision. Personally, I couldn't do it."

"That's not what happened." I look her in the eye, anger rising inside me at her accusations. "I wasn't testing the waters. I knew Derek was the one. I just made a mistake."

"Then tell him that." She folds her arms across her chest. "Fess up. Tell him what you did."

"Why would I tell him something that happened years ago? It doesn't matter now. We're happily married. We're planning on starting a family soon."

"Whatever you say." She walks past me and I see her going into the bathroom. "Hey, did you see this shower?"

I go into the bathroom as she's closing the shower door.

"It has dual jets." She smiles. "I know what Tyler and I will be doing tonight."

"Amber, about what happened that night, please say you won't tell Derek."

She shrugs. "I don't know, Beth. I mean, you did sleep with my boyfriend." She walks up to me. "And you and your friend treated me like shit that night. Then you left me like a five-dollar tip when your bill was over fifty."

"I'll make up for it," I say, scrambling for a way to keep her quiet. "I'll give you money. A hundred dollars. That should more than make up for that night."

"You mean for the tip, or for sleeping with my boyfriend?"

"The tip. I'm sorry about your boyfriend. I honestly didn't know." I grab her arm. "Amber, please. I'm begging you to keep quiet about this. Derek doesn't need to know."

She rips her arm from me. "Stop touching me. And don't tell me what to do. I don't take orders. And I don't respond well to threats. I suggest you keep that in mind this week or your little secret isn't going to be a secret anymore."

She goes past me out of the bathroom. I follow her and see her opening the bedroom door.

"Oh, hey," Amber says.

"I'm looking for my wife," I hear Derek say. "Have you seen her?"

"I'm right here." I walk up behind Amber. "I was just showing Amber her room."

Derek's eyes bounce between Amber and me. He's probably wondering why we were in here with the door closed. It does seem odd, given that we just met, or at least that's what Derek thinks.

"I just came to tell you I poured you some wine," Derek says to me. "And Olivia put out some appetizers."

"Sounds great!" I walk out to the hall, smiling at Derek.

"How long have you two been married?" Amber asks, even though she already knows the answer. That night at the bar, my cousin told her I was getting married in a week.

"Ten years." Derek takes my hand and gives me a kiss.

"Aww, you two are adorable," Amber gushes. She's being sarcastic, but Derek doesn't pick up on it.

"We got lucky," he says, gazing at me. "We found each other in college and are still going strong, ten years later."

"Let's go join the others," I say to Derek, wanting to get him away from Amber.

Derek looks back at Amber and smiles. "We'll see you down there."

"Tell Tyler I'll be down in a minute," she says, closing the door.

How am I going to spend all week with that woman, knowing she might tell on me? If she does, I'll deny it. She doesn't have proof that it happened. And Derek would believe me over her. Wouldn't he?

If, for some reason, he didn't, our marriage would be over. Derek's usually a very mild-mannered guy, but he gets extremely angry when he's jealous. One time in college I mentioned that a guy on campus was flirting with me and Derek blew up. I'd never seen him that angry. He yelled and threw things and punched his fist into the wall. And we weren't even married at the time. After we were, he told me that if he ever found out I'd cheated, it'd be grounds for divorce. He wouldn't give me a second chance.

I need to keep Amber quiet. Derek can't ever know what happened that night.

CHAPTER 5

"These cheeses are wonderful," I say to Olivia as I take some from the charcuterie board she set out.

We're all sitting around the fire, eating and having drinks. The wine is helping ease the stress I was feeling after finding out Amber knows my secret. She's sitting at the end of the couch, her legs draped over Tyler's lap. I really don't understand why he's dating her. She's not at all his type. It's not just because of her looks, but how she acts. She comes off as harsh with her negative comments and sarcastic humor. Tyler usually dates girls who are bubbly and sweet, almost to the point of being annoying. But I'd rather have one of those girls here than Amber.

"It's getting dark," Derek says, noticing the sun going down. "Shelby better get here soon or she'll never find the place."

"She's not arriving until tomorrow," Olivia says, before taking a sip of her wine.

"No, she's coming tonight," James says.

Olivia shoots an angry look at James. "And you didn't think to tell me this?"

"I thought I did." He shrugs. "Maybe I forgot."

"You most definitely forgot." She jumps up from the chair she was sitting in. "I'll set two more places for dinner. I just hope I made enough food."

"Two?" I look at James. "Shelby's bringing someone? Last I heard, she was single."

"She is." James picks up his phone and swipes through it.

I look at Derek. He looks back at me, then over at James.

"So who is it?" Derek asks. "Who's she bringing?"

James sighs and sets his phone down. "Let me start by saying he's changed. He's not like we remember."

"No," I say, my heart pumping faster. "Please tell me you did not agree to let him come here."

"I didn't have a choice," James says. "Shelby insisted. She didn't want him being alone all week."

"Ryan's coming?" Tyler says, not sounding the least bit concerned.

"Who's Ryan?" Amber asks.

"Shelby's younger brother," Derek answers.

"Her very *disturbed* younger brother." I set my wine on the table and turn to James. "Why would you agree to this? We're supposed to be having a fun, relaxing week together. This might be the last time we do this. And you invite Ryan?"

Olivia comes back and sits next to James. "As a nurse, I would think you'd have more compassion. Just because the poor man struggles with mental health issues doesn't make him a bad person."

"I didn't say it did. But I know Ryan well enough to know that he's unstable, and could be dangerous."

"Dangerous, how?" Amber asks. "What's he done?"

"He used to get in fights a lot when he was younger," Tyler says. "And he'd say all this dark shit, like that he had thoughts about poisoning people or pushing them off a ledge."

"He didn't mean it," James insists. "He was just saying that stuff to scare people. To get them to leave him alone. He used to get bullied a lot for being different."

"He did more than just that," I say.

"What else did he do?" Amber asks.

"Nothing," James says. "People made up stories about him, but none of them were true."

That's technically accurate, but just because you can't prove something doesn't mean it didn't happen. I'm almost certain Ryan was responsible for a sorority house fire that nearly killed three college girls. He was angry at one of the girls for making fun of him when he asked her out. The police didn't have evidence to charge him, but I'm sure Ryan did it. And I swear he took money from my purse one night when we were all hanging out at Shelby's apartment. I think he did it more than once. The money didn't just disappear, and nobody else would've taken it.

"Ryan's a decent guy," James says. "He just has some issues, but he's a lot better than he used to be."

Why is James sticking up for Ryan? He used to hate having Ryan around. He'd ask Shelby to get rid of him whenever we'd go to her apartment. Those bullies James talked about? He was one of them! So why the sudden change in how he feels about Ryan?

"That's it?" Amber says. "He got into fights and said inappropriate things?" She rolls her eyes. "Sounds like most of the guys I've dated. So Ryan went to college with you guys?"

"Shelby did," Tyler answers. "Ryan lived with her because her parents didn't want him."

"They were afraid of him," I mutter.

"They weren't afraid," Derek says. "If anything, it was the other way around." Derek looks over at Amber. "Their parents were abusive to Shelby and her brother when they were growing up. When Shelby went to college, she took Ryan with her to get him away from their parents. She became his legal guardian. Her parents didn't even care. It was a really sad situation. I felt bad for Ryan. He had to move away from his friends. Change high schools. That's a lot for a kid that age."

Now Derek's sticking up for Ryan? I don't understand this. None of us liked Ryan back in the day. We did everything we could to avoid him. He creeped us out whenever he was around.

"I spoke with him on the phone last week and found him to be quite nice," Olivia says. "And very polite."

"Why were you talking to Ryan?" I ask, thinking someone like her, who grew up wealthy and surrounded by rich, snobby friends, wouldn't want to be anywhere near someone like Ryan.

"He asked if he could bring something. A hostess gift." She gives me a smile. "Most people do."

She says it as though she's telling me I should've brought a gift. I feel my face getting warm. I glance at Derek, who's completely oblivious that Olivia just pointed out what I'm now realizing was a serious social blunder. I didn't even think about it. We never bring gifts to these reunions, so it didn't cross my mind to do it. But given that we're staying here, I should've brought something.

"That reminds me," Tyler says to Amber. "We left the cake in the car." He lifts her legs off him. "I'm going to get it before it freezes."

"You brought a cake?" Olivia asks, seeming pleased that at least someone in our group brought a hostess gift.

"And some bread," Amber says. "There's this really great bakery down the street from my apartment."

"Sounds wonderful," Olivia says. "And perfect, since I didn't have anything planned for dessert." She glances at James. "James is watching his weight so I've been keeping sweets out of the house."

Derek laughs. "You're on a diet?" he says to James.

"Just trying to lose a few pounds." James pats his stomach. "Got to get rid of this gut."

James is a big guy. Even ten years after college, he still looks like a football player. He's around six feet tall, and wide, with broad shoulders, a wide chest, and thick neck. He's muscular, but has put on a few extra pounds of fat over the years, mostly around the middle.

"You've had that gut for years," Derek says. "Why are you doing something about it now?"

"Yes," Olivia says, her brows rising. "Why now, James?"

He shrugs. "I'm just tired of it. And I'm getting older. Got to take care of my health."

"Then perhaps you should cut back on the whiskey." She eyes his glass, which he's refilled three times tonight.

"Could I get some help?" Tyler asks. I look back and see his hands are full and he's struggling to get through the door.

Olivia and I both jump up to help while Amber relaxes back on the couch, sipping her wine.

"I've got it," I say, taking the bread, which is set on top of the cake box.

"I'll get the cake," Olivia says.

Tyler hands her the box, then brushes the snow off his sweater. "It's really coming down out there."

I check out the window, but it's too dark to see anything.

"It wasn't supposed to snow tonight," James says, picking up his phone. "The weather app still says we're not getting any."

"The weather here is unpredictable," Olivia says, setting the cake on the kitchen island. "It can be sunny a few miles from here while we're getting snow."

"Have you ever been snowed in?" I ask.

"No." She shakes her head. "If we get a big storm, James has a vehicle that can get us out."

"What'd you get?" Tyler asks as he goes back to the couch.

"A big-ass truck," James says. "It's got four-wheel drive and extra-large tires. We keep it here. It wouldn't make sense to have it back home." He laughs. "I can't even imagine trying to drive a truck that big in Boston."

I go back to my place on the couch. "So you're saying we won't get stuck out here if we get a snowstorm?"

"We'll be fine," James says. "If your car gets stuck, I can pull you out with the truck."

"That makes me feel better," I say.

"She was worried we might be stranded here," Derek says to James. "She starts that new job a week from Monday and doesn't want to miss the first day."

"What's the job?" Amber asks. I really wish she wasn't here. I'll never be able to relax this week with her knowing my secret.

"I'm a nurse," I tell her. "A surgical nurse."

"How noble." She smirks.

"It's good she's here," Tyler says. "If anyone gets hurt, Beth's going to have to save us. The nearest hospital is like, what, fifty miles away?"

"Thirty," Olivia says. "But getting there on these roads would take at least an hour."

"An hour?" Derek says, sounding surprised. "You'd be dead by the time you got there. I mean, like if you had a heart attack or something serious like that."

"Thanks, Derek," James says, rolling his eyes. "Thanks for pointing that out."

"I'm just saying, you sure you want to live out here?"

"We're not. It's a vacation home." James smiles at me. "Maybe we could hire Beth to stay with us when we're here, just in case something happens."

"You'll be fine." I turn to Derek. "Would you stop worrying them? They just finished renovating the house. They don't want to think about ways they could possibly die here."

"It was just a comment." Derek takes a swig of his drink.

"He's right," Amber says. "I wouldn't want to live out here. Like Derek said, if something serious happens, you're screwed."

Why is Amber siding with my husband? Is she going to do this all week? Side with him every time we disagree? Try to drive a wedge between us?

The doorbell rings.

"That must be Shelby." James sets his drink down and gets up from his chair.

We all look back as James opens the door. From where I'm sitting I can't see who's there, but I can hear Shelby's raspy voice.

"Hey, big guy." Shelby steps into the house and I see her giving James a hug. She's wearing a bright pink coat and black knitted hat that she probably made herself. In addition to painting, she also knits and sews. She learned to sew out of necessity. Her parents were very poor so she had to make a lot of her own clothes or mend ones she got for free at the donation center. She's really good at making clothes. She'd probably make more money doing that than selling her paintings.

"Welcome," Olivia says, hurrying over.

"Hey, Olivia." Shelby hugs her. "It's good to see you."

"Where's Ryan?" James asks.

I shudder just hearing his name.

"Getting our stuff from the car." Shelby reaches into the bag she's holding and pulls out some dishtowels. "A little housewarming gift," she says, handing them to Olivia.

"How lovely," she says, but her expression is telling me she hates them. The towels are all very bright colors that don't at all fit Olivia's decor, which is mostly earth tones. "Thank you, Shelby."

"Hey, Shelby," Derek says, getting up from the couch.

"Derek!" She drops her bag and crocheted purse on the floor and runs over to him, then goes past him when she sees me getting up. "Beth!" She opens her arms to hug me. "Get over here!"

"You totally dissed me," Derek says, sounding hurt, as Shelby and I hug.

She lets me go and hugs Derek, laughing. "There. You happy now?"

"I guess," he mutters.

She lets Derek go and points to Tyler, who's still seated on the couch next to Amber. "You don't get a hug. I saw you a few days ago."

"You were with Shelby a few days ago?" Amber says to Tyler, pulling away from him.

"We met for lunch," he says, then says to Shelby, "Why'd you tell her? I told you it was supposed to be a surprise."

"Yeah. Sorry. I forgot."

"What surprise?" Amber asks.

"I had her make you some earrings," Tyler says.

"They're in my bag," Shelby says to Tyler. "I'll give them to you later."

"Shelby, where do you want this?"

I nearly jump when I hear Ryan's voice.

"Just leave them there for now," Shelby says.

"Hey, Ryan," Derek says, glancing back at him from the couch.

"Hey, how you doing?"

"Good. It's been a while."

"It has. How's it going, Beth?"

I turn back and look at Ryan. I almost don't recognize him. He looks completely different than he did ten years ago. He was really skinny back then, but he's filled out and looks much healthier now. His hair used to be long and straggly, but now it's cut short on the sides and a little longer on top. He always had a beard, but now he's clean-shaven. This is the first time I've seen his face without hair. He's not bad-looking all cleaned up. I might even say he's handsome, but that doesn't mean I trust him.

"Honey." Derek nudges me. "Say hello."

"Ryan. Hi." I force out a smile. "It's good to see you again."

It's a lie. I never wanted to see him again. I feel sick having him here. He may look different than he did ten years ago, but I'm sure he's still a psychopath.

I don't even want to imagine what horrible things will happen this week with Ryan in the house.

In the ... turned to each other and I sat back with a grin. ... not caught off guard, but I'm ... ing a little uncomfortable.

I don't even want to imagine what horrible things will happen ...

... point we're in the house.

CHAPTER 6

"Dinner was excellent," I say to Olivia as she gets up from the table. "Can I help you clean up?"

"I've got it," she says, glancing at James like she's waiting for him to help. He's too drunk to even notice. He's been drinking nonstop since we got here.

"Where'd you learn to cook?" Shelby asks Olivia.

"I spent a year in France." Olivia goes around the table, gathering up our plates. "While I was there, I took some cooking classes."

"What fun that must've been to live in France for a year," I say. "What did you do there? Besides the cooking classes?"

"I really don't remember," she says with a slight smile. "It was so long ago."

She reaches my end of the table and I hand her my plate. "It wasn't that long ago, was it? I assume you went there after college?"

"I was twenty-four, but that seems like ages ago. And I did indulge in a great deal of wine," she adds with a laugh. "Which I'm sure impacted my memory of that time."

How can she not remember what she did there? If I spent a year in France, I'd remember at least part of it.

"James and I are hoping to go back there this spring," Olivia says. "Right, honey?"

"I don't know. I'm not really interested in going overseas."

"Why wouldn't you go?" Tyler says. "You're not working, and you have the money."

"Doesn't mean I want to go hang out in a foreign country." James swigs the rest of his whiskey, then holds up his glass. "Babe, can you get me another?"

Olivia's lips purse as she lifts the heavy stack of plates from the table. "Don't you think you've had enough for tonight?"

"Why do you care? I'm not driving." He shoves his chair back and stands up. "I'll get it myself. Anyone else need a refill?"

"I'll take some more wine," Shelby says, raising her glass. James takes it from her and follows Olivia to the kitchen.

Why isn't he helping her? He was always a jerk in relationships, but I thought he grew out of that now that he's married.

This isn't right. I can't just sit here and let Olivia do all the work. She's been preparing food since we arrived, barely having time to sit down. She said she didn't need any help, but I feel terrible just sitting here.

I get up from the table and join Olivia in the kitchen. "Please. Let me do something," I say as she rinses off the plates. "You've been working since we got here."

She glances at me. "I suppose you could cut the cake."

"The cake." I search for the box, but don't see it. "Where did you put it?"

"On top of the dryer. It was in the way when I was getting dinner ready."

I go across the hall to the room I was in earlier with James. The boots he wore outside are sitting by the door in a puddle of melted snow. There's a waterproof mat right next to the door, which I'm guessing Olivia put there for snowy boots, and yet James left his directly on the wood floor. His coat is there too. He didn't bother to hang it up, even though there's a row of hooks above the mat.

The college version of James would've made a mess like this, but he's grown up now. He should know better.

Picking up the soggy, wet coat, I hang it on the hook, then I move his boots to the mat.

"Did you find the cake?" someone asks.

I whip around and see Ryan coming into the room. My heart slams against my chest and I feel my pulse speeding up.

"Ryan. What are you doing in here?"

"I came to help." He lifts his hand and I see he's holding a knife. A large chef's knife that looks sharp enough to cut through flesh and bone.

A chill goes through me as I stare at the knife.

"What are you doing with that?" I ask.

"I told Olivia I'd help you cut the cake."

My eyes rise to his. "I don't need help. I can do it. You can go back to the table."

He lowers the knife and steps closer to me. "I know you never liked me, Beth, but that was a long time ago. We're older now. Maybe we can forget about the past and try to be friends."

"Um, sure," I say, having no intention of being friends with him. "Let's go back to the kitchen. I'll grab the cake."

He backs away and I notice the cake box sitting on the dryer. I grab the box and get the hell out of there.

Why would Ryan be walking around with a knife? We weren't going to cut the cake in there, so what was he doing? Was he trying to scare me? Or was he warning me about what's to come? Is he planning to kill us all? Is that why he's here? He's going to kill us for not treating him well ten years ago?

Oh God, what if that's true? The guy is a psychopath. I'm convinced of it. James doesn't think he is, and neither does Tyler. Even Derek seems to think Ryan is harmless. I don't understand it. Did they forget what he was like? The guy spent months in a mental hospital. They don't lock people away like that unless they're seriously ill, or dangerous.

"There you are," Olivia says when she sees me coming back with the cake. "I was wondering what took so long."

"Beth and I were just catching up," Ryan says, coming over to stand by me.

I open the cake box. "Can I have the knife?" I say to Ryan, not looking at him.

"You sure you don't want me to help?"

"I can do it." I wait for him to set the knife down, but instead he takes my hand, places the knife handle against my palm, and closes my fingers around it.

"Be careful," he says in a voice so low only I can hear it. "It's really sharp."

Gripping the knife in my hand, I wait for him to take his hands off me.

"Ryan, would you get the plates?" Olivia says, as if he's just some normal guy. She has no idea what he's like. She didn't know him back then, and I'm sure James didn't tell her about him.

"Sure," Ryan says in a pleasant tone. "Where do you keep them?"

"The cabinet next to the stove."

He goes over there and I feel like I can breathe again.

"I really liked how you made the chicken," Ryan says to Olivia. "Could I get the recipe?"

"Of course. Do you like to cook?"

"I do, but I'm still learning. Shelby's a horrible cook, so I've been trying to learn how to do it myself."

"Hey!" Shelby yells from the table. "Did you just say I'm a horrible cook?"

"Yeah, and I was being nice," he yells back. "You know you suck at cooking. Nothing you make is edible."

She laughs. "It's so true," she says to everyone at the table. "I'd starve if it weren't for Ryan. And takeout. We get takeout a lot."

"So you and your sister live together?" Olivia asks Ryan.

"Yeah, in Brooklyn." Ryan sets the dessert plates next to me on the counter, then turns back to Olivia. "I'd like to get my own place, but the rent there is outrageous. For now, it's best for us to live together and split the cost."

"Where do you work?" Olivia asks.

"I'm just doing temp work until I find something better. Right now I'm walking dogs. It doesn't sound like much, but it actually pays well."

I don't get it. Ryan's acting normal. What happened to the crazy guy in the laundry room? Does he have a split personality? One minute he's a nice, normal guy, and the next he's a knife-wielding psychopath?

"I'd like a dog," Olivia says, "but James doesn't think we should get one."

"Why not?" Ryan says. "Dogs are great."

"He thinks it'd be too much of an inconvenience when we want to travel. I suppose he's right. It would make it harder for us to get away." She walks over to me. "How's the cake coming?"

"I'm not quite finished." I look down at the uneven slices and the crumbs that landed on the counter.

"Do you need some help?" she asks, noticing what a sloppy job I've done.

"No, I've got it." I'd normally be better at this, but I haven't been paying attention to the cake. I've been too busy listening to Ryan talk to Olivia.

"I'll start bringing them over," Olivia says, picking up two of the dessert plates.

As she takes them to the table, Ryan comes over to me. He laughs a little when he sees the mess I've made. "What happened?"

I tense up. "Nothing. I just wasn't paying attention."

He leans down to me, lowering his voice as he talks in my ear. "You sure you don't want some help? I'm good with knives."

"Derek!" I yell. "Could you come over here?"

"Why?" he yells back. "What do you need?"

Why can't he just come over here without needing an explanation?

"Nothing," Ryan answers, backing away. "We've got it."

I pick up two of the plates and shove them at Ryan. "Take these to the table, please."

He grins. "I'd be happy to."

He leaves, and I finish cutting the cake, then bring the remaining dessert plates to the table.

"Did I hear you say you walk dogs?" Amber asks Ryan when we're all seated again.

"Yeah, I've been doing it for about a year."

"He's always liked dogs," Shelby says. "But our parents wouldn't let us have one."

"Have you been home to see your mom?" I ask Shelby. It's been months since we've talked. I should've called her, but I didn't want to risk having Ryan answer her phone. He's done that before and I immediately hung up. I don't know why she still lives with him. He could find other roommates to share the rent, but whenever I mention that to her, she won't even consider it. I get that Ryan's her brother and she feels sorry for him, but it's really not her job to take care of him, and given how strange he is, I don't know why she'd want to.

"We stopped going to see her," Shelby says, glancing at Ryan. "She's always so out of it when we're there that Ryan and I decided it's not worth making the trip."

Their mother is an alcoholic and has been for years. Their father was too. They'd get angry and abusive when they drank, to the point that Shelby and her brother would hide from them or run away. They had a difficult childhood so I understand why Ryan has issues, but that doesn't mean I can overlook his behavior and feel comfortable around him.

"What about your father?" Olivia asks. "Do you ever see him?"

"He's dead," Ryan says in a nonchalant tone, as though he's talking about a stranger and not his father.

"He died a few years ago," Shelby says.

"I'm sorry to hear that," Olivia says.

"Don't be." Shelby looks at Ryan. "We hated him."

Awkward silence follows, none of us sure what to say.

Moments later, Tyler speaks up. "So what are we doing tonight?"

"Getting wasted." James holds up his bottle of whiskey. "I plan to finish this off."

Olivia clears her throat. "I think he was referring to an activity."

"Do you get internet here?" Amber asks. "We could stream a movie."

"We can try," Olivia says. "The connection cuts out when the weather's bad." She looks around the table. "What do you usually do when you have these little gatherings?"

The way she said 'little gatherings' sounded very condescending, like she thinks they're frivolous and a waste of time.

"It's usually summer," Tyler says. "So we do stuff outside. Golfing. Swimming at the lake. Going on a hike."

"I didn't realize you were all so athletic," Olivia says, again in that condescending tone.

"Did I mention we're usually drunk when we do this?" Tyler laughs. "One time, James and I were on the golf course and he was so drunk he hit his ball in the wrong direction. Almost hit a guy on the head."

"I got in so much trouble for that," James says, laughing. "Got banned for life from that course."

"They're giving you the wrong impression," Derek says to Olivia. "We don't just sit around and drink. We talk. Play games. And at night we hang out around the fire, reminiscing. Getting caught up on each other's lives."

"A game sounds interesting," Amber says.

"Like what?" Tyler asks.

Amber's eyes dart to me. "Truth or dare."

I stare back at her, knowing why she suggested that game and hating her for it. Why does she care that I never told Derek what I did at the bar that night? She doesn't even know Derek. And it was years ago. Over ten to be exact. Is she just trying to get back at me for sleeping with her boyfriend? She made it sound like he cheated on her all the time. She should be mad at him, not me. I didn't even know he *had* a girlfriend.

"What are we . . . twelve?" Tyler says to her. "Truth or dare is for kids. If we're playing kids' games, we might as well play spin the bottle. It's more fun."

"Hey, remember that time we played spin the bottle and I—" James stops suddenly, his eyes darting over to his wife. "Never mind."

"I want to hear this," Derek says. "What'd you do?"

"I'll tell you later," James says.

"You guys played spin the bottle?" Shelby scrunches up her nose. "In college?"

"Yeah," Tyler says. "Why are you looking at us like that?"

"I just didn't know people played spin the bottle at college. Seems more like a middle school thing."

"Excuse us for being fun." Tyler tosses his napkin at her.

"Fun for a twelve-year-old," she says, tossing the napkin back and almost knocking over one of the candles on the table.

"You're one to talk." He throws the napkin back at her. "You draw for a living."

43

She laughs. "Yeah, and you play make-believe." She tosses the napkin and it flies over the candle, nearly hitting the flame.

"Stop it!" Olivia yells, bolting up from her chair.

We all stare at her, shocked by her sudden outburst. She's so soft-spoken that I don't think any of us thought she was even capable of making her voice that loud.

"Honey," James says to Olivia. "You okay?"

She slowly lowers back to her seat. "Yes." Her lips rise to a smile. "Forgive me for reacting that way. I just didn't want the napkin catching fire. We'd all burn to death before a fire truck ever made it here."

"That's comforting," Amber mutters.

"Maybe we should call it a night," I say. "Everyone's had a long day and I'm sure we're all tired."

"I'm not," Tyler says. "Hey, James, you got any cards?"

"You know I do." James smiles at him. "You thinking poker?"

"Obviously."

"If you're doing that, I'm going upstairs," Amber says. "I'm going to try out the shower."

I get up from the table. "I'll help clean up."

"Beth, no," Olivia says. "You've done enough. Go up to your room and relax."

I think she's trying to get rid of me. Is it because I did such a bad job with the cake? Does she not trust me in the kitchen anymore? Or does she just not like being around me? I can't say I like being around her. She makes me nervous. She seems like one of those people who wants everything to be perfect. The type of person who freaks out over just the tiniest spill. If that's true, how is she able to live with James? He's clearly still a slob, given the mess he left in the laundry room.

"Are you coming?" I say to Derek.

"I think I'll stay down here and play cards."

"I'd really prefer if you went up with me."

He sighs. "Okay, fine."

"She's got you trained well," Amber says, smiling at Derek.

"She's had ten years to do it," he says in a kidding tone. But I don't find it funny. I find it insulting. I just want to talk to my husband without other people around. There's nothing wrong with that.

When we're up in our room, I shut the door and lock it.

"What are we doing up here?" Derek asks. "We should be with our friends. That's why we came here."

I go up to him. "We can't stay. We have to leave."

CHAPTER 7

"Beth, would you relax?" Derek says. "It's barely snowing. We're not going to get stuck here."

"This isn't about the snow. It's about being locked in this house with a psychopath!"

Derek rolls his eyes. "Ryan is not a psychopath. He's a nice guy. He's way better than he used to be. Whatever therapy or meds they gave him worked. He's totally normal now."

"No. He is not normal. Not even close. He came into the laundry room when I was getting the cake and was acting completely crazy."

"How? What do you mean?"

"He came in there holding a knife."

"It was probably to cut the cake. Isn't that why you went in there? To get the cake?"

"Yes, to bring it to the kitchen. I wasn't going to cut the cake in the laundry room."

"He's a guy. He doesn't know there's only certain places you can cut a cake. And that room is more than a laundry room. It's huge and has that long bench on the side. I would've cut the cake there and not thought anything of it."

"Derek, you're not getting it. If any other guy walked in there holding a knife, it probably wouldn't be a big deal. But we're talking about Ryan. The guy who used to creep us out back in college. The guy who spent months in a mental hospital."

"You're being too hard on him. He had a really shitty childhood. A lot of kids who grow up that way end up having mental health issues. A lot of them don't get help, but Ryan did. You shouldn't judge him for that."

"This isn't just a mental health issue. Ryan is dangerous! He hasn't changed. He's just as crazy as before. Maybe even crazier! We have to get out of here. I can't be in this house with him."

"Okay, just hold on." Derek takes my hand and leads me to the bed to sit down. "Tell me exactly what happened."

"I was in the laundry room to get the cake and Ryan came in there holding a knife."

"Was he just holding it? Or was he holding it up to you, like he was threatening to hurt you?"

"He held it up to show me he had it, but he wasn't near me when he did it. But he had this look on his face, like he was trying to scare me."

"Are you sure about that? Or were you just thinking that's how he looked because you were already scared of him?"

"Are you saying I'm making this up?"

"I'm just trying to figure out what happened. So then what'd he do?"

"He lowered the knife and stepped closer to me. Then he said something about wanting to be friends, which was odd because why would we be friends? We have nothing in common and don't live anywhere near each other."

"Okay, so then what?"

"I left. I took the cake and got out of there. Then later, when I was cutting the cake, he came over to me and asked if I wanted help. And here's where it gets really creepy." I look Derek in the eye. "He bent down to my ear and told me he's good with knives."

"Um, okay. That's a little odd, but it doesn't make him a psychopath."

"Derek, what is wrong with you?" I throw my hands up. "Why are you taking Ryan's side? You couldn't stand being around him when we were in college. You wouldn't even go to Shelby's apartment when he was there. And now you think he's this great guy, even after he cornered me in a room with a knife?"

"It doesn't sound like he cornered you. And I'm not sticking up for him. I'm just trying not to judge him for his past. He was just a kid when we knew him before. A teenage boy. Having been one myself, I can tell you, teenage boys say and do some pretty strange shit. A lot of times it's just to get a reaction out of people or to get attention. We used to ignore him when he was around. Maybe that's why he acted the way he did. He just wanted to be noticed."

I sigh in frustration. "That is not what he was doing. Remember all the stuff he used to say to us? How he fantasized about hurting people?"

"But was it true? Or was he just saying that to get a reaction from us?"

I get up and move around the room, trying to walk off my anger at Derek for not taking this seriously.

"Beth, I know he was messed up back then, but I really think he's better now."

"Then he has you fooled, because he is definitely not better. What normal person walks around holding a knife? And then whispers in your ear that he's good with knives?" I walk back over to Derek. "It was a warning. He was telling me he's going to do something."

"Like what?"

"Stab one of us with a knife? Who the hell knows?"

"Honey, there's seven of us and one of him. We could easily take him down if he tried anything."

That might be true, but even so, it doesn't mean Ryan wouldn't try to hurt one of us. He doesn't think logically. Knowing there are seven of us and one of him probably wouldn't even cross his mind.

"Why don't we talk to Shelby?" Derek says. "Or I will. I'll tell her we're concerned about Ryan and want to make sure he's not going to cause us any harm."

"She's his brother. She's not going to say anything bad about him. Back in college, she was always sticking up for him, saying we were being too hard on him."

"We were. We never should've treated him like that. Like there was something wrong with him."

"There *was* something wrong with him. There still is. Derek, I want to go. I want to leave first thing in the morning."

"No. We're not leaving. We came all this way to see our friends. Took time off from work. Drove hours to get here. We're not going home just because Ryan makes you uncomfortable. I honestly don't think that was his intention, but I don't want you to keep feeling this way so I'll have a talk with Shelby. See if we can figure this out."

I walk away, shaking my head. "I can't believe you're being this way. I'm your wife and I'm scared. You're supposed to make me feel safe, and the only way I'll feel safe is if we get out of this house."

Derek comes up behind me and puts his arms around me. "Honey, I know you're upset, but I don't think leaving is the answer. If Ryan really was trying to scare you or make you uncomfortable, then leaving is letting him win. Is that really what you want? For him to force us to leave a trip we've been looking forward to for months?"

"We could do something else." I turn to face Derek. "We're not far from Vermont. We could go there. Stay in a cute little inn. Or we could drive to Maine. Stay somewhere on the coast."

"In January? It's freezing, and there's nothing to do." He puts his hands on my shoulders. "I want to stay. I love seeing everyone again, and this house . . ." He looks around. "It's nicer than any place we've ever stayed. We may never stay at a place this nice again."

"We could come back some other time. Just the two of us. You know James would invite us back. Please, Derek, let's leave. I don't want to be here."

"Because of Ryan? Beth, I'm telling you, he's not going to do anything. And if he's bothering you, just walk away."

"It's not just Ryan," I say, thinking of Amber and the secret she's holding over me. "It's that girl. Tyler's girlfriend."

"What about her?"

"I don't like her." I fold my arms over my chest. "She's rude. I don't want to spend all week with her."

"Rude? What are you talking about? I thought she was nice."

"Did you hear that comment she made about me being noble because I'm a nurse? It wasn't a compliment, Derek. She was being sarcastic."

He sighs. "I don't know what's going on with you tonight, but you need to stop thinking everyone's out to get you."

"What about when you were talking about how hard it would be to get medical care living out here and I told you to stop so you wouldn't worry James and Olivia? Amber could've kept her mouth shut, but no, she just had to speak up and agree with you."

"She was just expressing an opinion."

I glare at him, wanting to strangle him for sticking up for some girl he just met. "Fine. Don't believe me, but the woman has something against me. I can't relax with her and Ryan here."

"Then you can stay up here in the room, because we're not leaving."

"Why are you being this way? You're not even listening to me."

"I am. And I think you're making something out of nothing. We'll see how tomorrow goes and discuss it again, but as of now, we're staying." He walks to the door.

"Where are you going?"

"Downstairs. I'm going to play poker with the guys."

He leaves, shutting the door behind him. I go over and lock it, feeling even more unsafe knowing my own husband doesn't have my back. I can't believe he thinks Ryan isn't dangerous, especially after what I told him. Maybe I didn't tell the story well enough, but even so, Derek still should've believed me.

I hear someone coming down the hall. Is it Derek? Is he coming back to apologize?

I'm about to unlock the door, but stop when I hear someone softly singing. I hear their footsteps stop just outside my room.

"Goodnight, Beth."

Oh God, it's Ryan!

"Sleep well," he says. "And be sure to lock your door."

I jump back, my heart pounding.

Where's Derek? Why isn't he here to witness this? He'd see for himself that Ryan is crazy.

Ryan's footsteps continue down the hall, then I hear him singing again.

I have to get out of this house. I had a bad feeling about this place the moment we walked through the door. It was almost like a premonition that something bad was about to happen. I tried to ignore it, but it wouldn't go away. I couldn't explain it. I didn't know why I felt that way. Until Ryan arrived.

CHAPTER 8

The next morning, I wake up alone in bed. I can hear the shower running in the bathroom. I take my phone from the nightstand and see it's after nine. I don't remember falling asleep. I was awake for most of the night, worrying about Ryan and what he might do.

Derek came up to the room just after midnight. He was angry when he found the door was locked. He started banging on it and yelling at me to let him in. He normally wouldn't act that way, so I knew he was drunk. When I opened the door, he reeked of alcohol. I decided it wasn't a good time to tell him what Ryan did so I said nothing and went back to bed.

"The shower's yours if you want it," Derek says, coming out to the bedroom, a towel wrapped around his waist.

His mention of the shower reminds me of the comment Amber made about taking a shower with Tyler. They probably had a romantic evening last night while I was up here alone, my husband more interested in getting drunk with his friends than spending time with his wife. Then again, I wasn't exactly in a romantic mood last night.

"Honey, did you hear me?" Derek says.

"Yes." I smile at him as I shove the down comforter off me and get out of bed. "How was the shower?"

"Great! It's got multiple shower heads and one of them has a massage setting." He walks over to his suitcase to get his clothes. "It's like being at a luxury spa. Not that I know what that's like, but you know what I mean." He takes out his boxers, a pair of jeans, and a T-shirt. "We should put our stuff in the dresser. Get these suitcases out of the way."

"Why don't we leave everything for now? In case we decide to leave."

He sighs. "Not this again." He walks to the bed and sets his clothes down. "We're not leaving. We came here to spend time with our friends and that's what we're going to do." He takes off his towel and starts getting dressed. "I talked to Shelby last night."

"And?"

"She said Ryan's doing really well. He's got that job walking dogs and makes a decent amount of money. She said everyone he works for loves him."

"According to who?" I say with a huff. "Ryan?" I walk over to Derek. "He's probably just telling her that. He probably made it up."

"He didn't make it up. Shelby knows some of the people he works for. They've told her how good he is with the dogs, how he's always on time to pick them up, how polite he is. A lot of them have recommended him to their friends."

"So he's good with dogs. That doesn't mean he's not insane."

"Beth, you really need to stop this," Derek says as he puts his shirt on. "You're letting the past cloud how you see him. Everyone agrees he's changed. You're the only one who thinks he hasn't."

"What do you mean everyone agrees? I thought you only talked to Shelby about this."

"I asked James and Tyler what they thought about Ryan and they both agreed he's not anything like how he used to be. Tyler even went to a baseball game with him last summer."

"Tyler invited Ryan to a game? Why? It's not like they're friends."

"He didn't invite him. Shelby got the tickets from a friend and couldn't go so she called Tyler. He said he had a great time with Ryan. And when James was in New York last summer to see Tyler, he hung out a few times with Ryan and Shelby and said Ryan was totally normal. He said if he didn't know anything about his past, he'd think he's just like any other guy."

"Then he's got everyone fooled, because I'm telling you, Ryan is not normal." I lower my voice. "He came by here after you left last night and stood outside the door. He told me to make sure to lock it."

I look at Derek, waiting for a response. Waiting for him to agree that no normal person would do that.

"Yeah? So?" Derek says. "He told you to lock the door. Big deal."

"Really? That's all you have to say? You don't find that even a little bit creepy?"

"No. I don't." He motions to the door. "It's been unlocked all night so if you're telling me he wanted to come in here and kill us, then why didn't he do it?"

"Just forget it," I say, walking away. "You've clearly made up your mind about him so it's no use talking to you." I go into the bathroom and shut the door.

I'm fed up with Derek. He won't even listen to me. I'm sure nobody else will either. They're all convinced Ryan is harmless, which is exactly what he wants. He wants them to feel safe around him so they won't be prepared to fight back when he turns on us.

"Good morning, Beth," Olivia says as I come down the stairs. I'm dressed for the day, but my hair is still wet. I just came down to get coffee, because without my morning coffee I get a headache that lasts all day.

"Hi," I say, noticing everyone sitting at the table having breakfast. I wasn't aware we were having a sit-down breakfast.

"Join us," Olivia says, getting up from the table. "I'll get you some coffee. Do you take it black?"

"No, with cream," I say, noticing everyone watching me as I follow Olivia to the kitchen.

Nobody is talking. Is it because of me? Were they talking about me before I came down? Did Derek tell them my concerns about Ryan and now they think *I'm* the crazy one? Looking back at the table, I notice Ryan isn't there.

"Here's your coffee," Olivia says, and when I turn back, she's holding out the mug.

"Thanks." I take a sip, desperate for a shot of caffeine.

"The cream is on the table," she says. "I made everyone eggs and bacon, but let me know if you'd like something else."

"I'll just have the coffee. I need to go finish getting ready."

"Honey, you should eat something," Derek says as I'm heading back to the stairs.

"At least come sit with us," Shelby says.

"We missed you last night," James says. "We had a whole party going on down here." He laughs. "You should've seen your husband. Amber had him dancing. I don't think I've seen him dance since your wedding."

My eyes go to Derek. "Why were you dancing? I thought you were playing poker."

"We were," Amber says. "But we also played a little truth or dare."

What is she up to? Why did she want to play truth or dare? I thought she was only suggesting that last night as a way to get me to tell Derek what I did that night at the bar. I never would, of course, so I don't know why she even suggested it.

"So what truths did you learn?" I ask, walking back to the table. I take a seat, deciding to join them. I need to find out what went on last night, since apparently my husband chose not to tell me. "And how did you convince Derek to dance?"

"He broke the rules," James says. "He chose truth, but then wouldn't answer Amber's question so we told him he either answers or has to dance."

"Your husband's a pretty good dancer," Shelby says, smiling at Derek.

Tyler laughs. "Only when he's drunk."

I help myself to some eggs. "What was the question?"

"It was nothing," Derek says.

"I really don't care for that game." Olivia dabs her lips with her napkin. "Perhaps we could talk about something else. Beth, would you like some bacon?" She holds up the platter.

"No, thanks." I look at Derek. "I want to know the question. You must've really not wanted to answer it if you chose dancing over telling the truth."

"I didn't choose to do the dance," he says. "They made me."

"I'll tell her," Amber says.

I look at her across from me, noticing the smirk on her face. "So what was the question?"

"I asked him if he was with anyone else when you two were engaged."

"Now that we're sober," Tyler says, "I'm realizing that was a really shitty question. You shouldn't have asked him that."

"Why not?" Amber says. "They're happily married now. Who cares if he was with some other girl when they were engaged? Derek, you wouldn't care if you found out Beth had been with someone, would you? I mean, it was so long ago, and you were both really young."

"This doesn't seem like a good topic for breakfast," Olivia says. "Why don't we discuss what everyone would like to do today?"

"Would you?" Amber asks Derek, ignoring Olivia's request to change the subject. "Would you be mad?"

"Amber, just drop it," Shelby says. "Let's talk about something else."

"I want to know. Derek, would you be mad or not?"

The room goes silent as we wait for his answer.

Derek finally looks at me, his expression serious, almost angry. "Of course I'd be mad. I wouldn't have married her if I'd found out she'd been with some other guy. I wouldn't have been able to trust her."

I swallow, my heart pounding, my stomach feeling sick.

"Isn't it funny how just one little thing could change your entire future?" Amber says.

"I'd hardly call cheating a little thing," Olivia says.

I look back at my plate and pick up my fork, but I have no desire to eat. Amber's going to tell Derek the truth. I know she is, especially now that she knows he'd divorce me if he found out. Why is she doing this? Why is she trying to break us up? I didn't intentionally sleep with her boyfriend. And she has Tyler now. Why does she care what happened with a guy she dated ten years ago?

"What about you, Beth?" Shelby says. "Would you have married Derek if you'd found out he'd been with someone else while you two were engaged?"

"I really can't say." I push the eggs around my plate with my fork. "I was a different person back then." I glance at Derek. "But I loved him, and I wanted a life with him, so I probably would've forgiven him."

"You wouldn't have had to," Derek says. "Because I was never with anyone else. I didn't even consider it."

"Then why didn't you just answer the question last night?" Tyler asks.

Derek shrugs. "I don't know. Probably because you guys always used to make fun of me for being a prude. I wanted you to think something might've happened. But it didn't. I was committed to Beth. After our first date, I never even considered being with anyone else."

"That's so sweet," Shelby gushes. "Beth, he really loves you."

I smile at her comment, but in my head I'm wondering if he really does. If Derek loved me, he'd believe me about Ryan.

Speaking of Ryan, where is he?

CHAPTER 9

"Where's Ryan?" I ask. "Is he still asleep?"

"He's out moving the cars," James says, adding more bacon to his plate.

"What cars?" I look at Derek. "He doesn't mean ours, does he?"

"Everyone's," James says. "They were blocking the garage. I wanted to get the truck out in case a storm comes. Ryan offered to move the cars around while we finish breakfast."

"You gave Ryan our keys?" I say quietly to Derek.

"He'll bring them back. He's probably almost done out there."

Derek's not the least bit worried that Ryan has our keys. Has he not even considered that Ryan could be out there tampering with our car? Draining the oil? Messing with our brakes so we go flying over the mountainside to our deaths?

"He misses having a car," Shelby says. "But we can't afford one living in the city. The parking alone would cost as much as our rent."

"Yeah, it sucks," Tyler says. "That's one of the things I don't like about living there. If I get a job in LA, the first thing I'm doing is getting a car."

"Hey, did you hear back from that audition?" Amber asks.

"I didn't get it," he says.

"Oh, babe, I'm sorry." She leans over to him and they kiss.

59

"What was the audition for?" Derek asks.

"A soap opera," Tyler mutters.

James laughs. "I would've loved to see that. Too bad you didn't get it."

"He'll get something else." Amber smiles at him as she messes with his hair. "Something better."

"Beth, do you not like the eggs?" Olivia asks, noticing I haven't eaten them. "I can make you something else."

"The eggs are fine. I'm just not very hungry."

The front door opens and Ryan walks in, his dark wool jacket and black stocking cap covered in snow.

"You get the truck out?" James says to him.

"Yeah, it's out." He looks at Olivia. "What should I do with my coat? I don't want to get your floor all wet."

She gets up. "I'll take it to the mudroom."

Mudroom? Does she mean the laundry room? I'm guessing they're the same, since she had that room set up with places to put wet coats and boots.

"I got it," Ryan says as she goes to take his coat. He takes off his boots and walks through the room. He spots me at the table and smirks at me. I glance at Derek, hoping he saw the interaction, but he wasn't paying attention.

James gets up. "You guys want to head down to the lake?"

"Yeah, just let me grab my phone," Derek says.

"You don't need your phone," James says. "Most of the time you can't even get a signal down there."

"What if we need to call for help?" Tyler asks.

"For what? We're just walking down there and walking back."

"What lake are you talking about?" I ask.

"James said there's a small lake about a half mile from here," Derek says. "We're going to check it out and maybe do some ice-fishing later."

"I'm staying here," Shelby says. "It's too cold to walk that far."

"She's right," I say to Derek. "I don't think you should be out in this weather."

The snow was just light flurries when I came downstairs, but now it's coming down so heavy it's hard to see.

"We'll be fine," Derek says.

"It's not that far," Olivia assures me. "You just go out the back and cut through the woods. James and I walked there yesterday. It's very pretty, and quite peaceful. You might want to consider joining them."

"You're not going?"

"No, I need to clean up breakfast and figure out what we're going to do for lunch."

"Let me do it," Ryan says, coming back to the table. "I can make lunch."

"You're not going to the lake?" she asks.

"Not today. Maybe later this week."

"Well, I suppose you could make lunch if you'd really like to."

There's no way I'm eating anything Ryan makes. He'll probably try to poison us all.

"I'm gonna get my coat," James says. "I'll meet you guys out there."

He takes off for the mudroom.

"Hey, Ryan, you got my keys?" Derek says.

"Oh. Yeah." Ryan digs into his pocket, pulls out the keys, and tosses them to Derek.

"Thanks." Derek turns to me. "What do you think? You coming with us?"

"I think I'll stay here with Shelby."

Amber notices Tyler heading to the stairs. "Tyler, wait up! I'm coming too."

Of course she is. So she can plant more doubts in Derek's head about our marriage.

Derek goes upstairs next, followed by Shelby. Olivia goes to the kitchen, leaving me alone at the table with Ryan.

"I'll help with the dishes," I say, getting up.

"How'd you sleep?" Ryan asks as I gather up the plates.

"I slept fine."

"I didn't." He reaches in front of me to pick up the platter of eggs. "I drank too much. I never sleep well when I drink a lot."

I nod, hurrying around the table to grab the rest of the plates.

"Shelby and I might take a drive later," he says. "Check out the area. You want to come?"

"No," I blurt out. I look at him. "I mean, I'd rather just stay around here."

He shrugs. "That's fine. Just wanted to ask."

"Thank you for helping," Olivia says, coming back to the table. "I didn't realize how much work it'd be to make so many meals." She laughs a little. "I'm not used to doing all this cooking."

"Liv!" James yells. "You know where my hat went?"

"On the washing machine," she yells back.

"Got it!"

She rolls her eyes. "He can't find things even when they're right in front of him."

Derek and Tyler come running down the stairs, followed by Amber.

"See you, honey." Derek gives me a peck on the lips on his way to the mudroom.

Moments later, I watch out the window as the four of them trudge through the snow, then disappear into the woods.

"Don't you have bears out here?" I say to Olivia.

She smiles. "They'll be fine. I've been coming here since I was a child and I've never once seen a bear."

I bring the plates to the kitchen. Ryan's following behind me with the platters of leftover food. Why is he always around me? Why can't he go do something else?

"Hey, Beth!" Shelby calls from upstairs.

"Yeah?"

"Would you come up here? I want to show you something."

"Go ahead," Olivia says. "I can finish up."

I'm almost afraid to leave her there with Ryan and a kitchen full of knives. But I don't think he'd hurt Olivia. He wants to hurt the people who hurt him ten years ago. And I think he's going to start with me.

When I get to Shelby's room, she's hanging up her clothes in the closet.

"What did you want to show me?" I ask.

"The earrings I made." She goes over to the dresser and takes out a small jewelry box. "I don't know Amber that well so I wasn't sure which pair to give her. I wanted your opinion."

"I don't know how much help I'll be. I just met her."

Shelby brings the box over to the bed and we sit down next to each other.

"This was my first choice." She takes out a pair of round silver earrings with a black stone in the middle.

"I think she'd like those. She seems like someone who wears black a lot."

"Everyone in the city wears black," Shelby says with a laugh. "But yeah, I think this is a good option. Here's the other one." She takes out earrings that look like small silver daggers.

"Those. Definitely. That's totally her."

"You think so?"

"Absolutely. You should get Tyler's opinion, but if I had to pick, it's those."

"Okay." She hands me the other earrings, the ones we didn't pick.

"What are you doing?"

"They're yours. For helping me."

"Really?" I get a closer look at them.

"What's wrong? I thought you liked them."

"I do, and they aren't dangly, so I could wear them to work."

"Try them on."

"We should wait until you show Tyler. He might want them for Amber."

"Yeah, I guess you're right." She takes the earrings. "But they're yours if he doesn't take them. If he does, I'll send you another pair when I get home." She brings the box back to the dresser.

"So how's everything going with your artwork?"

She shrugs. "Not great. I haven't sold a painting all year. That's why I started making jewelry. People buy it, but I don't make a lot. Not enough that I could quit my waitressing job."

"How's everything else going?" She comes back and sits beside me. "You think you'll stay in New York?"

"I kind of have to. If I'm going to sell my paintings, I need to be in a place where people will buy them, and people in the city buy art." She turns to me. "What about you? You think you and Derek will stay in Syracuse?"

"Yeah, we like it there, at least for now. I'm starting a new job when I get back."

"That's right. You told me that."

I glance around the room and see Ryan's duffle bag on the floor. I didn't realize he was sharing a room with Shelby, but now that I think about it, there aren't enough rooms for him to have his own.

"Where does Ryan sleep?" I ask, assuming they don't share the bed.

"He sleeps on the floor. He does it at home sometimes too. He said the floor feels better on his back than a mattress." She pauses. "Hey, um, Derek told me your concerns about Ryan."

"Oh. Yeah. I didn't mean to say anything against him. I just—"

"No. I get it. He had a lot of problems when you knew him before. I didn't see it back then, or I did, but didn't want to. I didn't want to believe there was anything wrong with him."

"That's understandable. I mean, he's your brother. Your only sibling."

"Which is why I've been so supportive of him over the years. Our parents did nothing but put us down. Tell us we're worthless. I was determined to prove them wrong, but Ryan was just a kid. He believed what they said. I think that's why he turned out that way. As his big sister, I couldn't let him go the rest of his life thinking he was worthless so I've worked really hard to build him up, make him feel better about himself."

"I can see how much you care about him. He's lucky to have you."

"I'm lucky to have him too. With my mom a mess and my dad gone, Ryan is really all I have left. Anyway, what I'm trying to say is that I know Ryan can be weird sometimes, but he's not the same guy you knew ten years ago. He's grown up a lot. He's responsible. Always shows up to work on time. He cleans up after himself. He's learning to cook." She smiles a little. "He's actually a really sweet guy if you give him a chance." Her eyes rise to mine. "That's all I'm asking. Is for you to give him a chance. So will you?"

CHAPTER 10

I don't want to give Ryan a chance. Maybe Shelby is right and I'm being too hard on him, judging him because of his past, but I know what I felt and I definitely felt threatened when he came up to me yesterday with that knife. And again, last night, when he told me to lock my door.

"Will you please just give him a chance?" Shelby asks.

I nod. "Sure."

"Thanks." She smiles. "It's so good seeing you again, Beth. I've really missed hanging out with you."

"You should come to Syracuse sometime. Spend a weekend there. We could go shopping. Relive our college days."

"I don't have a car."

"Oh, that's right. I guess I'll have to come to the city sometime."

"You totally should. We could meet up with Tyler. Go to dinner. See a show. Tyler is always getting free tickets to stuff. I guess it's a perk of being an actor."

"Speaking of Tyler, don't you think it's odd he's dating Amber?"

"Yes. I couldn't believe it when I saw her. She's not at all his type."

"I know, right? I get that he likes her for more than her looks, but she's just so different than the type of girl he normally dates. I've never seen him date a girl who isn't blonde."

"I haven't either. Last summer he dated three blondes."

My brows rise. "Three?"

Shelby laughs. "Not at the same time."

"Oh. Okay."

"I don't get it. I mean, Amber's not even that pretty. And Tyler is hot. He could have any girl he wants."

"I don't find her personality appealing either. I keep feeling like she's insulting me."

"Don't take it personally. I think that's just how she is. She was insulting everyone last night. The more she drank, the worse she got."

"So what exactly happened last night?"

"The guys played poker and Olivia and I watched a movie."

"What about Amber?"

"She played poker with the guys. They were mad because she kept winning."

"And after the poker, you played truth or dare?"

"Yeah, but not for long. It was getting late and everyone was tired."

"What did I miss? Did anyone reveal any truths I don't already know?"

"Only that Olivia had a miscarriage."

"She did? When?"

"Like a month after the wedding. I don't think Olivia wanted anyone to know. She seemed really mad when James blurted it out. But for her, mad is just giving him a dirty look. I can't imagine that woman getting angry. She seems so reserved."

"What was the question that made James tell everyone that?"

"Amber asked if he ever got a girl pregnant."

"And Olivia was the only one? I would've thought James got a girl pregnant before that. Remember how much he slept around in college?"

"Yeah, he was with a lot of girls. Including me."

I stare at her. "Wait, what? You slept with James?"

"Freshman year. We were drunk. It was just one time. He probably doesn't even remember."

"I can't believe you never told me this."

"It wasn't a big deal. Like I said, we were both drunk."

"But wasn't it awkward being friends with him after that?"

"Not at all. I'm friends with a lot of guys I've slept with."

Shelby is very nonchalant when it comes to sex. She sees it as just another form of personal expression, like her artwork. She can be with a man for a night and have no regrets, whereas I'm left feeling horribly guilty. Of course, it's different for me, since I was engaged to Derek when I had my one and only one-night stand, but even if I'd been single, I'm not someone who could sleep with a man and move on without feeling some regret.

"Did you and James talk about it?" I ask. "After it happened?"

"No, we just went back to being friends."

"Wow. I can't believe I never knew. You guys definitely hid it well."

"I didn't see a reason to tell anyone. We did it and it was over. We moved on."

"So going back to what James said about the miscarriage, did Olivia address it at all? Or did James say more about it?"

"No. We could all tell they didn't want to talk about it, so Amber moved on to Derek, which you already heard about."

"Yes, we don't need to talk about that," I say with a sigh.

"I wish she hadn't come."

"Who? Amber?"

"Yeah. She's really messing with our vibe. We always have so much fun when we get together, but I feel like Amber's bringing us down," Shelby says.

"I agree."

"He doesn't even act like he wants her here," Shelby continues. "Did you notice he never kisses her or puts his arm around her? Amber's always the one kissing him or touching him. Tyler goes along with it, but he never initiates it. Don't you think that's weird?"

"I guess I hadn't noticed," I say.

"Watch them together. You'll see what I'm talking about. It's almost like Tyler doesn't like her, at least not in a romantic way."

"Then why would he be dating her?"

Shelby turns to me, a sly grin on her face. "I think she might have something on him."

"What do you mean?" I ask, intrigued.

"Like maybe she knows something she shouldn't about him and she's keeping it a secret in exchange for him dating her."

"I doubt it. Why would she be blackmailing Tyler into dating her?"

"Maybe she thinks dating him will get her more work. Maybe she's using him for his connections."

"I don't think his connections are worth much. If they were, he wouldn't be struggling to get jobs. His last TV role — other than commercials — was years ago and he was only in one episode."

"Yeah, but he knows a lot of people in the industry."

"Maybe, but there are actors who are more successful and have better connections than Tyler. If Amber wants to advance her career, she should date someone else."

Shelby shrugs. "It's just a theory. I'm trying to figure out why he'd date her. Like we said before, she's not at all his type." Shelby glances at the door, then back at me. "I heard them fighting last night."

"All couples fight."

"Yes, but this was more than a disagreement. They were yelling, and I don't think Tyler stayed in their room last night."

"I didn't hear them yelling. How do you know all this?"

"Just after two in the morning, I went downstairs to get a drink and heard them in the garage. They must've gone out there so they wouldn't wake anyone up."

"Did you hear what they were fighting about?"

"No. I was worried they'd come back in the house and find me there, so I got my drink and left."

"How do you know Tyler didn't stay in their room last night?"

"I woke up at five and couldn't get back to sleep, so I went downstairs to watch TV. Tyler was on the couch. He made up this story about falling asleep there last night, but we all went up to bed just after midnight. And I knew he was lying because I'd heard him with Amber in the garage earlier."

"Did you tell him that?"

"No, but I did ask him how things are going with her."

"And what did he say?"

"He pretended like everything's good between them, which just proves there's something going on there. If you'd heard them fighting, you'd know things aren't good in their relationship."

"Maybe they're just going through a rough patch."

"Tyler doesn't stick around when things aren't working out. You know how he is. One fight with a girl and he's done."

"Maybe he's changed. Maybe he's realizing if he wants a relationship, he has to work through the tough times."

"He hasn't changed. I see him more than you do, and believe me, he hasn't changed. He told me he's focused on his career and doesn't want to waste time with a girl who just wants to create drama, which to him means even the smallest argument. And what I heard last night was more than an argument. It was a fight. So why is he still with her?"

"I don't know. It does seem strange. Maybe I could get Derek to talk to him. See if he can get him to open up."

"He could try." She gets up from the bed and shivers. "I'm freezing. I might take a bath. Try to warm up."

"I'll go see if the guys are back. I can't imagine they'd want to be out for too long in this weather."

I leave her room, thinking about what she said about Amber. I wouldn't be surprised if Amber had dirt on Tyler and was using it to her advantage. After all, if she's threatening to tell my secret, it's entirely possible she's doing the same to Tyler. But I don't know what kind of secret would be big enough for Tyler to make Amber his girlfriend.

Maybe she's not blackmailing him. Maybe Tyler and Amber are just having issues in their relationship and Tyler doesn't want to break up with her while they're here. When they're back in New York, he'll probably end it and move on to the next girl.

When I'm back downstairs, I don't see Olivia. Or Ryan.

I start to panic. What if Ryan did something to her? What if he grabbed a knife and took her out to the woods and killed her?

No. I'm being ridiculous. He wouldn't do that.

Would he?

"Olivia?" I call out as I search the house. "Ryan?"

Neither of them answers. I check the garage, then look outside, but I don't see them anywhere. And they weren't upstairs.

"Olivia?" I yell.

Where is she? And where is Ryan?

I'm getting a really bad feeling about this. Shelby told me her brother had changed, but I don't believe it. I think he's a monster with urges. Urges he can't control. Urges to kill.

CHAPTER 11

Maybe Ryan and Olivia decided to go down to the lake. I get out my phone and call Derek. It rings several times before he finally picks up.

"Hey, honey, you should check this place out. It's beautiful. And the walk here was—"

His phone cuts out.

"Derek? Are you there?"

"Yeah, I'm here."

"You cut out. I couldn't hear you."

"The service here is really bad."

"Is Olivia with you?"

"No. I thought she—" His phone cuts out again. ". . . staying home."

"What about Ryan? Is he there with you?"

"No. Why?"

"I can't find Olivia." My pulse races as I imagine what might've happened to her. "Ryan's missing too."

"I'm sure they're around. Maybe they're—" The phone goes silent. I look at the screen. The call disconnected. I call Derek back. It goes straight to voicemail.

If Ryan and Olivia aren't there, then where are they? What if I'm right and Ryan did something to her?

I have to tell Shelby. As I'm running up the stairs, I hear the front door open. I look back and see Olivia walking in.

"Olivia!" I race back down the stairs.

She stops as I go over to her. "Yes?"

"Where were you?"

"Out getting something from the truck. I was missing a glove and found it had fallen under the seat."

"So you're okay?" I ask, looking her up and down.

"I'm fine. Why do you ask?"

"I couldn't find you. I was worried."

She smiles. "That's sweet of you to be concerned, but as you can see, I'm fine."

"Where's Ryan?"

"He left," she says, taking off her coat. "He said he was going forest bathing."

"Forest bathing?" I ask, having no idea what she's talking about.

"It's a technique used to relax."

"I've never heard of that."

"You should try it. It's very calming. I usually do it at least once when I'm here. I've asked James to go with me, but the one time he did, he got bored and left."

"What exactly do you do?"

"Walk among the trees. Observe nature. Take deep breaths. I'm sure Ryan is still out there if you'd like to join him."

Is she insane? There's no way I'd be alone in the woods with Ryan.

"I'll pass," I say. "I'm sure some people enjoy it, but it doesn't really sound like my kind of thing."

She holds up her coat. "I'm going to put this away."

Now that I know she's safe, I'm able to relax, my heart returning to normal. I go to the couch to sit down. Olivia comes over and adds a log to the fire, then takes a seat on one of the chairs.

"Are you having a good time?" she asks, crossing her thin legs and adjusting the scarf around her neck.

"Um, sure." I glance around. "It's an absolutely gorgeous house."

"I wasn't asking about the house. I was asking if you're enjoying yourself. You seem tense."

I look at her. "I'm fine. Really. I just have a hard time relaxing sometimes."

"Is it because of Ryan?" She rests her forearms on the rounded arms of the chair. "I've noticed you two don't seem to get along."

"It's not that. I just didn't know he'd be here this week. He doesn't usually attend our reunions."

"I see." She nods, her gaze wandering to the fire. "He is rather odd."

"You think so?"

"I really shouldn't say. I just met the man. It's really not fair of me to make comments about him."

But I want her to. I want to know if she agrees that he's crazy. If she does, I'd at least have one person on my side, another set of eyes to keep watch on Ryan.

"Why do you think he's odd?" I ask. "You can tell me. I promise to keep it between us."

She checks to make sure we're alone, then says, "There was a mouse running around the laundry room and he, um . . ." She clears her throat. "Killed it with his bare hands."

I suck in a breath, my mind imagining Ryan wrapping his hands around the mouse, squeezing it to death. "How do you know this? Did you see him do it?"

"I walked in on him after the fact. It was while you were upstairs with Shelby. I put a load of laundry in, saw the mouse, and screamed. Ryan came in and I told him about the mouse. He said he'd take care of it so I hurried out of there. I assumed he'd use a broom to guide it out the back door to the outside." She pauses, her gaze returning to the fire.

"And? What happened?"

"I never heard the door open, so I went in there to see what was going on." She looks over at me. "I found Ryan holding the mouse. He'd squeezed the life out of it and was just staring at it." She shudders. "I found it very odd."

"Yes. That's . . . disturbing."

"I asked him to dispose of it outside, which he did. Then he came back in the house, washed up, and told me he needed to relieve some stress. That's when he told me he was going forest bathing."

"And he's still there? In the forest?"

"As far as I know."

Shelby comes down the stairs, smiling when she sees Olivia and me. "What are you guys talking about?"

"Forest bathing." Olivia smiles at Shelby. "Beth hadn't heard of it so I was explaining it to her."

"You should totally try it," Shelby says, joining me on the couch. "It's really relaxing. I used to do it when we were in college."

"You did?" I say. "I don't remember you doing that."

"I didn't do it that often. It wasn't a thing back then, but now it's really popular. Were you thinking of trying it?"

"No. I don't like being in the woods, especially in this weather."

"Ryan is out there," Olivia says to Shelby. "That's how the topic came up."

"Oh, yeah, he loves forest bathing," she says. "It was part of his therapy when he was in the hospital."

She says 'hospital,' but it was really a psych ward. Shelby has always insisted her brother is sane. Even when a judge decided he needed to be locked away, Shelby didn't think it was necessary.

"You mean when we were in college?" I ask. "Or was this more recent therapy?"

75

I'm asking because I'm wondering if Ryan is seeing anyone currently for his mental health issues.

"When we were in college," she says. "He really misses the forest. Being in the city, there's really no way to be around nature unless he goes to the park, but it's not the same as being out here. Surrounded by nothing but trees."

Olivia checks her watch. "I thought James would've been back by now."

"I talked to Derek a few minutes ago," I say. "I was going to ask when they'd be heading back, but the phone cut out."

"Yes, the service out here is spotty," Olivia says. "I don't even bother bringing my laptop here anymore. The internet is almost always down."

"So what do you and James do when you're here?" Shelby asks. "Just hang out in the house?"

"I usually read. James goes out exploring. We've really only been here twice since the renovations were finished."

"You don't get bored being here? I mean, the views are amazing and it's a nice break from the city, but I think I'd go crazy if I had to be here for more than a week."

I was thinking the same thing, but wasn't going to say it.

"James and I enjoy the solitude." Olivia's smile is strained. She's probably annoyed by Shelby's comment. But that's Shelby. She says whatever pops into her head.

We hear the back door opening and the loud clomp of boots. "We're back!" Derek calls out. "Anyone home?"

"We're by the fire," I call back.

There's more noise as they stomp the snow off their boots and shake out their coats.

"That was great," Tyler says, walking toward us, his handsome face still red from the cold. "You guys should've come with us."

"I'm perfectly happy by the fire," Shelby says.

Derek appears, still wearing his stocking cap, snow stuck to his neatly trimmed beard. "Beth, you missed out. We saw two bald eagles and a family of deer."

"Did you take some pictures?" I ask.

"Yeah, I sent them to you. You didn't get them?"

I check my phone. "I don't see them."

"Looks like they never sent," Derek says, looking at his phone. "My phone wasn't working out there."

Amber runs through the room to the fireplace. "I'm freezing." She shivers. "I need to warm up."

"I could make you some tea," Olivia offers.

"That'd be great," she says.

Tyler could've offered to make her some, but instead he sits down in the chair and looks at his phone.

"Where's James?" I ask.

"Here," Derek says. "Isn't he?"

"No. I don't think so."

"He's probably upstairs," Tyler says. "He was having stomach issues. He said he was coming back here to use the bathroom."

"Did you hear him upstairs?" I ask Shelby.

"No. There's nobody up there."

Olivia walks over to Amber. "Here's your tea."

"Thanks."

"Olivia, is James here?" I ask.

"I don't believe so."

"He should've been back by now," Derek says. "He left before we did."

"Maybe he had to stop and shit in the woods," Tyler says with a laugh. "The way he ran off, he was definitely having issues."

"I'm sure he'll be here soon," Olivia says. "Would anyone else like some tea?"

Nobody takes her up on the offer, so she excuses herself and goes upstairs. Maybe she's used to James not checking in with her, but if he were my husband, I'd be worried. It's freezing outside, cold enough to be dangerous.

Ten minutes later, James still isn't home. Ryan isn't either. Is that just a coincidence or did something happen? Even if James had to stop to relieve himself in the woods, he wouldn't still be gone. So why isn't he here?

CHAPTER 12

"You want some of this?" Derek asks as I join him in the kitchen. He's eating the cheese left over from the charcuterie platter.

"No, I'm not hungry." I stand beside him and quietly say, "Maybe we should go look for James."

"Why?" Derek asks, reaching across me to grab a box of crackers.

"He's not back yet. He told you he was coming back to the house, but he's still not here. Aren't you worried?"

"No. He's a grown man. It's not my job to keep track of him. Maybe he decided to go back to the lake."

"By himself?"

"We didn't tell him we were heading back. Maybe he went to the lake, thinking we'd still be there. I don't know, but I wouldn't worry about it. James can take care of himself."

That might be true if he were out there by himself. But he's not. Ryan's out there, hiding in the woods, doing who knows what.

I hear the back door open and the sound of someone coming into the house. I leave the kitchen and go to the mudroom.

"James, where—" I stop when I see it's not James, but Ryan. "Oh. Hi."

Ryan gives me his weird smile, which is really more of a smirk. "Hey, Beth. How's it going?"

"Fine." I remain where I am, keeping my distance from him. "Have you seen James?"

"Yeah, he's out in the shed." Ryan stomps his boots on the rug, sending snow everywhere. "Why are you looking for him?"

"I just wondered where he was. Derek said he was heading back to the house, but that was a half hour ago and he still isn't here."

"And you thought something happened to him?" Ryan yanks off his boots. "Like what? What did you think happened to him?"

"I don't know. Tyler said James wasn't feeling well. I just wanted to make sure he was okay."

Ryan walks up to me, that smirk still on his face. He leans down to my ear, his hot breath sending a chill through me. "Always worrying what people are up to, aren't you, Beth? You just can't stay out of people's business." He runs his index finger up the front of my throat to my chin. I go to yank it away, but he grabs my arm, stopping me.

"What are you—"

"Stop." He looks at me, his eyes dark, his jaw clenched. "Stop looking for things that aren't there. Stop getting in everyone's business. You're not helping anyone, Beth. You're only going to make things worse."

"Make *what* worse? What are you talking about?"

Just then, the door bursts open and James walks in, his arms full of firewood. "Damn, it's cold out there." He slams the door shut with his foot.

Ryan turns to James. "Want some help?"

"Yeah. Thanks, man," he says as Ryan takes the wood from his arms. "Just put it next to the fire."

Ryan leaves the room, not looking at me as he passes by.

"Did they get back from the lake yet?" James asks as he takes off his coat.

"Yeah, like twenty minutes ago. They said you weren't feeling well."

He shrugs. "It passed. I feel okay now."

"If you tell me your symptoms, maybe I could help."

"Really, I'm fine." He tosses his wet coat on the floor, even though the hook is right there. Then he yanks off his boots, not bothering to put them on the boot tray or even the mat. He just leaves them on the floor, chunks of melting snow leaving puddles behind.

"Hey, you're back," Derek says to James as he comes up beside me. "Beth was worried about you."

"Yeah, I was just telling her I'm fine. Whatever was bothering my stomach went away." He goes up to Derek. "So what'd you decide?"

"About fishing? I'm up for it."

"Fishing?" I turn to Derek. "It's freezing out."

"Ice-fishing," he explains. "James has all the equipment. We're just trying to decide when to go." He looks at James. "Maybe this afternoon."

"Why don't you go later this week?" I say. "That way we can all do something together this afternoon."

"That works," James says. "It's not a great day for it anyway. There's sleet coming down."

"James?" Olivia calls out.

"Right here," he says, going past Derek and me.

"Let's go," Derek says.

"Wait." I grab his arm. "I need to talk to you."

"About what?"

"Ryan," I whisper. "I think he was threatening me. Just now. Before James came in."

"Threatening you *how?*"

"He told me to stay out of people's business. That I'm going to make things worse. What do you think that means?"

Derek shrugs. "I don't know. He probably meant that he doesn't want you talking about him. You know how much he hated it when we used to talk about him in college."

"But how would he know I'm talking about him? He's never around when I'm doing it."

"Maybe someone told him, or maybe he just assumed you were." Derek puts his hand on my shoulder and looks me in the eye. "Beth, you gotta stop this. You've been on edge since he got here. I know you don't like him, but just ignore him. Otherwise, you're not going to have any fun this week."

"Oh, sorry," Olivia says, appearing at the door. "I didn't know you two were in here. I just wanted to put the clothes in the dryer, but I can come back."

"No, go ahead," Derek says. "We were just leaving."

She goes past us into the room, straight to James' coat on the floor, which she picks up and hangs. Seeing her clean up after him makes me grateful to have a husband like Derek, who always picks up after himself.

* * *

"Oh God, look at my hair," Shelby says as we're looking at photos later that afternoon. Whenever we have these reunions, I bring old photo albums of our college days and we go through them and reminisce. You'd think it would get old, doing it every year, but it never does. It's always one of my favorite parts of the trip.

"Look at that shirt I'm wearing," Derek says. "That pattern is so ugly. Why would I ever buy that?"

"You didn't." I swat his arm. "I did. I bought you that for your birthday."

"Oh," he says with a sheepish grin. "In that case, I love it."
Everyone laughs.

"Let me see," Tyler says, leaning over to look at the photo. "Oh, yeah, I remember that shirt. Sorry, Beth, but he's right. That shirt was hideous. I remember telling James you probably got it for Derek so that no other girls would want him."

"That is not why I got it," I insist. "I really thought it was a nice shirt."

"At least he didn't have it for long," Shelby says.

"That's right," I say to Derek. "That spark flew out of the bonfire and ruined it."

James laughs. "Is that what he told you?"

"What do you mean?" I ask.

"He gave it to Ryan," Shelby says, putting her feet up on the coffee table. "It actually looked good on him, way better than it looked on Derek."

"You gave that shirt to Ryan?" I ask Derek, shocked and a little angry that he never told me that.

"It didn't fit me right. And really . . ." Derek points to the photo. "Look at it. Did you really want me to wear that?"

"If I didn't, I wouldn't have bought it for you." I get up from the couch.

"Beth, come on. Don't be upset. It was ten years ago. More than that. You got me that shirt sophomore year."

"Yes, and it's taken this long for me to find out that you gave it away." I go to the bar cart Olivia set up and pour myself some more wine.

"What's the big deal?" Amber says. "Like you keep everything Derek gives you?"

I'm really getting annoyed with Amber. The way she keeps taking Derek's side, it's like she's determined to break us apart.

"She's right," Derek says, rubbing his chin. "What happened to that sweater I got you last year for Christmas?"

It was a horrible sweater. Bright orange with little white squares across the front. The orange looked terrible against my fair skin and the white squares didn't line up right. I wore the sweater once, then buried it in the back of my dresser.

"It's at home," I say. "In the dresser."

"Why haven't I seen you wear it?"

"I guess I just forgot about it." I sit back on the couch.

"Which means she didn't like it," Amber says.

I glare at her. "I didn't say that."

"You didn't have to. People don't wear stuff they don't like."

"You could've just told me you didn't like it," Derek says. "We could've exchanged it for something else."

"Yes, well, at least I didn't just give it away." I take a drink of my wine.

"Does Ryan still have it?" James asks Shelby, his lips sliding up to a smile. "Maybe he could give it back."

"He doesn't have it. It probably went in a donation box when we moved."

"Hey," James says, looking up at Olivia as she comes down the stairs. "You get any sleep?"

"Yes." She smiles. "I feel much better. I really needed that nap."

"Get over here." He pats his leg. "You should see some of these photos. I was actually in shape back then."

"I need to get dinner started."

"It can wait. Come on. Just sit for a few minutes."

She walks over to him, looking reluctant to sit on his lap, but there's really nowhere else to sit. He grabs her tiny body and sets her on his leg then gives her a kiss on the cheek. Her body stiffens and her smile seems forced. I wonder if she's angry at James about something or if it's more serious than that, like their marriage isn't going well.

"Where's Ryan?" Amber asks. "I haven't seen him since lunch."

"He's in our room," Shelby says. "Probably reading. He brought a stack of books with him."

"Ryan reads?" Tyler asks.

"Yes." Shelby shoots him a dirty look. "Don't be an ass. He's smarter than you think."

"I didn't say he wasn't. I've just never seen him read."

"He reads all the time."

"What kind of books?" Derek asks.

"Mostly suspense. Mysteries." She checks the time. "I guess he has been up there a long time. Maybe I should go check on him."

"I'm sure he's fine." I hope he stays up there. I'm having a much better time without him around.

* * *

Later that night, I get into bed and snuggle up next to Derek.

"Did you have a good day?" he asks, kissing my forehead.

"I did. It was fun to look at old photos and reminisce."

"You seem like you're finally starting to relax."

"It's because Ryan wasn't around. I wish he'd stay in his room for the rest of the week."

"I doubt that'll happen. You're just going to have to try to ignore him."

"I would, but he keeps bothering me. He won't leave me alone."

"You want me to talk to him?"

"No, that would only make things worse. If he knows something bothers you, he does it even more."

"When he was seventeen, sure, but he's older now. I think he'd leave you alone if I had a talk with him. Or I could talk to Shelby again, see if she can get him to back off."

"I already talked to Shelby. When you were at the lake. She asked me to give him a chance. She's convinced he's changed, but you know Shelby. She'd stand up for Ryan even if he killed someone."

"Maybe you should try giving the guy a chance. Don't keep assuming the worst of him."

Derek doesn't get it. He hasn't seen Ryan giving me that creepy smile or heard him talk to me in a threatening way. If Ryan had left me alone, maybe I'd be open to giving him a chance, but that's not what happened.

Ryan is purposely trying to scare me and make me suspicious of him. It's like he wants me to believe he's planning something. Something bad.

But why would he do that? Why is he being this way? And why is it only with me and nobody else? What is he up to?

CHAPTER 13

"Sleeping in?" Tyler asks as Derek and I come downstairs the next morning. "Or was something else going on?" He smiles.

"Stop it." I smile back. "We just wanted some extra rest."

The truth is, Derek and I did do what Tyler was implying, but he doesn't need to know that. Derek set the mood by turning on the fireplace, then he woke me with some gentle kisses that led to us doing more. Afterward, we took a long, hot shower together. It was very romantic and not something we normally do. We're always in such a rush in the morning that sometimes we don't even kiss each other goodbye before heading to work.

"You sure about that?" Tyler teases. "Because you two weren't smiling like that yesterday."

"At least someone got some," Amber mutters. She's sitting with her back to Tyler, staring out the window. They must not be getting along. I wonder if Tyler slept on the couch again.

"Would you like some coffee?" Olivia asks.

"I'd love some," I tell her.

"I'll bring it to the table. Breakfast is ready if everyone would like to sit down."

On my way to the table, I notice Ryan is already there. I feel him staring at me, but I don't look at him. I'm going to do as Derek suggested and try to ignore him.

"This looks great," Amber says as we pass the platters of food around. "You're a really good cook, Olivia."

"Thank you," she says, joining us at the table. "My mother said a wife should always know how to make a decent meal."

"That's sexist," Amber scoffs. "So James never cooks?" She glares at him.

"He will if we're grilling out."

"Why would I cook when she's better at it than me?" James says, before shoveling a forkful of eggs into his mouth.

Amber rolls her eyes. "Maybe so she wouldn't have to work herself to death."

"Let it go," Tyler says to Amber. "If it works for them, it's fine."

"Maybe it only works for them because he doesn't give her a choice."

"Amber, seriously?" Tyler looks at her. "Why do you have to turn everything into an argument?"

"I'm not arguing. I'm pointing out that it's not fair she has to do everything while he just sits around doing nothing."

"Hey," James says, his mouth full of pancakes. "I help out."

"Doing what?" Amber says. "Getting firewood? That you had delivered? You didn't even have to chop it. All you have to do is bring a few logs into the house."

"Would you stop?" Tyler sets his fork down and turns to Amber. "We're trying to have a nice meal together and you're ruining it."

"I'm ruining it by standing up for women?" She huffs. "Of course you would say that. You're a man. You hate the idea of a woman challenging the roles men put us in, like cooking all your meals and cleaning up after you."

He throws his hands up. "When have I ever asked you to make me a meal?"

"Maybe you guys could do this somewhere else," Derek says, clearing his throat. He can't stand conflict, even just watching it.

"See what you did?" Tyler says to Amber. "You're making everyone uncomfortable because you won't let this go."

"Amber, it's fine," Olivia says with a smile. "I really don't mind cooking. And James helps out in other ways."

Amber gets up to refill her coffee, shooting an angry look at Tyler. He doesn't even notice, his focus back on eating his breakfast.

"Does anyone want to see the dogs I walk?" Ryan asks, holding up his phone. It seems like an odd thing to say after what just happened, but at least it lightens the mood a little.

"That one is so sweet," Shelby says, pointing to a fluffy white dog in the photo. "The owner is this really old lady who lives next door to us. I'm thinking of doing a painting of the dog and giving it to her for Christmas."

"You really make good money doing that?" James asks Ryan. "Walking dogs?"

"Yeah, and it's easy money. I don't charge the old lady, but everyone else is willing to pay a lot to have someone walk their dog."

"Ryan and I would love to get a dog," Shelby says. "But we don't have the money right now. Maybe in a few years."

"You're going to keep living together?" I ask.

"We might as well." Shelby puts her arm around Ryan's shoulders. "We get along great, and honestly, I'd miss him if he left."

"The service up here is so slow," Tyler says, staring at his phone as Amber comes back to the table. "I was going to show you this dog I worked with on a commercial I did last year, but the website isn't coming up."

"I had the same problem," Derek says. "I couldn't even send Beth the photos from the lake."

"Oh, I finally got them," I say. "They showed up this morning."

"It's not working." Tyler swipes through his phone. "I don't think I'm getting my texts."

"Probably not," James says, helping himself to more bacon. "It's really windy today. That usually messes with the signal." He picks up his phone and swipes his fingers over the screen. "Yeah, mine's not working either."

"Maybe we should put them away," Olivia says. "We could stash them in a drawer and have a tech-free day."

"I think that's a great idea!" Shelby says. "Our phones aren't working anyway."

"I'd rather keep mine," I say. "What if there's an emergency?"

"The phones will still be here," Shelby says. "We just won't have them in our hands all day, letting them distract us." She looks at everyone around the table. "Come on, you guys. It's just one day. I went phone-free for a week last year and it was great. I've never been so relaxed."

"Here." Ryan slides his phone down the table to Olivia.

"And here's mine." Shelby puts her phone next to Ryan's.

Amber sets hers on the table. Tyler takes it and gives it to Olivia, along with his own.

"Might as well," James says. "I can go without it for a day." He hands it to Derek. "Pass it down."

I look at my husband, wanting him to back me up and agree this is a bad idea, but instead he takes his phone, and the one James gave him, and gets up from the table. He stands there, turned toward me, his hand held out.

I don't want to do this. Even if it's just for a few hours, I don't like the idea of not having my phone.

"Beth," Derek says. "Give me your phone."

"Where are you going to put them?" I ask Olivia.

She pauses a moment to think. "I have a drawer in the kitchen for odds and ends. I'll put them in there."

I guess I'm okay with that. We can all see the kitchen from the living room, and if I run upstairs for a minute, Derek can keep an eye out for anyone who might try to take our phones. I'm really only worried about Ryan. Nobody else would take them.

My gut is telling me this is a bad idea, but I feel pressured to go along with it. I'm sure it'll be fine. It's just for a few hours, and I'll make sure to keep an eye on Ryan the whole time.

"Beth, come on," Derek says, still holding out his hand.

I sigh and hand him my phone.

CHAPTER 14

"It's piling up out there," I say, noticing the snow coming down.

It's late afternoon and we've spent the day lounging around and watching movies. The fire has kept us warm while the sky outside has been dark and gloomy. It's one of those days where you feel like getting cozy under a blanket and taking a nap — which apparently is what I've been doing because I woke up to find I'd missed the end of the movie we were watching.

"It's been snowing like this for an hour," Derek says, kissing the top of my head as I lie in his arms. "You slept through it, along with most of the movie."

"We could barely hear it with your snoring," Tyler says.

I look over at him. "I don't snore."

"You did today," Amber says from her spot on the floor in front of the fire.

"Are they kidding?" I ask Derek. "Or was I really snoring?"

"Don't worry about it." He runs his hand over my hair, which is probably sticking up from me sleeping on it. "You needed your rest."

"Was I really that loud?"

"Yes," Shelby and James say at the same time.

"Sorry." I sit up. "I had no idea I snored. Why didn't someone wake me up?"

"Derek wouldn't let us," Amber says, lying down on the floor and staring up at the ceiling, seeming bored out of her mind.

I look around the room, noticing not everyone is here. "Where's Ryan?"

"Upstairs," Shelby says. "I think he's sleeping. He said he was tired."

"What about Olivia?"

"She's putting the laundry away," James says.

As he says it, Olivia comes racing down the stairs. "I should get to the store. I didn't realize how late it was."

"What do you need at the store?" James asks.

"We're running out of some things." She hurries to the closet to get her coat. "I'll just go to the local market. I won't be gone long."

"I'll take you," James says, going over to her. "You shouldn't be driving in this."

"Honey, you've been drinking. I'm not letting you drive."

"Why don't you just wait until tomorrow? We can go in the morning."

"I need some items for dinner tonight. I'll be fine. I've driven in snow before."

"Can I go?" Amber asks, getting up from the floor. "I really need to get out of here." She yawns and stretches her arms out.

"I'd prefer to go alone," Olivia says. "I'm better able to focus on the road. When other people are with me, I get distracted and worry I'll get in an accident." She slings her purse over her shoulder. "I'll see you all later."

As she leaves, I feel a chill in the air as the bitterly cold wind sneaks past her on her way out the door.

"Does your wife ever relax?" Amber asks James as she goes to the kitchen.

"No. She's always like that." He chugs his beer. "I don't mind. It means I don't have to do as much."

"Did you ever consider she might like some help?" I ask James.

"If she did, she could ask. But she doesn't, so that's on her." He gulps down what's left of his beer.

"Yes, but—"

"Beth," Derek says, giving me a look to keep quiet. I know I shouldn't interfere in James' marriage, but if he keeps acting this way, he may not have one.

"Amber, can you grab me a soda?" Tyler says to her as she opens the fridge.

"Get it yourself," she snaps.

He mutters something and shakes his head.

I glance at Derek and he gives me that look again, telling me not to say anything. I wasn't going to, but I do wonder why Tyler brought Amber on this trip. It's clear they don't get along.

Amber returns with a bag of chips and a bottle of soda.

"Can you make room?" she says to Shelby, who's seated next to Derek and me on the couch. James and Tyler are in the two chairs, leaving Amber nowhere to sit other than Tyler's lap. She was there before I fell asleep, but something must've happened because I woke up to find her on the floor.

We all move down on the couch, making a spot for Amber. It's a tight squeeze with all four of us sitting here.

"Be right back," James says, getting up. "Gotta use the bathroom."

While he's gone, Derek picks up the remote. "What does everyone want to watch next?"

"Are we really going to watch another movie?" Amber says with a sigh. "It's all we've done all day."

"What else are we going to do?" Tyler asks. "We can't go outside."

"So we're just going to sit here and watch movies until it stops snowing? And then what? We go outside? And do what?"

"Stop complaining," Tyler says. "I told you not to come. I knew you'd be bored."

So it wasn't his decision to bring her. She invited herself, but he could've told her no. I wish he had. The tension in the room rises whenever she's around, or maybe I'm just feeling that way because she knows my secret.

"I thought there'd be more to do," she says. "I didn't know we'd be so far from town. I mean, seriously, isn't anyone else wondering what we're going to do here all week?"

None of us answer, but honestly, I'm wondering that too. We've only been here a couple days and I'm already getting restless, wanting to go home. I love seeing everyone, but I don't know if I can take four more days of just sitting around, talking and watching movies.

"Anyone need another drink?" James asks from the kitchen. He's been drinking a lot more than usual.

We decline his offer and wait for him to return to his seat. He comes back with a glass of whiskey and the bottle, which is half full.

"I don't know how you do it, man," Derek says. "I'd be passed out if I drank as much as you."

James laughs. "You always were a lightweight."

"Remember when we got him drunk freshman year?" Tyler says to James. "And made him streak down the hall in the girls' dorm?"

"That was really mean," I say. "I can't believe you guys did that."

"Hey, he didn't have to agree to it," James says.

"He was drunk. He didn't know what he was doing."

"I didn't care." Derek smiles. "I got a date out of it."

Tyler laughs. "That's right. How many times did you go out with her?"

"Oh God, are you guys going to start telling stories again?" Amber leans over toward James. "Hand me the whiskey. I need it to get through this."

She takes the bottle and fills up her glass while Derek talks about his date with the girl who asked him out after he went streaking that night. I didn't know him back then. We didn't meet and start dating until sophomore year. I got to know Derek's friends, and soon we were all hanging out, pretty much all the time.

The stories continue and Amber falls asleep from boredom, or maybe it was the whiskey. Either way, it's nice to have her quiet for once.

"What time is dinner?" Ryan asks, coming down the stairs, his hair mussed like he just got out of bed.

"I don't know," James says. He checks his watch. "Shit, it's after six. Have we really been talking that long?"

"Guess so," Derek says. "Shouldn't your wife be home by now?"

"Yeah, you're right." He gets up. "I better call her."

He's on his way to the kitchen to get his phone when the front door opens and Olivia walks in, covered in snow, her face red from the cold.

James walks up to her. "What happened?"

"I got stuck on my way to the store." She yanks off her gloves. "I tried everything I could to get the truck back on the road, but I wasn't able to. So I left it there and had to walk home."

"You walked here?" I ask, getting up. "From where?"

She points outside. "Just down the road. Maybe a mile? It's probably less, but it felt like a mile having to walk in this weather."

"Why didn't you call me?" James asks.

"I didn't have my phone. I forgot I'd put it away with the others."

Ryan walks over to James. "You want me to go get the truck? I might be able to dig it out."

"No. I'll get it tomorrow. It's too dark out now, and the snow's really coming down."

"It'll be harder to get out tomorrow if it's buried in the snow," Derek says.

"I don't want you going out in this weather," Olivia says to James as she takes off her boots. "It's too dangerous. The wind is bitterly cold and the road is slippery from the ice. I'm surprised I made it back."

"Yeah, I'll wait until the morning."

I walk over to Olivia. "Could I get you something? Some hot tea?"

"No, but thank you. I think I'll go up and take a hot shower. That should warm me up."

"We'll take care of dinner," I say, not wanting her to worry about it after the ordeal she's been through. She was gone for almost two hours. She must've been scared to death being stuck out there, with no phone to call for help.

As Olivia goes upstairs, James puts on his coat.

"Where are you going?" Tyler asks.

"I'm going to walk down the road a little. See if I can see the truck. I want to know what I'm going to be dealing with tomorrow."

"I'll go with you," Tyler says, going to get his coat.

"I'll go too," Derek says.

"Are you sure?" I say. "Honey, it's dangerous being out in that cold."

"There's safety in numbers." He smiles. "And my wife is a nurse in case something happens."

I give up trying to change his mind, knowing he'll go even if I tell him not to. When he's around Tyler and James, he goes along with whatever they do and say.

"Care if I tag along?" Ryan asks.

James shrugs. "Sure. The more the merrier."

My concern over the frigid weather is replaced by panic as I think about Ryan going with them. These are the three guys who used to pick on him, exclude him, and make fun of him. What if Ryan sees this as his time to get revenge?

I calm down when I realize it's three against one, and James is much bigger and stronger than Ryan. He'd be able to fight off Ryan if he tried anything.

"Where is everyone?" Amber says, yawning as she wakes up from her nap.

"You slept through all that?" Shelby asks. "You must be a heavy sleeper."

"Why? What happened?"

"Olivia got the truck stuck in the snow somewhere along the road and had to walk back. The guys left to go see where the truck is and how bad it's stuck."

"So she never made it to the store?"

"Doesn't sound like it. I think she got stuck on her way there."

I walk over to Shelby and Amber. "Are either of you up for helping make dinner?"

"I will," Shelby says. "But I need to go up to my room first."

"Go ahead," I tell her. "I'll see what there is to make."

"I'm going back to sleep," Amber says, lying down on the couch.

Shelby goes upstairs while I look through the refrigerator for something to make.

"There's a package of chicken in there," Olivia says.

I turn around and see her dressed in jeans and a sweater, her hair wrapped in a towel.

"Oh, I wasn't going to start anything yet," I tell her. "I was just seeing what you had. You should go sit by the fire. I'm sure you're still trying to warm up after being out in the cold."

She glances at the fireplace. "It looks like we need more wood. Where did James go?"

"He and the other guys went to see if they could find the truck."

She sighs. "I wish he would've waited until morning. It's too cold to be out there, and now he's not here to get the wood."

"I could do it. It's in the shed, right?"

"Yes, but you're our guest. I can't ask you to go out there."

"Really, I don't mind."

"Are you sure?"

"Yes. You go relax. I'll be right back."

"Be sure to turn the light on. It's dark out there."

I put on my coat and boots, flip the back light on, and go out the door, the wind nearly yanking it out of my hand. Icy flakes of snow hit my face as I trudge through the backyard toward the shed. I've never liked sheds, even new ones. It's probably because I've seen too many movies where people are locked in sheds, or killed in sheds, or go into one and discover a dead body. At least Ryan isn't around. I feel safer knowing he's not here to scare me.

With the high wind, it takes a lot of effort to open the shed door. When I finally pry it open, I have a hard time seeing what's inside. The light from the house doesn't reach into the shed. If I had my phone, I'd have a flashlight. I should've brought it with me. I've played along with the no-phone experiment long enough. I want my phone back.

I step into the shed and feel around for the wood. The door behind me slams shut and I nearly jump out of my skin. I whip around, feeling for the door. I push on it, letting out a sigh of relief when it opens. For a moment, I thought someone was trying to trap me in here, but it was just the wind. It's going to keep slamming the door shut, leaving me in darkness. I need to get my phone so I'll have some light.

When I'm back in the house, I see Olivia wrapped in a blanket, sitting by the fire. Shelby is in the chair across from her, reading a book. I'm guessing Amber's still asleep on the couch, but I can't see her from here.

"Olivia, where did you put the phones?" I ask.

She looks over at me. "Are we taking them back now?"

"I am. I don't know about everyone else. I need a light so I can see in the shed."

"There's a flashlight in the mudroom. It's in the cabinet above the washer."

"I'd rather use my phone." I start opening drawers. "You put them in the kitchen, right?"

"Yes. The first drawer. To the right of where you're standing."

Opening the drawer, I see rolls of tape, some pens, a pad of paper, but no phones.

"They're not here," I say. "It must be one of the other drawers."

"No, it's the first one, where we keep pens and scratch paper."

"I just looked. They're not there."

"Are you sure?"

"Yes." I open the drawer again. "They are definitely not here."

Olivia gets up and joins me in the kitchen as I continue to search through the cabinets and drawers.

"That's odd," Olivia says, staring at the drawer she said the phones were in. "They were here the last time I looked."

"When was that?"

"This morning. When I put them here."

I look at her. "This doesn't make sense. They didn't just disappear."

"I don't know what happened." She points to the drawer. "I'm certain this is where I put them. And now they're gone."

CHAPTER 15

"There must be some kind of mix-up," I say, yanking open the drawers I just looked in. "Someone must've moved them."

"But who would do that?" Olivia asks. "There's no reason to."

"I bet Ryan did it," I say, seething with anger as I search under the sink. "He used to do stuff like this when we were in college."

"What do you mean?" Olivia asks. "What did he do?"

"He'd hide things, like our car keys or apartment keys. He did it to mess with us. He'd let us search for hours or days, and then suddenly, the keys would just appear, usually right where we'd left them." I turn around and search the cabinets near the stove.

"That sounds like a teenage prank. Ryan's a grown man now. I'm sure he didn't hide our phones."

I look at Olivia. "You don't know him like I do. Ryan isn't normal. James told you about him, right? How he spent all that time in the mental hospital? And you saw what he did with that mouse. I'm telling you, Ryan did this. He didn't want us having our phones."

"What are you guys talking about?" Shelby yells from across the room. She must've heard me say Ryan's name.

"We seem to have misplaced the phones," Olivia says.

They weren't misplaced. Ryan took them. It had to be him. Who else could it be?

Amber sits up, looking over at us from the couch. "I thought they were in the drawer."

"They were, but now they're gone," I say, continuing to search the cabinets.

"I'm sure they're around here somewhere," Olivia says. "There's no need to panic."

"Can you guys help us look?" I say to Shelby and Amber.

They get up and walk over to the kitchen.

"Maybe James moved them," Shelby says. "He was messing around in here earlier."

"Why would James move the phones?" I ask. "That doesn't make sense."

Olivia nods. "She's right. James wouldn't do that. He doesn't even look in the drawers."

"Who else was in here?" Amber asks.

"All of us were," Shelby says. "We've been in and out of here all day, getting drinks and snacks. And Beth and Derek were in here making lunch."

"Well, I certainly didn't take them," I say, halting my search as I think of where they might be. "Shelby, could you check your room?"

"My room?" She scrunches up her face. "Why would they be in there?"

I don't want to say it. I shouldn't have to. She knows her brother and the tricks he used to play on us.

"Wait, are you saying Ryan did this?" she asks, with anger in her tone.

"Shelby, you know he used to hide our things. You don't think it's possible he's doing it again?"

"He was a kid when he did that. He's grown up now. He doesn't do those things anymore."

"How do you know? He wouldn't tell you if he did."

She storms up to me. "You know, I'm really getting tired of you accusing my brother of being some kind of monster. He had some issues in the past, but who doesn't?"

"Yes, everyone has issues, but most people don't get locked away for months."

"If you knew what Ryan and I went through, how horrible our parents were, you'd understand why he ended up there. Our parents treated Ryan even worse than me. How can you not have even a little compassion for him? You're a nurse. Aren't you supposed to care about people?"

"This is getting out of hand," Olivia says, coming over to Shelby and me. "We shouldn't be making assumptions until we know what actually happened. One of the men must've moved the phones. Let's not discuss this any further until they get back."

Shelby storms off to the hall bathroom while Olivia gets the teakettle from the stove.

"They should be home soon," Olivia says, filling the teakettle with water. "I'm sure one of them will be able to straighten this out."

"There's nothing to straighten out. Ryan did this. I know he did. This is exactly the type of thing he would do."

Amber leans against the counter. "Why do you hate him so much?"

"I don't hate him. I just don't like the games he plays. Shelby thinks he's changed, but he hasn't." I point to Olivia. "She saw him squeeze the life out of a mouse."

"Seriously?" Amber looks at Olivia. "You actually saw him do it?"

"I walked in after he'd done it. The mouse was already dead."

"Did he admit to doing it?" Amber asks.

"We didn't discuss it." Olivia takes a mug from the cupboard. "Would either of you like some tea?"

"None for me," I say.

103

Amber shakes her head. "Me either."

Shelby returns, passing by the kitchen without looking at us. She sits on the couch and stares at the fire. It needs more wood, but I'm not going out to the shed without my phone.

The teakettle screeches, startling me so much that I jump.

Olivia removes it from the stove and pours the water into the mug. "I suppose we should think about starting dinner."

Dinner? How could she be thinking about dinner when our phones are missing? What if there was an emergency? What if someone was hurt or the house caught on fire? We'd have no way to call for help.

I hear the front door open and look over to see James walking in, followed by Derek and Tyler. They're covered in snow and their faces are bright red.

Olivia and I race over to them.

"James, I told you not to go out in this," Olivia says, taking his coat.

"I just wanted to see where it was," James says. "But we couldn't find it. It must be farther down the road."

"Yes, it was after the turn."

"I can't feel my face," Derek says. "It's so damn cold."

I take his coat. "You should go warm up by the fire."

"We need more wood," Olivia says to James. "Could you go out and get some?"

"Yeah, I'll go right now." He tromps through the house with his boots, leaving a trail of snow and slush on the shiny wood floors.

Olivia sees it and purses her lips, but doesn't say anything.

"Where's Ryan?" Shelby says, still seated by the fire.

Tyler looks back at the door. "Shit, I don't know. He was right behind me." Tyler opens the door. "Ryan! Get your ass in here before you freeze to death!"

He leaves the door open and Ryan comes in, a big grin on his face.

"What's so funny?" I ask, thinking the grin is because he hid our phones and finds it humorous.

"I'm not laughing," he says. "I just like the snow. I like being out in it."

"When it's ten below zero?" Tyler shakes his head. "You're nuts."

Ryan takes his boots off and shakes the snow from his hair.

"I was just about to start dinner," Olivia says, smiling at the men. "How does baked chicken sound?"

Again with the dinner. What is wrong with this woman? Why isn't she asking about the phones?

"Anything sounds good," Tyler says. "I'm starving."

"Before we worry about dinner," I say, "an issue came up that we need to discuss."

"I'll be upstairs," Ryan says, taking off.

"Ryan, wait," I tell him. "This involves you as well."

Shelby jumps up from the couch. "No. Actually it doesn't." She comes over to us. "Ryan didn't do it. How could he? He was in our room all afternoon."

That's true. He was, but he was down here for lunch. Maybe he did it then, although if he did, we would've seen him do it. I had my eye on him the whole time.

"Didn't do what?" Tyler asks. "What's going on?"

Amber saunters over. "Beth thinks Ryan took our phones."

I glare at her. Why can't she keep quiet instead of always interfering?

"I don't know who did it," I say. "But the phones are missing, so someone took them."

"Did you check the drawer?" Derek asks.

"Of course I checked the drawer! I checked every drawer and cabinet in the kitchen and they're not there!" I take a breath, hearing how loud my voice is and telling myself to calm down.

Derek places his hands on my shoulders. "I'm sure they're around here somewhere. It's okay. We'll find them."

James comes in with the wood and brings it over to the fire.

"James, did you happen to move the phones from the drawer?" Olivia asks.

"Why would I move the phones?"

"I didn't think you would, but we can't seem to find them. I thought maybe you moved them."

"Or someone else did," I mutter, glancing at Ryan.

I feel him staring at me. "Why do you think I did it, Beth?"

"I was thinking back to when you used to hide our things," I casually say, trying not to upset him. I'm worried about what he might do to me if I did. "I thought maybe you were doing it as a joke. To remind us of those times."

"Why would I do that?" He folds his arms over his chest. "I was a different person back then. A messed-up kid. I regret a lot of what I did back then, so why would I still be doing that stuff now?"

"You wouldn't," I say, sensing his anger. "I mean, unless it was a joke."

"She's lying," Amber says, rolling her eyes. "She totally thinks you did it. She was telling us all that before you got here."

My eyes dart to Amber. "Would you please stop speaking for me?"

"I'm not. I'm just repeating what you said. Tell him, Shelby."

She goes over to Ryan. "Beth doesn't want to accept that you've changed. She still thinks of you as an immature teenager, which is completely unfair." She shoots me a dirty look.

"Okay, everyone just stop for a moment," Derek says. "Let's go sit down, take a breath, and calm down."

Derek doesn't get it. This is not the time to calm down. We need to find out who has our phones and get them back.

"He's right," Olivia says, agreeing with Derek. "We should all sit down and see if we can figure this out."

Derek leads the way as we all follow behind. When we're seated, with Amber and Ryan on the floor, since there aren't enough seats, Derek begins.

"Okay, so when was the last time someone saw the phones in the drawer?" he asks.

"I don't think anyone saw them," I say. "Except whoever took them. We all just assumed they were there."

"The last time I saw them was this morning," Olivia says. "When I put them in the drawer."

"I saw them in there when we were having lunch," James says. "When I got up to get a fork. I forgot where we keep them so I opened all the drawers until I found one."

"And you saw the phones?" I ask.

"Yeah, in the first drawer."

"Has anyone seen them since lunch?" Derek asks.

Nobody answers.

"We came in here and watched movies after lunch," Tyler says. "If someone had been messing around in that drawer, we would've seen them, or heard them."

"So then it had to be after that," Derek says. "While we were out looking for the truck."

"You're saying one of us did it?" Amber says, gesturing to the women. "It wasn't me. I was asleep on the couch."

"I was next to her on the chair," Olivia says. "Trying to warm up by the fire."

"And I was upstairs," Shelby says.

"I was outside," I say. "I found out the phones were gone when I came back in the house."

"It was probably you," Amber says. "You took them, and now you're blaming us so we don't suspect you."

"If it was me, I wouldn't be upset that they're gone."

"Beth wouldn't take them," Derek says. "She hates being without her phone. I'm surprised she let me take it from her this morning."

"I shouldn't have given it to you. I knew taking the phones away was a bad idea."

"This is stupid," James says. "Whoever did it, just fess up so we can move on."

"They're not going to fess up," Shelby says. "Not when everyone's mad at them for doing it."

"Okay, how about this?" Tyler says. "Whoever took the phones puts them back in the drawer tonight after everyone's gone to sleep. In the morning, we get our phones back and we forget it ever happened."

"I'm good with that," James says.

We all agree to it, knowing we don't have a choice. The guilty person clearly isn't going to step forward.

I know it's Ryan, but what if he doesn't go along with the plan? What if he doesn't return our phones? What if he's keeping them for a reason? Like to make sure we can't call for help?

CHAPTER 16

"We're never getting out of here," I say to Derek as we get into bed that night.

"Honey, you're overreacting. Everything's going to be fine. We'll wake up tomorrow and you'll have your phone back."

"Not if it's Ryan who did this. What if he took our phones so we'd be helpless if anything happened? Like if he tried to kill us in our sleep?"

"Ryan is not going to kill us." Derek turns to face me. "If he took our phones, he did it as a joke, like when he used to take our keys."

"This isn't a joke. This is serious, Derek. We're out in the middle of nowhere with no way out."

"We have our car."

"Yes, but we can't get to the main road with James' truck in the way."

"We don't know if it's blocking the entire road. And tomorrow I'll help James get it out of the way." Derek kisses my cheek. "Try to get some sleep." He rolls onto his side. "Goodnight. Love you."

I stare up at the ceiling. "We shouldn't have come here. I had a feeling something bad would happen."

"Nothing bad has happened. Everything's going to be fine. Stop thinking about your phone and go to sleep."

Several hours go by before I finally drift off.

When I wake up the next morning, I don't feel any better. I almost feel worse knowing I'm going to go downstairs and our phones will still be missing.

"You up?" Derek asks, turning toward me.

"Yes. I didn't get much sleep."

"I slept great." He kisses me, lingering at my lips as his hand slides down to my chest.

"Derek, no." I push him away. "I'm not in the mood."

"Beth, come on. We're on vacation. We don't have to rush off anywhere." He pulls me toward him and kisses the side of my neck.

My body stiffens. "Derek, I said no." I sit up. "I can't believe you'd even want to after everything that happened last night."

"Nothing happened," he says with a frustrated sigh as he lies on his back. "It was just a stupid joke. Why are you letting it ruin everything?"

"Because it isn't a joke. This is serious. We need our phones. It's the only way to call for help."

"We could use the computer. James has his laptop. We could use it to email or send a text. We could even use it to make a call."

"I hadn't thought about that. I guess that makes me feel a little better. We should've brought ours."

"I was going to, but James said the internet doesn't always work up here. I told him he needs to get a satellite connection. That tends to work better in the mountains."

I check the time. "It's after nine. Everyone's probably up. Let's go see if our phones are back."

"Aren't you going to get dressed?" he asks as I head to the door. "I can see right through that shirt."

It's an old T-shirt I wear to bed. I've washed it so many times, it's almost see-through by now.

"Fine, I'll put something on." I go to the dresser and pull out some clothes. "Derek, come on. Get up."

He yawns and takes his time getting out of bed. I toss some clothes at him.

"What's the rush?" he asks.

"I need to know if they're back. I won't relax until I have my phone again."

I'm dressed now and waiting impatiently for Derek to put on his jeans and sweatshirt.

"Okay, let's go," he says, opening the door for me.

When we get downstairs, Olivia is in the kitchen making breakfast.

"Are the phones back?" I ask, racing over to the drawer.

"I'm afraid not," she says as I open the drawer, feeling sick to my stomach when I confirm that the phones aren't there.

"Maybe they're somewhere else," Derek says, looking around the room. "Have you checked?"

"James did," Olivia says. "He checked everywhere he could think of, except the bedrooms, of course."

"That has to be where they are," I say. "Whoever has them is hiding them in their room."

"Where is everyone?" Derek asks. "Usually everyone's down here by now."

"They must be sleeping in," Olivia says, putting bread in the toaster. "Maybe I shouldn't be making all this food if no one is going to show up."

"I'll have some," Derek says. "I'm starving."

How can he have an appetite at a time like this? Whoever has our phones took them for a reason. They're obviously planning something, and they want to make sure we can't call for help. How is Derek not seeing this? I used to admire my husband for his calm, reasonable nature, but right now, it's making me furious.

"Where's James?" I ask Olivia.

"Out in the shed, getting whatever it is he needs for ice-fishing." She takes the butter and jam from the fridge. "He plans to go to the lake today and get everything set up for whoever wants to join him."

"I'm in," Derek says, filling a mug with coffee.

I stare at him like he's crazy. "You're going ice-fishing?"

"Sure. Why not?" He glances out the window. "Looks like the snow has stopped."

I walk up to him. "Someone took our phones and isn't giving them back. That's not a concern to you?"

"I still think it's a prank. Or maybe James did it, to force us to spend time together instead of being on our phones. That is why we're here, after all."

"That doesn't sound like something James would do. He wouldn't care if we had our phones." I pause a moment to think. "But Shelby would. She's all about being in the moment. Connecting with others. And she's the one that got us all to go along with it."

"Well, there you go," Derek says. "This is just Shelby being Shelby. Wanting us to be present with each other instead of distracted by our phones. It makes sense. She's always been that way. Remember when she'd try to make us draw our feelings?" He laughs. "It was so stupid. And then James actually did it because he had a crush on her." Derek realizes what he said and his eyes dart to Olivia. "That was a long time ago. He obviously doesn't feel that way now."

James had a crush on Shelby? I never knew that. But I also didn't know he'd slept with her in college until Shelby told me the other day. I'm sure Derek knew about that, so why didn't he ever tell me? What else hasn't he told me?

"How exactly do you draw your feelings?" Olivia asks, setting the toasted bread on a plate.

"According to Shelby," Derek says, "feelings have shapes and colors. You're supposed to draw whatever comes to mind when you're having the feeling."

"And why would you do this?" Olivia asks as she adds more bread to the toaster.

"You're supposed to do it when you can't verbalize your feelings. Again, this is Shelby's reasoning, not mine. She said if you don't express emotions, especially negative ones, they get stuck in your body and cause problems. So you have to get them out somehow."

Olivia smiles. "That's an interesting theory, although I don't believe psychology experts would agree with her."

"My point is, Shelby does stuff she thinks is helpful, not considering that others don't want to go along with it. Even if they tell her that, she'll do it because she thinks it's for their own good. Beth, remember when she was putting that supplement into Tyler's drinks without telling him?"

I nod. "That's right. He kept saying his soda tasted off, but none of us knew what he meant."

Olivia's brows rise. "She drugged his soda?"

"It wasn't a drug," I explain. "It was an herbal supplement. A powder you mix into drinks. The herbs were supposed to help you relax. She gave them to Tyler so he'd relax before an audition. He used to get really nervous before auditions. But whatever she gave him didn't work."

"And when he caught her stirring that stuff into his drink," Derek says, "he was furious. He didn't speak to her for a couple weeks."

"Which didn't bother her," I add. "Because she insisted she did it to help him, and that it would've worked if he hadn't blocked its effects with anger."

Derek laughs. "That's right. She tried to get him to draw his anger, but he wouldn't do it."

"Given what you've told me," Olivia says, "it sounds like she might be the one who took the phones. Not to harm us in any way, but to bring us all together. Like you said, she probably believes she's doing this for our own good."

"Yeah, I bet it's her," Derek says. "She knows this will probably be our last trip together, at least for a while, so she wants us to make the most of it."

"Then she needs to tell us that," I say. "She needs to let us know she has the phones so we can all stop worrying."

Derek sips his coffee, then says, "She's not going to admit she has them. If she did, she'd have to give them back, ruining her plan to make us all be in the moment or bonding or whatever."

"She doesn't get to decide that without input from the rest of us. We let her have a day without our phones, but now it's over. We're not doing this for the rest of the week."

Olivia continues making breakfast while Derek goes to refill his coffee. They don't seem the least bit concerned about the missing phones. Even if Shelby has them hidden in her room, I still don't feel safe not having mine with me. Why am I the only one who feels this way?

CHAPTER 17

"If Shelby has my phone," I say, "I'm making her give it back as soon as she gets down here."

"Honey, come on," Derek says. "Do you really need it? Isn't it kind of nice not always having to check it?"

I put my hands on my hips, eyeing him with suspicion. "You know, the way you keep making light of this makes me think *you* might be the one who took them."

He laughs. "That's ridiculous. I think your lack of sleep is affecting your judgment."

"You didn't sleep?" Olivia says as she transfers the scrambled eggs from the skillet to a platter.

"No, I was up for most of the night."

"I'm sorry to hear that. I always sleep amazingly well when we're here. I think it's because it's so quiet, and so dark without any streetlights shining through the windows."

We hear the back door open and the stomping of boots, then the sound of them being tossed on the floor.

James appears, a big grin on his face when he sees us. "Derek, what do you think about ice-fishing today?"

"Sounds great. How cold is it? Did it warm up at all?"

"Not really, but the wind died down so it feels warmer. I was thinking we could go to the lake after breakfast and get everything set up."

"I'm up for that."

"What about the truck?" I ask. "I thought you were going to go get it."

"That can wait until later," James says, getting himself a cup of coffee.

"But what if we need to leave?"

James looks at Derek. "You guys are leaving?"

"No. Beth just means if any of us had to go into town, we need to be able to get to the main road."

"Even with the truck out of the way, you won't be able to get there until the plow comes," James says. "And it probably won't come today. They'll be too busy doing the main roads."

"But that's not safe," I say. "What if you have to get out for an emergency?"

"That's why I have the truck. It can get through anything."

"And yet it's stuck," I point out.

James chuckles. "Yeah, ironic, huh?"

Why isn't anyone taking this seriously? What if one of us gets hurt and needs medical care? Being a nurse, I'm more concerned about these things than others, knowing what can happen if medical care isn't given within a certain amount of time, but I would think at least someone here would be worried that we can't get to the road.

"Beth is right," Derek says to James, finally sticking up for me. "We should go see what happened to the truck and try to get it out of the way."

"Olivia," James says as she arranges the food on the table. "Is it the back tires that are stuck or the front?"

"I think it's both, but I really don't know," she says, setting napkins beside each of the plates. "The wind was blowing the snow around so much that I couldn't really see."

"What exactly happened?" Derek asks Olivia.

"I hit a slick spot, and before I knew what was happening, the truck spun to the side." She walks back to the kitchen. "I panicked and slammed on the brakes, not wanting it to slide off the road. Luckily, it didn't, but then when I tried to turn it so it was back facing the road, I couldn't. It was stuck."

"Stuck on the road?" Derek asks. "I'm not picturing this."

"It's perpendicular to the road," Olivia explains. "So yes, it's positioned so that no one can get past it."

"Unless they drove around it through the snow," I say.

"I wouldn't even try doing that," Derek says. "The snow is too deep. There's no way our car would get by there without getting stuck."

"Which is why we can't leave the truck there," I say. "We need to be able to get to the main road."

"We'll go shovel it out," James says. "Once it's turned around, we'll be able to get it back here so we can use it if we need to."

"You should really attach a plow to it," I say. "Living out here, you need it."

"We're going to," James says. "We just haven't gotten around to it yet."

Why in the world would they wait to do that? They're in the mountains. In the winter. Living miles away from the main road. Putting a plow on the truck would've been the first thing I did before coming here.

"Hey," Tyler says, coming down the stairs with Amber following behind. I guess that means they shared a bedroom last night. "Why didn't anyone wake us up?"

"There's no set schedule." Olivia smiles at them. "You can sleep as late as you'd like. Would you like some coffee?"

"Yes." Amber groans. "My head is killing me."

"Are you regretting that whiskey?" Derek jokes.

"Today I am," she says. "Yesterday I loved it."

James chuckles. "Funny how that works."

"Everything is ready if you'd like to eat," Olivia says.

We all sit down at the table, except for Olivia, who's racing around the kitchen. She hardly ever sits down. I keep offering to help, but she keeps turning me down. She seems like someone who likes things done a certain way. It's probably easier for her to just do it her way than try to explain how she wants it done. I bet she'll be glad when we leave so she can finally relax.

"Did we get our phones?" Tyler asks, scooping some scrambled eggs onto his plate.

"No," I say, "but we might have figured out who has them."

"Yeah. So who is it?"

"We think it might be Shelby," Derek says. "We think she wants us to be together without being distracted by our phones. We were remembering how she used to do all that stuff to supposedly help us, but it really just annoyed us."

"Like when she put that stuff in your soda," I say.

"Shit, that's right." Tyler shakes his head. "I was so mad when she did that."

"What'd she put in your soda?" Amber asks.

Tyler tells her the story, then says, "You guys are right. It was totally Shelby. And she's not going to fess up until the week is over, after we've had whatever so-called bonding time she thinks we should be having."

"Why does she get to decide this?" Amber says, gnawing on a piece of dry toast.

"She doesn't," I say. "She's giving them back. I'm not going all week without my phone."

"I thought Shelby was done doing stuff like this," Tyler says. "She knows we all hate it."

"Her intentions are good," Derek says. "I think she's worried this will be the last time we're all together like this, so she doesn't want us wasting time on our phones."

"Do you really think this will be the last time we do this?" Tyler asks.

Derek shrugs. "I don't know. I guess it depends. I mean, you could have a job in LA next year and not be able to come out."

"I wish," Tyler mutters.

"And everyone knows Beth and I are trying to start a family," Derek says. "If all goes well, we'll have a baby by next year."

I glance at James, thinking he'll mention that he and Olivia also hope to have a baby by next year, but he doesn't speak up.

"We can still get together like this," Derek says. "Just not every year."

"I'm honestly surprised we've kept it going this long," Tyler says. "Even though we said we'd do this, I didn't think it'd actually happen."

"I'm going to do all I can to make sure we keep doing these trips," James says. "It's hard to find friends like you guys. That's not something you just give up."

Olivia comes over with the coffee pot. "Would anyone like some more?"

"Yes, please." Amber weakly holds up her mug.

"Why don't you go lie down?" Tyler says to her.

"I just got up. I'll be fine. I just have to keep drinking coffee."

"So what are we doing today?" Tyler asks.

James grins, a gleam in his eyes. "Ice-fishing. I can't wait to get out there. I got the stuff all set out. We just need to bring it down to the lake."

"But first, he's going to get the truck," I remind James.

"That shouldn't take long," he says. "We just need to shovel around the tires."

"I can help with that," Tyler says.

"Good morning," I hear Shelby say.

We all watch as she comes down the stairs, dressed in black leggings and a long knitted sweater.

"Good morning." Olivia smiles at her. "Can I get you some coffee?"

"Not today. I think I'll make some tea."

"I can make it for you. Go ahead and have a seat."

As Shelby sits at the table, Ryan hurries down the stairs.

"We didn't know it was so late," he says, bumping the table as he sits down. "I guess we were tired."

"I slept great," Shelby says, taking a piece of toast. "It's the clean mountain air. I'm convinced it makes me sleep better."

Nobody says anything. I'm not sure how to bring up the phones to Shelby. I don't want to harm our friendship, but I don't know how to say this in a nice way when I'm angry at her for not giving us the phones back.

"Why is everyone so quiet?" she asks.

"They want their phones," Amber says, before stuffing more toast in her mouth.

I should've known Amber would blurt that out. She has no filter, and no sense of timing when it comes to bringing up difficult topics.

"They're not back?" Shelby asks.

"No," I say, hoping she'll fess up. "They weren't in the drawer."

"So what are we going to do? Obviously, someone has them."

The table is silent, then Amber says, "Are you really not getting this? They think it was you. They think you took the phones."

"Me?" Shelby laughs. "Why would I take the phones?"

"Because you don't want us being distracted by them," Derek says. "You want us to make the most of this week and you're worried we won't if all we do is stare at our phones."

"I wasn't even thinking about that. And I promise, I did not take them."

"Shelby, come on," I say. "It's fine if you took the phones. We'll forget it even happened. We just want them back."

"I don't have them." Her eyes bounce around the table. "You all really think I did this?"

120

"You had a chance to," Amber says. "Yesterday. When I was asleep and everyone was gone."

"Maybe you did it," Shelby says to Amber. "Maybe you were pretending to sleep and took them when I was in the bathroom."

"Yeah, okay," Amber says, rolling her eyes.

"This is ridiculous," I say, getting angry. "Shelby, just give us the phones."

"I don't have them!" she says, raising her voice.

"If you don't believe her, go check our room," Ryan says. "But you're not going to find them."

"Then where are they?" I ask Ryan. "Where did you hide them?"

"He didn't," Shelby says, glaring at me. "And stop accusing my brother. He wasn't even here when they disappeared."

"We're not getting anywhere with this," James says. "We're just talking in circles. Whoever has the phones will put them back eventually. Until then, I'm not going to worry about it." He gets up. "Derek? Tyler? You ready? Let's go dig out the truck."

"You need me to help?" Ryan asks.

"If you could, then yeah," James says.

"I'm going back to bed," Amber mumbles, pushing away from the table.

Shelby gets up. "I'll be in my room."

She sounds angry, and she won't even look at me.

Derek quickly finishes his eggs and swigs his coffee. "I'll see you later." He kisses my cheek, then whispers in my ear, "Everything will be fine. Stop worrying."

As I watch him go to get his coat, I start to wonder if he knows something I don't. Why else would he not seem to care about this? Does he know who has the phones, and isn't telling me? He wouldn't do that, would he?

CHAPTER 18

"We're back," Derek announces, coming into the house. The other guys follow behind, their boots covered in snow.

They were gone for over an hour. During that time, I helped Olivia clean up breakfast, then she went upstairs to rest while I sat on the couch, looking out the window at the gently falling snow. I was hoping I'd find it soothing, but it just made me more anxious, worried the snow will make it harder to get out of here.

"So the truck is back?" I ask, going over to them.

"No," James says, pulling off his stocking cap. "I think we might need a tow truck to get it moved. And the battery is almost dead. I need to charge it."

"We can't call for a tow truck until we get the phones back," I say, glancing at Ryan.

"Shelby doesn't have them," Ryan says. "Go ahead and search our room if you don't believe me."

"We'll use the laptop," Derek says, taking off his coat. "We can use that to call for a tow."

"We can try," James says. "But it wasn't working last night. I couldn't get a connection."

"You may need to restart your router, especially after a storm."

"It's behind the TV if you want to try."

Derek walks over to the flat-screen TV and pushes it out from the wall so he can get behind it. "You said behind the TV, right?"

"Yeah, on the shelf," James says.

"I don't see it."

"What do you mean? It's right there." James walks over to Derek and looks behind the TV. "What the hell? Where is it?"

"Did you move it?" I ask, walking over to them. "Or maybe Olivia did."

"She wouldn't move it," James says. "She doesn't like dealing with tech stuff. She makes me handle it."

"Then where is it?" Derek pushes the TV farther out from the wall so he can get a better look. "It's definitely not here."

"It was there yesterday," Tyler says, joining us in the living room. "We streamed movies all day."

Derek pushes the TV back in place. "So the router was here yesterday and now it's gone."

"Someone took it," I say, feeling sick as I realize what's happening. "They didn't want us using the laptop to get help or send any kind of message. If something happens, we're—"

"Honey, calm down." Derek pulls me into his arms. "This doesn't mean anything. It's probably just a prank."

"And I think we can all guess who's behind it." I pull away from Derek and look at Ryan, who's in the kitchen getting a glass of water. "There's only one person here who likes hiding things, but he won't admit that he did it."

"God, let it go," Ryan says. "I was a teenager when I did that. Teenagers do stuff like that all the time."

I glare at him. "Then tell me, Ryan, who do you think did this?"

He shrugs. "I have no idea. Maybe Tyler's new girlfriend. She seems to like stirring up trouble."

I hate to admit it, but he does have a point. We really know nothing about Amber, and she does like causing trouble.

"How well do you know her?" I ask Tyler. "I mean, obviously you're dating her, but it hasn't been long, right? Didn't you say a couple months?"

"More like a month and a half." He sits down on the chair. "I wouldn't say I know her well. We don't talk much. We're both busy with work so I usually only see her a couple times a week, more if she's on a shoot with me, but that's only happened once since we started dating."

"Don't take this the wrong way," Derek says, "but why are you dating her? She doesn't seem like your type."

Tyler glances at the stairs, making sure Amber isn't there. "She knows the casting agent for this movie I'm trying to get. I know it's wrong, but hey, that's how this business works. It's all about who you know, and people have done a lot worse than date someone to get a job. I don't know if I'll get it, but I'll at least get an audition."

"So you're using her," I say.

"Yeah, but like I said, this happens all the time in entertainment. And she's using me too. She's hoping my connections will get her more jobs."

"I knew you two weren't really dating," James says. "I couldn't see you with someone like her."

"Why'd you bring her here?" Derek asks.

"Because she wanted to come. She said she needed a break from the city. I wanted to tell her no, but I didn't want her getting mad and telling her friend to cancel my audition." He rubs his jaw. "I need to get some real work or I can't keep doing this. I've been trying for ten years and all I've had are commercials and a couple side gigs on TV shows nobody watches. I've started writing screenplays, in case the acting thing doesn't work out."

I sit on the couch, turned toward Tyler. "Do you think Amber would do this? Take our phones and the router?"

"It's possible. She likes creating drama, and this has definitely caused drama in the house."

"Would you talk to her? See if you can get her to admit she did it?"

"I can try."

"Go do it right now. She's upstairs."

"I can't do it when she's hungover. When she doesn't feel well, she gets angry. Every little thing sets her off. I'll talk to her tonight, when she's feeling better."

Ryan joins us, sitting on the couch and picking up the TV remote.

"You can't use it," James says. "We can't stream anything without the router."

"Yeah, I forgot." He sets the remote down.

Shelby comes down the stairs, not looking at us as she heads to the kitchen.

"Still mad at us?" James says, smiling at her.

"Only if you're still accusing me," she says, filling a glass with water.

"Now they think it's Amber," Ryan says. "Tyler's going to talk to her tonight."

Shelby comes over to us, holding her glass of water. "You guys think Amber did it?"

"She's not part of our group," James says. "I could see her doing it, just to mess with us or ruin our week."

"Yeah, I could see that. She doesn't seem to like any of us, except maybe Derek." Shelby takes a drink of her water.

"Yeah, what's going on there?" James asks Derek. "Why is she nice to you and nobody else?"

"She's not," he insists.

"She's always sticking up for you," James says. "Taking your side."

Tyler looks at Derek with suspicion. "He's right. She's nicer to you than she is to me."

It's because Amber feels sorry for Derek for marrying a woman who cheated on him and never told him. But that's none of her business. She needs to stay out of it. It happened years ago. Derek and I weren't even married.

"What are you guys talking about?" Amber asks, coming down the stairs. She looks better than she did at breakfast. She fixed her hair, put makeup on, and has changed out of her sweats and put on jeans and a sweater.

"The router's missing," James says. "We can't watch anything on TV."

"You don't have cable?" she asks.

"No, we're never here. This is a vacation home."

"Yeah, I guess." She sits down on Tyler's lap and I notice him tense up. "Hey, babe. You get the truck out?"

"No. It's still stuck. We need to call a tow truck, but we can't because someone has our phones." He gives her a look like he's urging her to confess.

"This is so dumb." She rolls her eyes. "I feel like I'm back in high school. This girl at cheerleading camp stole our phones and wouldn't give them back until the end of camp."

"Why'd she do it?" I ask.

"She didn't want us taking pictures of her because she thought she looked fat." Amber laughs. "A few weeks later, she found out she wasn't fat. She was pregnant."

Olivia comes downstairs, smiling at James. "You're back."

"Yeah, but we didn't get the truck. I'll have to call for a tow."

"Oh." She walks over to him. "I was really hoping to get to town today. We're running low on groceries."

"You hear that?" James says to us in a stern tone. "Everyone should eat less." He laughs, but I don't find it funny.

What if we don't get our phones back? How will we get out of here? Maybe the plow will come by and the driver will call a tow truck to get the truck out of the way. Or it's possible he'd turn around, deciding to let the truck owner deal with it. That's the more likely scenario.

"Who's up for some ice-fishing?" James asks.

"I'm in," Derek says.

I am so frustrated with him. How can Derek just continue on as if nothing has happened?

"I'll give it a try," Tyler says. "But I need to change my socks. They got wet trying to dig out the truck."

"What am I going to do?" Amber says to Tyler as he moves her off him and gets up. "There's no TV. And I don't have my phone."

"Maybe you could look for it," he says, sounding annoyed. "Our phones are around here somewhere."

She doesn't say anything.

Tyler goes upstairs with Derek. I follow behind, going into our room just as Derek was about to close the door.

"What are you doing?" he asks.

"You're seriously going fishing?"

"Yeah. Why?"

"Why?" I stare at him. "Are you kidding? We're stranded here with no way out and no way to call for help."

"Beth, there's nothing I can do about that. Do you expect me to just sit here and worry all day? I only get two weeks off a year and this is one of them. I'm not going to waste it sitting in this room, staring at the wall." He goes to the dresser and takes out a sweater. He puts it on, then walks back to me and gives me a kiss. "You sure you don't want to try ice-fishing?"

"Positive." I sigh, frustrated with him for not taking this seriously.

"Honey, come on." He rubs my arm. "Try to make the best of it. Maybe go talk to Shelby. She doesn't seem mad at you anymore. Or talk to Olivia. She seems nice. Have you two talked much?"

"We have a little. She's nice, but she's very proper. Sometimes I feel like she's judging me."

"Judging you for what?"

"For not being as sophisticated as her. Did you see the look she gave me when I didn't know the designer she was talking about?"

"No. I didn't notice."

"Maybe you weren't there. It was the other day, probably when you were at the lake. Anyway, she was telling me about a purse she bought from some designer and I had no idea who she was talking about. She gave me this look like I was stupid for not knowing."

"I think you're reading too much into it." He kisses me. "I need to go. They're probably waiting for me. Call me if you—" He stops, realizing I can't call him. "I'll see you later."

He goes out to the hall and I hear him talking to Tyler as they go downstairs.

Realizing I didn't shower this morning, I go into the bathroom and take a long, leisurely one. I get dressed, then take my time doing my hair and makeup, figuring I have nothing else to do.

Just before noon, I decide to go help Olivia with lunch. I assume she started making it. The guys should be back soon.

"Hey, Beth," Ryan says as I'm leaving my room.

"Ryan." I turn to him. "I was just going downstairs. Do you know if the guys are back?"

"They're not." He smiles a little. "I hope nothing happened to them."

My pulse speeds up. "Why would you say that? Did you do something?"

"Like what?" He smirks.

I don't answer, furious that he thinks this is funny.

"I'm going downstairs," I say, annoyed with myself for letting him get to me.

"Beth. Before you go . . ."

"What?" I snap.

He grabs my arm, leans down to my ear, and whispers, "I know who has your phone. You're not getting it back. And you're not getting out of here . . ." He pauses. "Alive."

CHAPTER 19

I yank away from Ryan. "Is this some kind of joke? Do you think this is funny?"

He doesn't answer me. He just smiles, then walks down to his room.

He's joking. He has to be. He's just trying to scare me like he did when we were younger. But I'm older now and not putting up with it.

I storm down to his room and knock on the door. "Ryan, open the door!"

He doesn't, so I knock again, then try the handle. It's locked.

"Tell me why you're doing this," I say. "If it's a joke, it's really immature. You said you'd changed, but clearly you haven't."

There's silence on the other side of the door. I don't even hear footsteps.

"Ryan, please give us back the phones. I promise I won't tell anyone you took them. Just leave them in the drawer tonight."

"What's going on?" I hear Shelby say. I look down the hall and see her coming toward me.

I point to her room. "Ryan's in there. He has the phones and he said he's not giving them back."

"He told you he has the phones?" she asks with concern.

"Well, no, he said he knows who has them, but I'm assuming he's referring to himself."

129

She shakes her head. "He doesn't have them. I talked to him last night. He promised me he didn't take them."

"He was lying."

"He wasn't. I can tell when he's lying. He doesn't have the phones. I even searched our room and didn't find anything."

"Then why did he say that to me?"

She folds her arms over her chest. "Are you sure that's what he said, or are you twisting his words to make him look bad?"

"Shelby, I am not trying to make him look bad. I'm just trying to get our phones back. I need to find out who has them."

"Yeah, well, it isn't Ryan, and if you don't stop accusing him, I don't think we can stay friends."

"Shelby, I—"

"Ryan, open the door." She jiggles the handle.

The door opens and she sneaks inside. Then it slams shut and I hear the lock turn.

I've always thought I could trust Shelby, but I don't anymore. She'll do anything for Ryan, including lie to cover up what he did. I didn't even tell her what he said about me not leaving here alive. If I had, I'm sure she would've either denied he said it or told me he was joking.

I go back to my room and lock the door, deciding I'm not coming out until Derek is back. I get into bed and pull the covers over me, feeling a chill in the air I didn't feel a few minutes ago.

What if Ryan wasn't joking? What if he really does plan to kill me? Or all of us?

There's a knock on the door. "Beth? Can you let me in?"

It's Derek.

I throw off the covers and race to the door.

"Get in," I say as I open the door. "Hurry up!"

When he's in the room, I shut the door and lock it.

"What's going on?" he asks.

"Ryan told me he knows who has the phones and that we're not getting them back. And then he said I'm not getting out of here alive."

"When did he tell you this?" Derek asks as he takes off his sweater.

"A few minutes ago. I was leaving our room to go downstairs and he stopped me in the hall."

"Did anyone else hear him say this?"

"No, it was just him and me."

Derek brings his sweater to the dresser and puts it in the drawer. I thought he'd be as upset as I am, but instead he's his usual calm self.

"Derek, we have to get out of here! Before something happens!"

He walks back to me. "Honey, nothing's going to happen. Ryan was just messing with you. He obviously hasn't matured as much as we thought."

"He wasn't joking. He was serious. It had to be him who took the phones and the router. He probably drained the battery in the truck too."

"That was Olivia's fault. She told James she thinks she left the overhead light on when she got out of the truck."

"Okay, fine, but Ryan definitely took the phones and he's not giving them back."

"He wasn't even here when they went missing."

"Yeah, so maybe he had Shelby do it for him. I don't know how it happened, but he clearly did it. Why else would he stop me in the hall and say he knows who has the phones?"

"Maybe because he knows how upset you are that they're missing, so he said something that would make you even more upset. I'm telling you, Beth, if you weren't getting so worked up about this, Ryan would leave you alone. He gets off on scaring people. Or he did when he was younger, but he clearly still does."

"Why do you keep dismissing me? This is serious, Derek! I'm not overreacting. We're not safe with Ryan here."

Derek puts his hand on my shoulder. "If Ryan tries anything, I'll protect you, but I really don't think he will." He kisses my cheek. "Let's go downstairs. Lunch is going to be ready in a few minutes."

"I'm not hungry."

"I am. I'm starving. If you don't want to eat, at least come down with me. You'll feel better being with the group than up here alone in the room."

He's right. Even with the door locked, I don't feel safe here alone.

When we get downstairs, James, Tyler, and Amber are sitting down at the table.

"Did you tell Beth what you caught?" James says as Derek and I take our seats.

"No, we were talking about something else." Derek helps himself to the casserole Olivia made. It looks wonderful, but I feel too sick to eat.

"He thought he caught a fish," James says to me. "But when he pulled it up, it was a shoe."

Tyler laughs. "You should've seen his face. He was so disappointed."

"This casserole is really good," Amber says to Olivia.

"Thank you." Olivia smiles at her. "Does anyone know if Shelby and Ryan will be joining us?"

Derek glances at me. "I don't know. They're in their room."

"Beth, aren't you going to eat?" Olivia asks.

"I'm not hungry."

Olivia looks down the table at James. "Honey, I really need to get to town to get groceries. Is there any way you could get the truck working again?"

"Yeah, if I had my phone." His eyes dart to Amber. "Hey, Amber, any idea where the phones are?"

She looks over at him. "Why are you asking *me?*"

He shrugs. "You were here when they disappeared."

"Oh, so you think I did it?"

He doesn't answer.

She turns to Tyler. "Do you hear this? Why aren't you sticking up for me?"

He pauses, looking like he's unsure what to say.

"Great. So now you're believing your friends over me?" Amber shoots up from the table. "I'm done. This whole trip has been a disaster!"

"Amber, wait!" Tyler says.

She ignores him and races up the stairs.

Tyler looks at James. "Why the hell did you say that? I told you I'd talk to her later."

"I didn't want to wait," James says. "I'm tired of this shit. We need the phones back. We're running out of food. Everyone's fighting. This has to end."

"I agree," Tyler says. "But accusing people isn't going to bring our phones back."

"Let's do a search of the house," Derek says. "After lunch, let's search every possible place they could be, including everyone's room."

"That's a good idea," Olivia says. "They have to be here somewhere, and if we all spend time looking, we're bound to find them."

"What if someone won't allow us to search their room?" I ask, the someone I'm referring to being Shelby and Ryan.

"It's my house," James says. "I can go in any room I want."

After lunch, we scour every inch of the house. I stay downstairs with Derek and Tyler. James and Olivia search the upstairs. I was certain the phones would turn up, but after an hour of looking, nobody can find them.

* * *

At dinner, I can feel the mood has shifted. People are no longer thinking the missing phones are some kind of prank, but are realizing we might never get them back, and wondering what that will mean for our chances of getting out of here.

"Ryan was right," I say to Derek when we're in bed later. "We're not getting out of here alive."

"Beth, you're—"

"No. Don't say I'm overreacting. I can feel it. Something bad's about to happen. And I'm not the only one who thinks this. When I was helping Olivia clean up dinner, she admitted that she and James are worried too. They've been trying to act normal to keep us from panicking, but she told James she can't do it anymore. She can't keep pretending everything's fine when it's not."

"I'll talk to James tomorrow. Maybe I could drive our car down to the truck and try to jumpstart it. I'm sure the battery's completely dead by now."

"Our car will never make it. There's probably a foot of snow on the road from the storm last weekend."

"Then we'll have to shovel our way out."

"That would take days. You can't be out there long when it's this cold outside."

"We'll figure something out." He gives me a kiss. "Try to get some sleep."

Hours pass before I finally doze off.

I wake up when I hear a noise. It sounds like people arguing.

"Derek." I push on his shoulder. "Derek, wake up."

"What?" he asks, sounding groggy. "What's wrong?"

"Listen."

He sighs. "I don't hear anything."

"Just wait."

The voices start up again, coming from the room next to ours. "I never said that! I never accused you of taking the phones!"

"Then why didn't you stick up for me?"

"It's just Tyler fighting with Amber," Derek says. "Go back to sleep. I'm sure they'll quiet down soon."

Tyler's talking again, his voice getting louder. "What do you want me to do? We're stuck here. We can't leave."

"We haven't even tried," Amber says. "Let's just get in the car and go."

"Are you insane? Have you seen how high the snow is out there? We have a rental car. A cheap one. There's no way it's getting through that snow. I'm not talking about this. Just go back to bed."

"I'm going downstairs. I can't be near you right now." I hear one of them stomping around the floor, then the door opening. "Oh, and forget your stupid audition! When we get out of here, I'm calling my friend and telling her to cancel it!"

"Amber, no." I hear Tyler race to the door. "I'm sorry, okay? You were right. I should've stuck up for you about the phone thing."

"Too late. This is over. It never should've started. I thought we could help each other out, but you're the only one benefitting. Those connections you claimed to have? I called them. They don't even know who you are."

"That's a lie. I've worked with everyone on that list."

"Yeah, and they forgot about you. Because you're forgettable. And a horrible actor. You might as well quit and do something else."

"You know what?" I hear him stomp around, then stop. "Go ahead. Cancel the audition. I don't need this bullshit. Just go. Get out of here." The door shuts and I hear Amber storming down the hall.

"I figured they'd break up this week," Derek says. "All they do is fight."

"I can't believe she said he was a horrible actor."

"Well, to be honest, he really isn't very good. It's his looks that get him jobs." Derek turns on his side. "Goodnight."

Checking the clock, I see it's two in the morning. I've had less than an hour of sleep. Another hour passes before I drift off again.

* * *

In the morning, Derek and I shower and get dressed before going downstairs for breakfast. Everyone's already at the table except Tyler and Amber.

"Good morning," Olivia says to us, but it's not her usual upbeat tone and she's not smiling.

"Good morning," I mutter as we join them at the table.

Shelby and Ryan don't even acknowledge us. James is staring down at the table as he mindlessly shovels food into his mouth.

The mood has definitely shifted. It seems even darker than last night. The sky is dark too, making it feel like it's evening instead of nine in the morning.

It's Wednesday and we're supposed to head home on Saturday. I'm supposed to start my new job on Monday and Derek has to be back at work. If we don't show up, will someone look for us? Both our families have moved out of the area and we don't talk to them as often as we should. If they don't hear from us, they just assume we're busy and don't have time to call. Weeks could go by before they'd get worried.

"It's getting chilly in here," Olivia says. "James, would you mind adding some wood to the fire?"

He doesn't respond. I don't think he heard her.

"James?" she says.

This time he hears her and looks up. "Yeah?"

"The fire. Could you add some wood to it before it burns out?"

"Yeah, okay." He sets his fork down and pushes his chair back. "Looks like we're out. I'll have to go to the shed."

"I forgot to get your coffee," Olivia says to Derek and me as she gets up from the table. Her mind is definitely elsewhere today. She's always quick to give us coffee the moment we come downstairs.

"The door is stuck," James calls out from the mudroom. "The snow must've drifted in front of it."

"Should I get the shovel?" Olivia says as she pours our coffee.

"No, I'll just try to shove it open."

Olivia brings our coffee to the table. I pick mine up and take a sip.

"Amber!" James yells, so loud I almost drop my coffee. "Help! Someone help!"

We all burst up from the table and hurry into the mudroom. The back door is partially open and just outside of it is Amber, lying face down, her arm stretched out like she was reaching for the door. Her body looks stiff, frozen, like she's been out there for hours.

She's dead. Amber is dead.

CHAPTER 20

I gasp, my hand clamped over my mouth as I try to take in what I'm seeing, not wanting to believe that it's real.

"Oh my God," I hear Shelby say.

"We have to get her inside." James bends down to Amber. "Derek. Ryan. Go out and get her legs."

They hurry outside, then the three of them carefully carry Amber into the house, gently turning her onto her back.

"Beth, get down here," James says. "See if she's still alive."

I kneel down to Amber.

"She can't be dead," Olivia says, her voice shaking. "Please say she's not dead."

But seeing Amber's pale skin and lifeless body, I know she's dead before I even check for a pulse. I do it anyway and confirm that she's gone.

"Do you feel anything?" James asks.

I shake my head.

Shelby breaks down crying. "Oh my God. We're all going to die!"

"Hey, don't say that," James says in a stern tone as he stands up. "We don't know how this happened. Maybe it was an accident."

"How?" Shelby cries. "How could it be an accident? Obviously, she was locked out and couldn't get back in."

"Maybe the door was stuck," Derek says. "Maybe it was frozen shut and she wasn't strong enough to pull it open."

I stand up and look at Derek. "But why would she be out there? In the middle of the night?"

"Exactly." Shelby sniffles. "Amber wouldn't go out there. Someone put her out there, then locked the door."

"This can't be happening," Olivia mutters as she stares down at Amber.

James goes over to her and puts his arm around her.

"Where's Tyler?" Ryan asks.

"I assumed he was still upstairs," James says. "I thought Amber was too."

"Someone go check," Derek says. "Ryan, go knock on his door."

Ryan nods and takes off, but soon after he leaves, I hear him talking. "Hey, Tyler."

"Hey," Tyler says. "Where is everyone?"

"They're back there."

James walks past us out of the mudroom. "Tyler. Have you seen Amber?"

"Not since last night. Why?"

"When's the last time you saw her?"

"I don't know. Maybe two or three in the morning? Why?"

"She didn't stay in your room last night?"

"No. We had a fight and she left."

"And you didn't see her again after that?"

"No. Why? What's going on?"

James brings Tyler to the door of the mudroom.

"Holy shit," Tyler says, staring at Amber's body. "Is she . . ."

"Yes," I tell him. "James found her outside, right next to the door."

Tyler rubs his hand over his face. "What the hell? Amber wouldn't go outside in the middle of the night."

My gaze goes back to her body. "We think someone put her there. And left her."

Tyler turns to Ryan and gives him a shove. "You did this! You sick bastard, you killed her!"

"It wasn't him!" Shelby runs over to Tyler, getting between him and Ryan. "He was in our room last night. He never left."

"You really think I'll believe that?" Tyler yells at her. "You'll say anything to protect him! Anything to keep him out of trouble!"

"I wouldn't protect him if he killed someone!" Shelby yells.

"Yeah, you would," Derek says.

Shelby whips back to him. "Shut up, Derek. You don't know what you're talking about."

"Sophomore year. You covered up for him then. And I know you'd do it again."

I look at Derek. "What are you talking about? What happened sophomore year?"

"Nothing," Shelby says. "He's making it up."

"I was on my way home," Derek says. "It was late. The road was dark. I almost hit a car that was stopped in the road. It was Shelby's, but Ryan was holding the keys. They were in front of the car, looking at something. A body in the road."

Shelby races over to Derek. "He was already gone! Ryan didn't do it!"

"Then why were you there?" Derek says. "And why didn't you call the police?"

"And have them blame my brother for something he didn't do? He already had a history of arrest. They never would've believed that he didn't do it."

"Forget it, Shelby," Ryan says. "Let him believe what he wants. You can't change his mind."

"That's what happened that night?" James asks Ryan. "You're the one who hit that guy?"

The night they're talking about happened before I met Derek, but I remember the story. A car slammed into a drunk guy who was wandering down the road. The police ruled it a hit-and-run.

"I didn't hit him," Ryan says. "I stopped to see what was in the road."

"Yeah, right," James mutters.

"Why have you never told me this?" I ask Derek. "That you were there that night? And saw Shelby and Ryan?"

"Because Shelby had me convinced they didn't hit him. She made me promise not to tell anyone."

"And you just went along with it?"

"In exchange for me getting him together with you," Shelby says. "That night you met wasn't an accident. I told Derek to be there. And then I made sure you saw him."

Derek and I met at a party off campus. He never went to parties. He was an introvert who would rather stay home and play video games than go to a party. He had his small group of friends he'd met in the dorms and that was enough for him. He wasn't looking to meet people, other than me, apparently.

Derek comes over to me. "I know I should've told the police what I saw, but I was just a kid. I wasn't thinking straight."

"How could you have gone all these years and never told me this?"

"I didn't think you needed to know. It was a long time ago, and I couldn't prove Ryan did it." Derek's eyes go to Shelby. "But if he did, Shelby covered it up. Just like she's doing now."

"We need to stop this," Olivia says. "We only become weaker if we turn against each other."

"She's right," James says. "We need to stick together."

"How do we do that when we don't know who we can trust?" I ask. "I can't even trust my own husband to tell me the truth."

"Beth, that's not fair," Derek says. "That happened before I even met you."

How can he think this was something I didn't need to know? If he'd told me Shelby had covered up a hit-and-run, I never would've been friends with her. I probably wouldn't be with Derek now if I knew he'd hid what he saw that night from the police. If he'd told them, there's a good chance Ryan would be in prison now instead of here in this house, terrorizing us.

Shelby claims Ryan was in their room all night, but why would we believe her? Like Tyler said, she'll say anything to protect her brother.

"I think Beth did it," Shelby says, staring at me with hate in her eyes.

"Shelby, come on," Derek says. "You know Beth didn't do this."

"She would if it was the only way to keep Amber quiet."

"Quiet about what?" Derek asks.

"Amber knew her secret," Shelby says, glaring at me. "And Beth was terrified you'd find out."

My heart pounds as I stare at Shelby, wondering if she's bluffing or if she really knows. But if she didn't, how would she know to even say that?

Derek looks at me. "What secret?"

"There isn't one," I say, my eyes on Shelby. "She's just saying that to take the blame off her brother."

"Amber told me what you did," Shelby says to me. "I was shocked. I mean, you were always such a prude, or you pretended to be."

"What is she talking about?" Derek asks.

"Are you really going to listen to her?" I say. "You know Shelby lies."

"The week before your wedding," Shelby says. "Beth—"

"Shelby, stop!" I run up to her. "Please. Don't do this."

"No, tell me," Derek says. "I want to know. What'd she do?"

"She slept with some guy at a bar," Shelby says. "Who just happened to be Amber's boyfriend at the time."

"Beth?" Derek says from behind me. "Is that true?"

I turn to him and see the shock on his face, the disbelief that I would do such a thing.

"It was a mistake," I blurt out. "I'd been drinking. It never should've happened."

"You cheated on me?" he says, his voice getting louder. "Just days before our wedding?"

"Derek, it was years ago. I—"

"Do any of you give a shit that my girlfriend is dead?" Tyler pushes his way into the room and kneels down to Amber. "She's dead! And you assholes are talking about shit that happened ten years ago!"

The room gets quiet. We watch as Tyler runs his hand over Amber's lifeless face.

"I'm so sorry," he says, his eyes tearing up. "I never should've brought you here."

"Let's give them some time," Olivia whispers to James.

They leave the room. The rest of us follow behind and gather by the fire.

"What are we going to do?" James asks.

"About what?" Derek asks. "The dead body? The missing phones? The truck blocking the road? This whole week has gone to hell."

"Dealing with the truck should be our first priority," Olivia says. "We'll never get out of here if we can't get it out of the way and running again."

"I can try to get our car down there," Derek says. "But there's a good chance it'll get stuck. It's too low to the ground to make it over the snow."

"Yeah, I know," James says. "I went out last night to look at it. Your car will never make it down there unless we shovel a path. Same with Tyler's rental, and Shelby's."

"So maybe that's what we do," Derek says. "We shovel a path. We could at least try."

"What about Amber?" Shelby whispers. "We can't leave a dead body in the house."

"We'll put her outside," James says.

"James, that's horrible," Olivia whispers. "We can't just throw her outside."

"What else can we do? I know it sounds harsh, but it's our only option. When we get out of here, we'll contact Amber's family and they'll give her a proper burial."

"Someone needs to tell Tyler," Shelby says. "Before we put her out there."

"I'll do it," I say. "After he's had some time with her."

"How did this happen?" Olivia says, her eyes scanning over us like she thinks one of us is responsible. "Who would do this?"

"Babe, we don't know if anyone did," James says, putting his arm around her. "It could've been an accident. Maybe she went outside to get some air and couldn't get the door open."

"Was it locked?" Olivia turns to James. "When you found her, was the door locked?"

He pauses to think. "I don't know. I can't remember if I unlocked it or just opened it. It was one of those things you don't think about."

"James, this is important," Olivia says, sounding frustrated with him. "Was it locked or not?"

He rubs his jaw. "I think so. I mean, if I had to bet, I'd say yes."

"Then someone did this," Shelby says. "They locked her out."

"We heard them fighting last night," Derek says, lowering his voice. "Like around two in the morning."

"Tyler was fighting with Amber?" James asks.

Derek nods. "I don't know who started it, but they were definitely fighting. We heard Amber leaving Tyler's room, but didn't hear anything after that."

"What were they fighting about?" Ryan asks.

I wish Ryan wasn't here. I feel like we shouldn't say anything when he's around. We shouldn't be giving information to the enemy, which I'm convinced is Ryan.

CHAPTER 21

"It was nothing," I say, answering Ryan's question. "Just typical stuff couples fight about."

Derek looks at me. "What are you talking about? Don't you remember?"

"Remember what?" Ryan asks.

"Amber wanted to leave," Derek says. "And Tyler told her they couldn't."

I grit my teeth, wishing my husband would keep quiet. Telling them what we heard will make them think Tyler killed her. But it wasn't him. Just seeing the shocked look on his face when he saw her lifeless body tells me he had nothing to do with what happened to her.

"Leave?" James says. "Like go back to New York?"

"Yeah," Derek says. "Amber wanted to go and Tyler told her they couldn't, that the car wouldn't make it through the snow. Then the fight heated up and Amber told Tyler she was going to cancel the audition she'd set up for him."

"So he was angry at her," Olivia says. "For threatening to harm his career."

"That doesn't mean he killed her," I say, glancing back at the room where Tyler is still with Amber.

Shelby shrugs. "It sounds like a motive to me."

I look at her. "Shelby, he's our friend. We've known Tyler forever. You see him more than the rest of us. You know he wouldn't do this."

"Just because you know someone doesn't mean you can trust them," she shoots back. "We all have secrets. Isn't that right, Beth?" She smirks at me, obviously still angry at me for accusing her brother of things she claims he didn't do.

I'm about to say something back, but decide not to when I see Tyler coming into the room. His head is down and his shoulders are slumped as he makes his way to the stairs.

"Tyler," James calls out. "Where are you going?"

He stops in front of the stairs, shaking his head. "I can't be around anyone right now. I need to be alone."

"Let us know if you need anything," James says.

We all watch as Tyler goes up the stairs.

When he's gone, Shelby whispers, "We didn't tell him what we're doing with the body."

"We'll tell him later," James says. He looks at Derek. "Let's go move her."

Olivia shudders. "This is so horrible. I feel like I'm going to be sick." She walks to the couch and sits down.

Shelby joins her, while James and Derek head for the mudroom.

"Wait!" I race up behind them as they go into the room. "We should wrap her in something, not just throw her out there."

My gaze goes to Amber's body. Her shirt, which was bunched up and wrinkled, has been pulled down and straightened, and her arms are crossed over her chest. Tyler must've done it, maybe in an attempt to give her a more dignified death. He clearly cared about her, which proves he didn't do this.

"We have some old blankets in the garage," James says. "If you want to grab one."

I nod and hurry down the short hallway to the garage. I flip the light switch on and notice our car sitting there. I'm tempted to get in it and try to drive through the snow, but I know I'd never get out. I'd barely make it out of the driveway. Derek and I keep saying we're going to buy an SUV that can get through the snow, but we haven't saved up enough money to do it.

Looking around the garage, I notice a see-through plastic storage bin with blankets piled up inside. I hurry over to the shelf and reach up to get the bin.

"Need some help?" I hear Ryan say.

Turning back, I see him at the door, a creepy grin on his face. I don't care what Shelby says. I still think Ryan is dangerous. I'm sure he's the one who locked Amber out of the house last night, although I don't know why he'd want to kill her. He doesn't even know her.

"I got it," I tell him.

"It's too high up," he says, coming over to me. "You won't be able to reach it."

I move out of the way and watch as he takes the plastic bin from the shelf and sets it down. He takes off the lid. "Go ahead."

"Just grab one. I'll be inside." I turn to leave.

"I didn't do it," I hear him say. "Shelby wasn't lying. I was in our room all night."

I whip around to face him, trying to hide my fear of him. "Then who did? Who else here has fantasized about killing people?"

He shrugs. "Honestly? I think everyone has. They just don't admit it."

"No. You're wrong." I look him in the eye. "Normal people don't think that way. You only think we do because that's how *your* mind works. You think everyone is like you, but we're not. I've never once thought of harming someone. I became a nurse to help people."

He laughs a little. "Whatever you say." He takes a gray wool blanket from the bin and tosses it at me. "Hold it up. See if it's big enough. It should be. The body isn't very big."

The way he refers to Amber as just a body sends a chill through me. I've heard that murderers dehumanize their victims to relieve any guilt or shame they might feel for what they've done. They think of them as objects — bodies — instead of actual people.

"I'm going inside," I say, hurrying back into the house.

Why does Ryan keep showing up when I'm alone? Is he just trying to scare me, or is he planning on making me his next victim?

"There you are," James says as I come back to the mudroom. "Did you have trouble finding it?"

"No." I hand him the blanket. "I hope it's big enough. I didn't check."

He unfolds the blanket. "It'll work." He nods at Derek. "I'll lay it down, we'll put Amber on it, then wrap it around her."

"Yeah, okay." Derek glances at me. "You should go."

His tone is cold. He's barely looked at me since he found out what I did. Why would Shelby tell him that? He didn't need to know. I understand she's upset with me because I keep accusing Ryan of things, but that isn't reason enough to try to destroy my marriage.

As I'm leaving the room, I run into Ryan, stopping abruptly before I slam into him.

"We meet again," he says with a smirk.

"Stay away from me," I mutter, before hurrying back to the living room.

Shelby's still on the couch, but Olivia isn't there.

"Where's Olivia?" I ask.

"She went upstairs to rest. She's really upset."

"We all are." I look back and see Ryan isn't behind me. He must've gone into the mudroom to help James and Derek. I walk over to Shelby and sit beside her. "Can we talk?"

She won't look at me, her gaze on the fireplace. "Go ahead."

"I know you're upset with me. About Ryan. But why couldn't you have just talked to me instead of telling Derek what I did?"

"I *did* talk to you." She turns to me. "I told you to stop accusing him. I told you to give him a chance. But you wouldn't. You've been saying bad stuff about Ryan since we got here."

I sigh. "Shelby, I know you only want to see the good in him, and I know you believe he's changed, but you don't know the whole story. You don't know what he's done to me since we've been here."

Her brows draw together. "What has he done?"

"He's been making all these strange comments."

"Like what?"

"Like telling me to lock my door at night. It's like he's warning me something's about to happen. Like he's planning something. And he told me he knows where the phones are, but then he denies it when everyone else is around."

"I already told you, he didn't take the phones. He doesn't know where they are."

"Then why did he say that to me? And why would he tell me to lock my door?"

"To keep you safe. Why are you making this into something it isn't?" Her voice rises as her anger at me returns. "If I was the one who'd told you to lock your door, would you accuse me of being dangerous?"

"No. Of course not. You're not getting what I'm saying."

"I am. You're saying Ryan can't win. That no matter what he does, you'll still turn against him. You'll still make him the enemy." She bolts up from the couch. "I can't believe you're being this way. When did you get so judgmental? You used to stand up for Ryan when the guys used to pick on him, and now *you're* the one attacking him."

Shelby doesn't know this, but I wasn't actually sticking up for Ryan back in college. It's true I told the guys to leave him alone, but it wasn't because I was trying to protect Ryan. It was because I was worried about what he might do if they weren't nice to him. Even back then, I thought Ryan was dangerous. Derek was convinced he was harmless, but I didn't believe it. I still don't.

"I'm not attacking him," I say. "I'm just—"

"Forget it. I don't want to hear it." She walks off. "I'm going up to my room."

She runs up the stairs.

"Where'd everyone go?" James asks.

I get up and see him coming toward me, with Derek and Ryan following behind.

"They're all upstairs. Did you . . ." I almost said 'dispose of the body' but realized how bad that sounds.

"We put her in the boat," James says. "There's a fishing boat on the side of the house. It's on a stand and covered with a tarp. Animals shouldn't bother it there, but just in case, I'll keep an eye on it until we can get someone out here."

I wasn't even thinking about that, but James is right. Leaving Amber's body outside in the open could attract animals. It's bad enough she's dead. It'd be even worse if we went out there later and found her body had been eaten by vultures or some other wild animal.

"Should we head down there?" Derek asks James.

"Down where?" I ask.

"We're going to try to dig out the truck again," Derek says.

"Is there anyone around who could help?" I ask James. "Any neighbors?"

He shakes his head. "Our closest neighbors are this old retired couple that only come here in the summer. Even if they were there, we couldn't get to their cabin without going back to the main road."

"That's it for neighbors?" I say, thinking that can't possibly be true, although I don't remember seeing any houses once we turned off the main road to get to James' place. "There's no one else?"

"Not that we could get to. They all live off the main road, and most of them aren't here this time of year. They come in the summer. This area is mostly vacation homes. The locals live in town."

"We should get going," Derek says to James.

"I'll get the shovels," Ryan says.

"Hold on." James turns to Ryan and Derek. "The shovels aren't going to do shit to that ice."

"What ice?" I ask. "Are you saying the truck is stuck in ice?"

"It's a mix of snow and ice," James says. "I'm guessing when Olivia was trying to get the truck out, the tires were spinning, making enough heat to melt the snow and then it froze."

"What about the ice auger?" Ryan asks. "We could try using it to break up the ice enough that we'd be able to shovel it away from the tires."

"It's not a bad idea." James looks at Derek. "What do you think?"

Derek shrugs. "It's worth a try. Is it still at the lake?"

James nods. "Yeah, I'll run down and get it."

"I'll go with you," Derek says.

"You don't need to. It won't take me long." James goes over to the fire and stands in front of it. "I need to warm up before I head out there again."

"I'm going to go put something warmer on," Derek says.

"Good idea," Ryan says, following Derek upstairs.

I'm about to go up there too, but then James starts talking.

"You doing okay?" he asks, glancing back at me.

"Honestly?" I walk up beside him, gazing at the flickering flames of the fire. "No. I'm not."

"Stupid question. I don't know why I asked. None of us are okay. I just put a dead body in my boat." He sighs. "I'm really sorry about this."

"James, it's not your fault," I say, then wonder if it is, if he's apologizing because he's the one behind all this. The missing phones. Amber dying.

What am I thinking? James wouldn't do that.

"I'm the one who invited you all here," he says. "If we'd just done like we always do and met somewhere next summer, we wouldn't be in this mess."

He's right. I wish we'd never come here. But what's done is done. Now we just need to find a way out of this.

CHAPTER 22

"Can I ask you something?" I say to James.

"Go ahead." He holds his hands up to the fire.

"Do you think Ryan did it? Do you think he locked Amber out of the house?"

James pauses before answering. "I don't know, Beth. I really don't. I'd like to think he didn't, but I wouldn't rule it out."

"Did you hear him leave his room last night?" I ask, knowing James' room is next to the one Shelby and Ryan are staying in.

"I didn't, but I sleep like a log. They could've been playing the drums and I wouldn't have heard it."

"If it wasn't Ryan, who else could it be?"

He shrugs. "Maybe no one. Maybe it was just an accident. Maybe Amber went outside and couldn't get back in. If snow blows up around the door, it can freeze and make it feel like it's frozen shut. You really gotta yank on it to get it open. Maybe Amber didn't have the strength to do it."

"But why would she go out there at night? It's dark. It's freezing cold."

"I don't know. It's hard to say. Maybe she smokes." He glances at me. "You ever see her with a cigarette?"

My mind goes back to that night — the night I cheated on Derek. I remember Amber telling one of the bartenders she was going out for a smoke.

"She used to smoke. Or she did that night. When I first met her." I look down, feeling the shame and regret of that night all over again.

"So it's true?" James says. "You were with some other guy?"

"I'd rather not talk about it."

"I'm not judging you. Technically, you weren't married. I get that it's still cheating, but if doing that was what you needed to make sure Derek was the one, then maybe it was the right thing to do."

"It wasn't. I never should've done it."

James is quiet a moment, then says, "I cheated on Olivia."

I look at him. "When? You mean before you got married?"

"And after," he mutters.

"You're saying you cheated twice?"

He nods toward the couch. "Let's go sit down."

When we're seated, I say to him, "Was it the same person? Or two separate women?"

He leans toward me, lowering his voice. "If I tell you this, you need to keep it between us. Olivia knows, but it's not something she wants me telling people."

"Are you saying I can't tell Derek?"

"He already knows about one of them." James leans back on the couch. "He overheard me talking to Shelby."

"Wait, so Shelby knows too?"

"Well, yeah. She and I . . ." He looks down.

I stare at him in disbelief. "You didn't."

He nods. "It was a few months after I met Olivia. We had a fight and I drove down to New York to get away. Clear my head. I stayed with Tyler, and Shelby came over. We all went out, had too much to drink, and . . . things happened."

"So Tyler knows?"

"No. He took off with some girl. Stayed at her place that night. Shelby and I went back to his apartment. We got to talking about college, reminiscing about the past, and before we knew it, we were . . ." He shakes his head. "It was a mistake. It felt good at the time, but we shouldn't have done it."

"Did Shelby agree? That it was a mistake?"

"She never said. We didn't really talk about it. Or we didn't that night. She brought it up at our last reunion, when we all met up at Lake Placid. Derek overheard me talking to Shelby about that night. I didn't know he'd heard us until he asked me about it later."

"I can't believe he didn't tell me."

"I asked him not to. I wanted you to think I'd changed. That I'm not still the guy I was in college. The dumb jock who slept with as many girls as he could."

"I never thought you were a dumb jock. School just wasn't your thing. That doesn't mean you weren't smart. Look how well you did after college."

"Yeah, well, I always felt like I wasn't good enough." He glances upstairs. "Then I met Olivia and felt like things had changed. That I wasn't a screwup anymore. How else could I get someone like her? Someone who's smart, beautiful, rich. If she chose me, I couldn't be that bad, right?"

"James, you're not—"

"But there were times when I felt like Olivia was better than me. Like she was looking down on me. With Shelby, I never felt that way. We both came from shitty homes. Struggled for most of our lives. I could be myself around her. That night I saw her in New York, I needed that. I needed to be able to feel like myself again." James' eyes rise to mine. "But the next day, I told her it was over. That it would never happen again."

"And did she accept that? Because back in college when you two were together—"

"How did you know I was with her in college?"

"She told me. A few days ago."

His brows furrow. "Why would she tell you that?"

"It just came up while we were talking." I move closer to him and keep my voice low. "Do you really think it's a good idea to keep seeing her? Even as a friend? I mean, given your history?"

"I'm over it. It won't happen again." He glances upstairs. "She's, um, got some issues. Even if I was single, I wouldn't get involved with her."

"What issues?"

"Same things as in college. All that dark shit she was into. I'm sure it's just part of her artistic expression or whatever, but I'm not into that stuff."

"I'm not sure what you mean. What was she into?"

"I don't want to get into it. Actually, I'm surprised you don't know. You were one of her closest friends." He gets up. "I need to get out there and get the auger. We need to work on getting the truck out before it gets dark. Tell Derek I'll be back in a half hour or so."

"Are you sure you don't want him to go with you?"

"No, I'll be fine. If you see Olivia, tell her I went down to the lake."

James goes off to get his coat. I get up from the couch and go upstairs, deciding I need to talk to Derek. When I go into our room, I find him standing by the dresser, putting on one of his old college sweatshirts.

"James headed down to the lake," I say. "He said he'll be back in a half hour."

"Yeah, okay," Derek mutters, not looking at me. "I'll wait for him downstairs."

I walk up to him. "Derek, we need to talk."

"About what? About how you cheated on me? Lied to me? Made me feel like a fool in front of our friends?" He goes past me, shaking his head. "I can't do this now. There's too much other shit going on. We need to get the truck out of the way so we can get the hell out of here."

"Derek, don't be this way. Don't shut me out. We need each other now more than ever. We need to stick together."

"You lied to me." He turns to me, his eyes locking on mine. "You've been lying to me for years. What else haven't you told me? Were there others? Other men you were with?"

"No!" I say, shocked that he would even think that. "It was one time, and it was a mistake. I'd had too much to drink."

"So it's okay because you were drunk?" He huffs. "I'll remember that the next time I drink too much."

"Derek, stop it. You know what I mean."

"Do I? Because right now, I'm thinking you didn't want to marry me. That you were having second thoughts the week before our wedding and had to convince yourself I was the right guy. If that's the case, then we never should've gotten married."

"Honey, don't say that." I step up to him and take his hand. "Of course I wanted to marry you. I was just really young and unsure of myself. It was more about me than you."

"That's bullshit and you know it." He yanks away from me. "It was absolutely about me, and how you felt about me. If you had no doubts about us getting married, you wouldn't have felt the need to be with another man."

"I was drunk. I wasn't thinking."

"Being drunk is when the truth comes out. When your inhibitions are down and you let yourself do what you really want. And then you didn't even fess up and tell me what you did! I don't know what's worse. You cheating on me, or keeping this secret for ten years?"

"You want to talk about secrets?" I say, my voice rising along with my anger. "How about the secret you kept about finding Ryan and Shelby on the road, standing in front of a dead body?"

"That wasn't my secret to tell. It was theirs. I don't even know what happened. Maybe they hit the guy or maybe they didn't. All I know is what I saw when I got there."

"You could've called the police."

"And made myself a suspect? You really think I was going to do that? I was nineteen. I was just a kid. I was scared of what might happen if I got involved. So I kept my mouth shut."

"You still could've told me. If I knew that about Shelby, I probably wouldn't have been friends with her."

"Why are we even talking about this? So you can take the focus off you and what you did, and make me the bad guy?"

"No! I'm just making the point that we were both hiding things."

"I didn't even know you when that happened!" he says, raising his voice. "You lied to me when we were *engaged!* About to get married! You looked me in the eye and said your wedding vows, knowing you'd been with another man just a week before." He walks away, to the other side of the room, mumbling something under his breath.

"I'm sorry." I remain where I am, sensing he doesn't want me anywhere near him right now. "I'm sorry for what I did, and I'm sorry I didn't tell you. I don't know what else to say. I can't go back and change it."

"I can't do this right now." He walks to the door and leaves.

"Derek," I hear Tyler say from the hall. "You got a minute?"

"Yeah, of course. What do you need?"

I hear them go into Tyler's room and shut the door. I assume they're talking, but can't hear what they're saying. And I'm sure Derek won't tell me later, given how angry he is with me. I've never seen him like this. He usually wants to talk things out, and he rarely raises his voice. I don't know what this means. Is he thinking of ending our marriage over this? Over something I did ten years ago? I hope not. I hope his anger is more about the situation we're in, and that once we're out of here and back home, he'll be able to see that what I did was just a stupid mistake and didn't mean anything.

Derek's in Tyler's room for almost an hour. When I hear the door open and the sound of them going downstairs, I leave my room and go out to the hall.

There's a creepy silence in the house that sends a chill through me. When we arrived here, the house was alive with energy and noise as we celebrated being together again. But now, just a few days later, the house is silent and there's a feeling of dread in the air, as though we know this isn't over. That more bad things are about to happen.

Or maybe that's just me. I have this horrible feeling that Amber's death won't be the only one. That someone else isn't going to make it out of here alive.

CHAPTER 23

"Hey, Beth," Tyler says as I come down the stairs. He's sitting on the couch, pouring bourbon into a glass.

"Hey." I walk over to him. "How are you feeling?"

"Not great." He swigs the bourbon. "I can't believe she's gone."

I sit beside him. "Is there anything I can do?"

He shakes his head, then stares down at the glass. "What the hell am I going to tell her family?"

"Have you met them?"

"No, but they know about me. She told them we were dating." He pauses. "I feel like it's my job to tell them. I don't want them hearing this from the police."

"Do what you think is right, but if you decide that you can't, it's okay to let the police do it."

The shrill sound of the teakettle startles me, its high-pitched ring piercing through the otherwise silent room.

"Sorry about that," Olivia says. I look back and see her hurrying over to the stove to get the teakettle. "I was doing laundry and forgot about the tea." She looks over at Tyler and me. "Can I get either of you some?"

"No, thanks," I say. Tyler just shakes his head.

I watch as Olivia pours the boiling water into a mug. She changed out of the dress pants and cashmere sweater she had on earlier and is now wearing jeans and a black turtleneck with a long knitted cardigan over it. It'd be a dressy look for me, but it's casual for her. Since we arrived, she's dressed like she's going to work or to a nice restaurant. I'm guessing that's just her style. Coming from wealth, she probably grew up having to always look her best.

"Where's Derek?" I ask, noticing he's not around.

"He's in the garage," Tyler says. "He's checking your car to make sure it's ready to go. He wants to be prepared if we're able to get the truck out today."

"But we can't get down the road. Our car would never make it."

"James would drive the truck into town and get a plow to come out."

I feel a sudden spark of hope at the thought that we might actually get out of here today.

"Is that really possible?" I ask. "Do you really think you guys can get the truck out?"

"If we're able to use the auger to break up the ice around the tires, then yeah, I think we'll get it out."

"Is James back?"

"I don't think so. I haven't seen him."

I check the time. "He's been gone for over an hour. He should've been back by now." I look over at Olivia, sitting at the table, sipping her tea. "Olivia, have you seen James?"

"I believe he's out shoveling a path around the truck."

"By himself? Derek was going to go with him."

"Derek will probably head down there after he's done messing with the car," Tyler says. He finishes his bourbon and reaches for the bottle. "I'll go down with him when he's ready."

"That's probably not a good idea when you've been drinking. You could get hurt."

"Good thing we've got a nurse here," he says, glancing at me before refilling his glass. He sets the bottle down and sits back, swirling the bourbon around the glass as he gazes at the fire.

"Did you and Derek have a good talk?" I ask.

"Yeah." Tyler nods. "He told me what they did with her."

"It isn't what any of us wanted. It's just that we couldn't really leave her in the house."

"Yeah, I get it." He swigs his drink.

I feel bad for him. I don't think he loved Amber, but I can tell he had feelings for her. At the very least, they were friends, and now she's gone.

"Would you like me to pack up her things?" I ask. "I'm sure it's hard to see them there, in your room."

"I already put them away. Everything's in her suitcase." He glances at me. "You can have the earrings I got her. They're really nice. Shelby did a good job."

"She showed them to me." I pause. "I'm sure Amber would've loved them."

He wipes his eyes. "It's all my fault. If I hadn't been fighting with her—"

"No. Tyler, don't blame yourself." I rub his arm. "This isn't your fault. All couples fight."

"But it didn't have to end this way." He looks at me. "I told her to go. I kicked Amber out of our room. If I hadn't done that, she'd still be here."

"You didn't tell her to go outside. She could've stayed in the house, but she didn't. That was her decision." I pause. "Do you have any idea why she might've gone outside?"

"I'm guessing she went out there to smoke. She told me she'd quit, but I don't think she had."

So maybe it really was an accident. Amber went outside to smoke, the door iced up, and she couldn't get back inside.

"Did you see any cigarettes in her suitcase?"

"No, but she wouldn't put them in there. She'd hide them in the car. Somewhere I wouldn't find them."

I'm tempted to go search his rental car for a pack of cigarettes. Or maybe they're still with her, in the pocket of the hoodie she had on over her pajamas. Why wasn't she wearing a coat? If she went outside to smoke, wouldn't she put a coat on? It's freezing outside and it was snowing last night.

Olivia appears beside the couch, holding her mug of tea. "It's getting close to lunch time. I'm sure nobody is hungry, but do you think I should make something, just in case?"

"I wouldn't," I say. "If one of us wants lunch, we can make it ourselves. You should rest, Olivia. You've been working nonstop since we got here."

"It's just how I am." She sits down in the chair next to the couch. "I've always been that way. I find it hard to relax." She smiles a little. "That's one of the reasons I fell for James. He was the one person who could make me sit still long enough to watch a movie or linger at the table after dinner."

"Yeah, James is an expert at doing nothing," Tyler jokes.

"He's getting better," Olivia says. "He's been helping out more around the house. Doing the lawn work. Running errands for me."

"You two seem really happy," I say, although it's not entirely true. I've caught Olivia looking annoyed with James on more than one occasion, and James admitted to being unfaithful to her at least once during their marriage, and to sleeping with Shelby when he was dating Olivia. I can't believe he did that. I wonder who the other woman was, the one he was with after he was married.

"We're very happy," Olivia says. "James and I are opposites in many ways, but as the saying goes, opposites attract." She sips her tea. "James has been good for me. And I hope I've been good for him."

"I think you have," Tyler says. "Not that my opinion counts for anything."

"It does," Olivia says, looking at Tyler. "Thank you for saying that. Sometimes I can't always tell if James is happy being married. But you know him better than me, having been friends with him since college."

"He wasn't someone we thought would ever settle down," I say. "But he's changed. You've clearly been a good influence on him."

She gives me a smile, then her expression turns serious as her gaze moves to the fire. "I'm so sorry for how this week has turned out. I feel terrible about it."

"Why?" Tyler says. "It's not your fault."

"James and I invited you all here." She looks at Tyler. "We have this big house, and it's so beautiful up here in the winter. I thought it'd be nice to have you all here to enjoy it. But instead it's become a nightmare."

"Olivia, please don't think we blame you for that," I say. "You've done everything possible to make us feel welcome. And it wasn't just your idea that we come here. We all agreed to it. Personally, I was excited to see the house, and Derek and I have been talking about taking a winter trip to the mountains for years."

"I just wanted to get together with everyone," Tyler says. "I didn't care where we went."

The door from the garage opens and I see Derek coming down the hall.

"Everything good with the car?" I ask.

"Yeah." He unzips his coat as he walks over to us. "Is James back yet?"

"Olivia said he's already working on the truck," I say.

"I assume he is," Olivia says. "He said he was going there to try to dig it out."

"When?" I ask. "Did you see him after he got back from the lake?"

165

"The lake?" Olivia sets her mug down. "When was James at the lake?"

"This morning. He left after you went upstairs. He went to get the ice auger to break up the ice around the truck tires. I was supposed to tell you, but you were upstairs and I didn't see you until now."

"He shouldn't still be down there," Derek says. "That was over an hour ago. Maybe he came back when we were all upstairs, and decided to take the auger down to the truck."

"Without telling anyone?" Tyler says. "That doesn't sound like James. He would've told at least one of us."

"Oh God," Olivia whispers, panic in her eyes. "What if something happened to him?"

"I'm sure he's fine," I rush to say, but I don't actually believe it. If James was fine, then where is he? Why isn't he back?

CHAPTER 24

"Tyler's right," Olivia says. "James wouldn't come back here and then leave without telling anyone where he was going. He knows how dangerous it can be in the mountains, especially when he doesn't have his phone." Her eyes dart between Tyler, Derek, and me. "We have to find him! Please, help me find him!"

"We will." Tyler gets up. "I promise you, we'll find him. We'll go right now." He looks at Derek. "You go down to the lake. I'll go check the truck."

"I don't want you going alone," I say to Derek. "I'm coming with you."

"Someone should go with Tyler," Olivia says. "The road to the truck is covered in ice. I don't want him falling and hurting himself and not able to get help."

Plus, he's been drinking, putting him at a greater risk of falling.

"I'll see if Ryan can go with me," Tyler says, hurrying upstairs.

I go over to Olivia and kneel beside her. "I'm sure James is fine. He was probably in such a hurry to get to the truck that he didn't think to tell anyone where he was going."

She nods.

"Can I get you anything before we leave?"

"No." Her thin body is trembling. I grab a blanket from the basket near the fire and drape it over her shoulders. "Thank you," she whispers, her eyes welling up with tears.

Tyler runs down the stairs with Ryan right behind him.

"We're heading down there," Tyler says, putting on his coat. "Since we don't have phones, let's meet back here after we find James so we know everyone's okay."

"Sounds good," Derek says, getting our coats from the closet.

"What can I do?" Shelby asks, running down the stairs.

"Stay here with Olivia," I tell her.

Shelby glances at Olivia, sees the state she's in, and looks back at me, giving me a nod to let me know she'll take care of her.

"Here's your coat," Derek says, tossing it to me. "Let's go."

We hurry to the mudroom, pulling on coats as we go. When we've put on our boots, hats, and gloves, we go out the back door into the frigid wind and swirling snow.

"What are you doing?" Derek asks as I stop to search around the door.

"Tyler thinks Amber came out here last night to smoke. I was seeing if I could find her cigarette to see if that's really what she was doing."

"You can look for it later. We gotta find James."

Derek takes off through the snow, not waiting for me as I struggle to keep up.

"Could you slow down?" I call out.

He looks back, continuing to trudge through the snow. "I can't. James could be in trouble. Just keep up the best you can. I'll meet you there."

"I don't know where we're going. I've never been to the lake."

I hear Derek sigh. He stops and looks up at the dark gray clouds overhead. "It's going to start snowing again. We're not going to be able to get the truck out today."

"You could still try," I say, finally catching up to him. "Even if it's snowing."

We continue down the path, dense patches of trees on both sides of us.

"What if the truck doesn't start?" Derek says. "It barely started the last time we tried."

"If it started, it means the battery's not dead."

"It could be by now."

"Derek, we need to stay positive. It's not helping to assume the worst."

"I'm just preparing you for what might happen. We may be stuck here until a plow comes down that road and sees that it's blocked."

"That has to be soon, right? It's been snowing since we got here. I'm surprised the plow hasn't already cleared the road."

"James said they're really slow getting to the side roads. He said most people have plows attached to their trucks so they can clear a big enough path to get to the main road."

"So why doesn't James have a plow? He had to have known something like this could happen."

"I don't know." Derek stops and points down a steep slope. "The lake is down there. You think you can make it?"

"I can, but I might need some help."

He offers me his arm. I grab hold of it and we carefully make our way down the slick, snow-covered rocks jutting out of the ground. I can see the lake just up ahead. It's larger than I was imagining. I thought it'd be more like a small pond.

"How was James going to get the ice auger up this hill by himself?" I ask. "Aren't those things heavy?"

"It's probably around thirty pounds, which isn't much for someone like James. But it's awkward to carry. And the blades are really sharp. You gotta be careful."

We're at the bottom of the slope now, back on another snow-covered path.

"The place we were fishing is just around this cluster of trees," Derek says. "James! You out here?"

We listen, but all we hear are some crows cawing in the trees above us.

"He must not be here," I say as Derek races ahead of me. It's not like him to do that. He'd usually wait for me to make sure I'm safe. He's clearly still angry at me, angry enough to make me fend for myself.

"Beth!" Derek yells, sounding frantic. "Beth, get over here!"

"I'm coming!" I try to run through the snow, but it's too deep.

"Oh God," Derek cries out. "Beth!"

"What? What is it?" I finally make it around the trees and see Derek staring down at the ice, his body shaking.

I race over to him and see James, face down on the ice, his chest on top of the auger. His torso has been ripped to shreds and blood is splattered all around him.

"James!" I kneel down to him and start checking for signs of life, even though I know it's pointless. There's no chance he's alive.

I hear Derek behind me, vomiting. I close my eyes and take a breath, trying to remain calm. It was an accident. A horrible, tragic accident. Nobody did this to James. I won't let my mind even go there. We were all at the house when it happened. It was an accident.

"Beth," Derek says, his voice trembling. "What . . . what are we going to do? He's . . . there's nothing left of him."

I turn to Derek. His face is pale and he looks like he's going to be sick again. "Turn away. Don't look at him."

As a surgical nurse, I'm used to seeing disgusting things, but seeing James, one of my closest friends, like this, is harder than anything I've ever had to face as a nurse. His head and limbs are still intact, but his torso is nothing but pieces of flesh scattered across the ice.

"How did this happen?" Derek says.

I get up and go over to him. "He must've slipped and fallen on the auger while it was running."

"But why would it be running? He didn't come here to use it. He was getting it to take to the truck. And he knew how dangerous it was. He even showed us how to take the battery out so it doesn't accidentally turn on when you're not using it."

So then how did this happen? Was it really an accident?

CHAPTER 25

"I should've gone with him," Derek says, tears running down his face. "I knew I shouldn't have let him come here alone. Why did I listen to him?" Derek wipes his face. "He'd be alive right now if I'd just come down here with him."

"You can't think that way. This isn't your fault." I put my arms around him. "It was an accident. A horrible accident."

Derek's body trembles as he quietly sobs over the loss of our friend. I'm too shocked to cry. I feel like none of this is real. Like it's all some kind of nightmare I'm going to eventually wake up from.

"What are we going to tell Olivia?" Derek asks.

"We'll tell her there's been an accident."

"And that her husband's body is spread all over the lake?" Derek yanks away from me and walks back to the trees, taking deep breaths as he stares up at the sky. "I can't believe this. First Amber, now James? What the hell is happening?"

"I don't know, but we have to get out of here. We have to find a way." I go over to Derek. "Maybe we just start walking. We'll walk to the main road and hope a car goes by."

"That's miles from here, and the wind chill has gotta be below zero. We'd never make it without someone getting frostbite. And it's almost noon. It's going to be dark in a few hours."

"Then you and Tyler need to work on getting the truck back on the road. I guess Ryan could help, although I still don't trust him. I'll help too. The four of us can try chipping away at the ice where it's stuck, then if we're able to start the truck, maybe we'll be able to get some movement in the tires."

"I don't want you out in this." He rips his gloves off and feels my face. "You're freezing. You need to get back in the house."

"I don't care how cold it is. I'm going to help with the truck. It's our only way out of here."

He glances back at James. "We need to cover him. We can't leave him like that." He takes off his jacket.

"Derek, no. You need that. We'll get a blanket from the house." I look around. "Or maybe we could cover him with some branches."

Derek tromps through the snow and picks up a fallen branch. It's large enough that he has to drag it through the snow.

"Take the other end," he says.

I pick it up and we carefully place it over James.

"This isn't right," Derek says, his voice cracking. "He deserves more than this. He deserves a proper burial."

"And he'll get one when we're able to get help. But until then, I don't know what else we can do. We can't take him back to the house like this."

"Beth, he's going to get eaten!" Derek yells. "Animals are going to smell the blood and he'll be gone! There'll be nothing left of him!"

"Then what do you want to do?" I yell back. "Just tell me and I'll do it!"

Derek leans down, his hands on his knees, staring at the ground. "I want my friend back. This wasn't supposed to happen. This week was supposed to be our last trip together before everything changed. Before James and Olivia had a kid. Before *we* had one. And now . . ."

"Now what?"

"I don't know. I don't know anything anymore. I'm questioning everything I thought I wanted."

"Are you talking about us having children?" I pause. "Or about *us?* About our marriage?"

He stands back up. "I'm saying I need time to think." He looks up toward the house. "We should get back. It's freezing out here and everyone's waiting for us."

"We haven't decided what to tell them. And who's going to do it."

"I think you should. You're a nurse. You have experience giving people bad news."

That's not really true. The doctors usually do that, but I *am* better than Derek when it comes to saying difficult things.

We get back to the house, but stop before going inside.

"I'm going to say there was an accident," I tell Derek. "I'm not going to go into details. She doesn't need to know what we saw."

"I agree, but you know Olivia will have questions. What if she asks to see him?"

"I'll handle it if she does. I might even take her aside and talk to her privately. Actually, maybe that's what I'll do. She should know what happened before anyone else."

Derek nods. "You sure you can do this?"

"I don't have a choice."

We go into the house and take off our coats and boots. I'm unraveling my scarf from my neck when Olivia appears at the door to the mudroom.

"Where's James?" she asks. "He was there, right? He had to be. Tyler checked the truck and he wasn't there."

Derek goes past me to Olivia. "Beth needs to talk to you. I'm going to leave you two alone."

She watches him leave, then looks back at me. "Talk about what? What . . . what does he mean? Did something happen to James?"

I go over to her and gently take hold of her arm. "Let's sit down."

"No! Just tell me! Tell me what happened!" She's already crying. I feel terrible for her. I can only imagine how awful I'd feel if someone were to give me this news about Derek.

"There was an accident," I tell her. "James was . . . injured."

"Injured how? What happened?"

"It was the ice auger. I don't know exactly what happened but—"

"We have to help him!" She races past me, but I grab her arm, stopping her.

"Olivia, stop. It's too late."

She turns back to me, shaking her head. "No."

"I'm sorry," I say, my heart breaking for her.

"No!" She collapses to the floor, sobbing. "No! He can't be gone!"

"I'm so sorry." I kneel down to comfort her, but she pushes me away.

"Fix him!" she yells at me. "You're a nurse! Go save him!"

"Olivia, if there was anything I could've done, I promise you, I would've done it."

She's rocking back and forth, tears streaming down her face. "What am I going to do? James was my life. My future. We had everything planned out. And now he's gone."

"Hey." Ryan appears. "Can I help?"

What is he doing here? He's the absolute last person who could help. He'll just make things worse.

"She needs some time," I say. "Please, just go."

He nods and walks away.

Shelby rushes into the room and kneels down in front of Olivia. "I just heard. I'm so sorry." She yanks Olivia into her arms. "Whatever I can do, just tell me. We're all here for you."

"I need to get up," Olivia says, her voice trembling. "I think I'm going to be sick."

"Let me help you to the bathroom," I say.

"I'll do it," Shelby says, helping Olivia up from the floor. They head to the bathroom down the hall.

I leave the mudroom and see everyone standing around the fireplace, staring down at the floor, in utter shock that James is gone.

"Come here," Derek says, motioning for me to join him.

I walk over to him and collapse into his arms. Telling Olivia about James was the hardest thing I've ever had to do. I can only imagine how awful this must be for her, what she's feeling, knowing the man she loved, the man she'd planned her future with, is gone.

They have this beautiful house where they were going to take their children someday, and a home in Boston where they'd planned to raise those children. And now, none of that will happen. Olivia is alone. She has no siblings. Her parents are gone. If something happened to Derek, I'd at least still have my parents and sister. But Olivia has no one.

"I'm going to take her upstairs," I hear Shelby say.

I look over and see Shelby with her arm around Olivia, walking her toward the staircase. We all watch as they slowly make their way up each step, Olivia looking like she's struggling to remain standing.

When they're finally upstairs, Tyler says, "She looks horrible."

"She just lost her husband," I say. "I'd look the same way if something happened to Derek."

"What should we do?" Ryan asks. "Are we going to go get him? We can't just leave him at the lake."

I look at Derek. "You didn't tell them?"

"I didn't go into details. I wanted to wait until you told Olivia. How much did you tell her?"

"Not much. I said there was an accident and that James was injured and didn't make it. She broke down before I could say anything more."

"So what exactly happened?" Tyler asks.

Derek tells him what we saw. Hearing him describe it makes me feel sick to my stomach, which is strange because I didn't feel that way when I was actually there, looking at it. I was too much in shock, not believing what I was seeing was real, but now it's hitting me that it really happened. James is dead. And his body is splattered across the ice.

"Shit," Tyler mutters as he collapses down on the chair. "You can't tell Olivia that. She doesn't need to know."

"I agree," I say, going to the couch to sit down. "I'm just worried she's going to ask, once she's had time to let this sink in. Or even worse, what if she asks to go see him?"

"Tell her no," Ryan says. "Say he was badly injured and there's a lot of blood."

"The blood," Tyler says, sounding panicked. "It's going to attract animals. What if we go there later and he's gone?"

"Beth and I talked about that," Derek says, looking at me. "We didn't have an answer for what to do. I mean, it's not like we can bring him back here. There's not much left of him."

Tyler shudders. "I can't even imagine. I'm sorry you guys had to see that. But I'm kind of glad it was you and not me. I don't think I could've handled seeing that."

"I didn't handle it well," Derek says. "If Beth wasn't there, I might've passed out."

Shelby comes down the stairs. "Olivia's in her room. I'm worried about her. Her whole body is shaking."

"It's the shock," I say. "The shaking should stop when the shock wears off. But we should keep checking on her. She shouldn't be up there alone for too long."

"I feel so bad for her," Shelby says. "And for James. I can't believe he's gone."

"None of us can," Tyler says. "He was the one who kept us all together. The one who insisted we do these reunions every year. Without him, we probably wouldn't all still be friends."

"He valued our friendship more than anything else," Derek says. "He told me he could always count on us to be there for him, which is something he didn't have growing up." Derek blinks the tears from his eyes. "He said we were his family, and that he never wanted to lose what we had together."

"And now he's gone," Shelby says, sitting down on the floor, hugging her knees to her chest.

Ryan sits next to her, putting his arm around her. I watch him, looking for any signs that he might've had something to do with this. But if he did, how would he do it? He would've had to get the auger going and somehow cause James to fall on it. That couldn't have happened. James is bigger and stronger than Ryan. James would've overpowered Ryan and fought him off.

It was just an accident. A terrible, tragic, horrific accident.

So why does part of me still not believe that?

CHAPTER 26

"What about the truck?" Ryan says. "Are we still going to try to dig it out?"

Tyler shakes his head. "I can't. Not after what happened." He looks over at Derek. "I'm sorry, but I can't do it. I got nothing in me."

"It's okay," Derek says. "I get it. I don't think I could do it either. I say we try to get through today and maybe go out there in the morning." He glances out the window. "The sky's getting dark. It looks like it might start snowing again."

"We'd know if we had our phones," Tyler mutters. He sits up straighter and looks at us. "Let's end this bullshit with the phones. Whoever has them needs to give them back. If keeping them from us was some kind of joke, it's not funny anymore. People are dead. Animals are going to take what little is left of James if we don't get someone out here to get his body. Same with Amber. We covered her the best we could, but it's just a matter of time before an animal finds her."

"He's right," I say. "We need the phones. Someone here has them and needs to give them back."

"It wasn't me," Shelby says.

I look at Ryan, not able to help myself.

Shelby notices and jumps up from the floor. "It wasn't him! Stop blaming him, Beth! He didn't do this!"

"Then why did he tell me he knew where the phones were?"

She looks at Ryan, who's still sitting on the floor. "Did you tell her that?"

"No. I don't know what she's talking about."

"He's lying!" I point at Ryan. "He came up to me in the hall when I was leaving my room and told me he knows where the phones are."

"Or maybe you made it up," Shelby shoots back. "To make everyone *think* Ryan did it."

"Shelby, you know I wouldn't do that." I get up from the couch. "I'm telling you, Ryan knows where the phones are. You just don't want to believe it because he's your brother."

"And you don't want to believe that he's changed! Everyone here has accepted Ryan except for you. You're determined to make him the villain." She narrows her eyes at me. "Which makes me think you're the one who took them."

"Are you serious?" I shake my head incredulously. "You think I took the phones?"

"I wouldn't put it past you. You'd do it just to make Ryan look bad. You want everyone to turn against him, so you took the phones so you could blame him for it."

"I did not take the phones! That is the most ridiculous thing I've ever heard!"

"Beth." Derek grips my hand, pulling on me to sit down. "This isn't helping. Fighting about this isn't going to fix anything."

"Accusing people isn't helping either," Shelby says.

"And yet you just accused me," I point out.

"Okay, everyone just calm down," Tyler says. "The phones are here somewhere. They didn't just disappear. We just need to find them."

"We've already searched the house," Derek says. "They aren't here."

"Maybe Amber took them," Ryan says. "Or Olivia."

"Why would they take our phones?" Derek asks.

"It wasn't Amber," Tyler says. "Ever since they went missing, she was complaining about not having hers."

"And Olivia's been freaking out about the road being blocked," Derek says. "James said that's why he's been trying so hard to get the truck working again. He said she hasn't been sleeping, knowing we're stuck here."

"Then who does that leave?" Shelby asks.

"It has to be one of us," Tyler says.

The room gets silent. Whoever has the phones isn't going to admit to it.

"Okay, so obviously nobody's going to fess up," Tyler says. "But I think we all agree we need the phones back. So whoever has them, just put them back tonight. We'll all be in our rooms. Nobody will know who did it. We stop accusing people. Stop asking questions. At this point, it doesn't matter who took them. We just need them back. Agreed?"

We all nod.

"I'm going to go check on Olivia," Shelby says.

"Let me do it." I hurry past her and go up the stairs to Olivia's room. "Olivia?" I knock on the door. "Can I come in?"

"Just a minute," I hear her say.

She opens the door, holding a wad of tissues in her hand. Her eyes are red and her cheeks are streaked with mascara. She looks terrible, not at all like the put-together, seemingly perfect woman I'm used to seeing.

"I just wanted to check on you," I say. "How are you doing?"

"Awful," she says, her voice cracking. She turns away from me and goes over to the bed to sit down. "He was all I had left. My whole world."

I go over to her and sit beside her. "I can't imagine how difficult this is for you. I know you're feeling alone right now, but you're not. When you married James, you became part of our group. Our family. We'll always be here for you, for whatever you need."

"That's kind of you to say." She sniffles. "But I want James. I want my husband back."

"I know." I rub her arm. "Tell me what I can do. How I can help."

"There's nothing you can do." Her eyes rise to mine. "Actually, maybe there is."

"Anything. What is it?"

"Take me to see him. I need to tell him goodbye."

"Um, I don't think that's a good idea."

"Beth, I have to." She grips my hand. "I need to see him. Where is he? Did you . . ." She swallows. "Bring him up to the house? Is he . . . with Amber?"

"No. He's, um, still at the lake."

She stands up, looking alarmed. "We can't leave him down there! Someone needs to go get him!"

"Olivia, I'm sorry, but we can't." I take a breath and try to put myself in work mode, as the nurse who has to tell a patient's family bad news. If I make this personal, I'll never be able to say it. I need to use my training to say what needs to be said and try to keep my emotions out of it, for Olivia's sake.

"Why?" she asks, tears streaming down her face. "Why can't we go get him? What are you not telling me?"

"The accident. It did a lot of damage." I describe what happened in the fewest words possible, trying to leave out the details as best I can, while also making it clear that James' body can't be moved.

Olivia falls to the floor and sobs. It kills me to see her suffering, but there's nothing I can do. She needs to feel the pain of her loss to accept that James is gone.

"How's she doing?" Derek asks when I come back downstairs. He's by himself, sitting on the couch.

"She's struggling." I go over to Derek and sit beside him. "She wanted to see him. I had to tell her why she couldn't."

"Sorry." He rubs my hand. "That must've been tough."

"It was horrible." I wipe my eyes. "But at least now she knows." I take a breath. "Where is everyone?"

"In their rooms. We agreed to meet down here in an hour to have kind of a memorial for James. And also for Amber."

"What do you mean by memorial?"

"Just talk about them. Reminisce about the time we had with them. Obviously, only Tyler really knew Amber, but it didn't feel right to leave her out. She deserves to be remembered as much as James."

"I can't believe they're both gone." I turn to Derek. "Do you really think their deaths were accidents? Be honest with me, Derek. It's just you and me here. Tell me what you really think happened to them."

"I think they were accidents. Amber went out to smoke and couldn't get back in, and James slid on the ice and fell on the auger."

"But why would the auger be running if he was only there to get it and bring it back here?"

"Maybe he was testing it. Making sure the battery was charged."

"You really don't think someone was involved?"

"No, and you need to stop thinking that way. All you're doing is scaring yourself and making this whole situation more difficult. You need to quit making accusations. I know you hate Ryan, but you need to stop making him the bad guy. If we want to get out of here, we need to stick together. But that's not going to happen if you keep accusing people of things they didn't do."

"Ryan told me he knew where the phones were. I wasn't lying about that. Are you saying you don't believe me?"

"I don't know what to believe. I'd like to think you wouldn't lie about that, but knowing how much you hate Ryan . . ."

"Really, Derek? You're believing Ryan over me? You're taking his side over mine?" I get up and head to the stairs.

"Beth, wait! I didn't mean it that way."

I continue up to our room. I close the door but don't lock it, thinking Derek will come up here, wanting to talk and hopefully apologize. But he doesn't. He doesn't believe me, which makes me question the strength of our marriage.

This isn't the first time I've felt this way, like Derek and I are drifting apart. It's been like this for a couple years now. We've become consumed with our jobs, trying to save up money to buy a bigger house and start a family. We no longer have date nights. We do our own things on the weekends. We rarely even sit down for dinner together anymore.

This trip was supposed to bring us back together. A time for us to relive our college days, when we fell in love. With no work or household duties to distract us, we could spend the week focused on each other, and our relationship, while being surrounded by our closest friends.

But instead this week is proving that our relationship isn't as strong as we thought. It has cracks and crevices that get deeper each year, driving us farther apart. The fact that Derek doesn't believe me about Ryan just proves that he doesn't see me like he used to. The Derek I married would always take my side. The Derek I know now won't.

What does that mean for us? Is this trip going to end with us breaking up? We came here talking about having a baby. Are we going to leave here talking about getting a divorce? I don't want it to come to that, but I need my husband to support me. If he's not willing to do that, I don't know if our marriage can survive.

CHAPTER 27

"What time is it?" I ask, waking up the next morning to find I'm alone in bed.

"It's just after eight." Derek's standing at the dresser, putting a sweatshirt on over his flannel shirt. "I'm going to eat something, then get to work on the truck."

"Alone?"

"No, Tyler and Ryan are going with me. They're probably already downstairs."

I hurry out of bed. "I'll go too. Just let me get dressed."

"Beth, you're not going. Just stay here."

"Why? I'm not helpless. I've shoveled snow before."

"The snow is packed with ice. You'll hurt yourself trying to lift it. Plus, we don't have enough shovels for you to help. Just stay here and pack up our stuff."

"You really think we're getting out of here today?"

"Probably not, but if there's even a chance, I want to be prepared." He goes to the door. "I'll see you down there."

I skip the shower and get dressed, wanting to hurry downstairs to see if the phones were returned. We all went to bed around ten, giving whoever took them plenty of time to put them back.

"Are they here?" I ask, running down the stairs.

"What are you talking about?" Shelby asks.

185

"The phones. Are they back?"

"No," she says, heading to the table, where Ryan, Tyler, and Derek are sitting. Derek's helping himself to the eggs while Ryan passes Tyler a platter of toast.

Did Olivia make breakfast? I hope not. Given what she's going through, she shouldn't be worrying about feeding us.

"Did anyone look?" I ask. "Like check around to make sure they aren't here?"

"I looked," Tyler says, putting a piece of toast on his plate. "I couldn't find them."

No one seems concerned by this, which I find infuriating.

"And you're all okay with this?" I say. "That our phones are still missing?"

"Of course not," Derek says. "But what are we going to do? Being upset about it isn't going to help us get out of here. We need to stay focused on what we have control over, which as of now is getting the truck working and driving it to town to get help."

"Why don't you join us?" Shelby says. "Try to eat something."

Shelby and I are back to being friends, or we're pretending to be. We reconciled last night when we were all gathered around the fire, reminiscing about the past. It was a reminder to both of us of how close we used to be, how much fun we used to have, and how we were once best friends. I wish we could be like that again, but I don't see it happening. She's too protective of Ryan. She'll always take his side, no matter what he does. I don't trust him, and never will, which makes it hard for Shelby and me to be as close as we once were.

"Did Olivia make all this?" I ask, taking a piece of toast.

"Yeah, she said keeping busy helps take her mind off what happened."

I look around. "Where is she?"

"I'm not sure," Shelby says. "Maybe upstairs?"

"Last I saw her, she was in the laundry room," Tyler says.

"Olivia?" I call out. "Are you here?"

She doesn't answer.

"She was saying we needed more wood for the fire," Tyler says. "Maybe she went out to get it."

"How long has she been gone?" I ask.

"I don't know," Tyler says. "Maybe a few minutes? I wasn't paying attention."

"She shouldn't still be out there." I push my chair back. "We need to go check on her."

"I'll do it," Derek says, hurrying to get up.

I follow him to the mudroom and look out the small window in the door while Derek puts his boots on.

"I don't see her," I say.

"She's probably in the shed."

"I don't think so. The door is closed."

"Check upstairs. Maybe she went up there without anyone noticing."

"I'll wait until you get back."

Derek goes outside, tromping through the snow to the shed. I leave the back door open and scan the area around it for remnants of a cigarette. I don't see anything, but it's been snowing. If Amber's cigarette was here, it'd be buried by now.

"Olivia?" Derek yells.

I hear her voice, but it's muffled.

"I'm trying!" Derek pulls on the shed door. "It's stuck!"

Olivia's in the shed, and apparently can't get out! I yank on my boots and grab my coat, putting it on as I run out to the shed.

"I can't get it open," Derek says to me, yanking on the door.

"Please hurry!" Olivia yells. "I'm freezing!"

"The latch," I say to Derek, pointing to the wood board lodged in it. "You have to move the board."

"Shit, I didn't even see that."

He shoves the board out of the way and opens the door.

"Thank you," Olivia says, collapsing in Derek's arms. "I thought I was going to die in there."

"What happened?" I ask.

Olivia notices me behind Derek and pulls away from him. "I went to get the wood and the door slammed shut. I couldn't get out."

"Someone locked you in?" I say, my pulse racing.

"It was probably just the wind," Olivia says. "It must've blown the door closed."

"What about the latch? The board was over it, like someone put it there."

"Maybe the wind caused it to fall." She pauses. "At least, I hope that's all it was."

"We need to get you inside," Derek says, taking her by the arm and leading her back to the house.

"What happened?" Tyler asks when he sees us with Olivia.

"She was locked in the shed," I say.

"It was an accident," Derek says, giving me a look to go along with it. Does he really believe it was an accident, or does he think someone was involved?

"The wind must've blown the door closed," Olivia says as I wrap a blanket around her.

"You couldn't push it open?" Shelby asks.

"Beth said the wood board was secured in the latch," Olivia says. "I suppose the wind did that too. It's extremely windy today."

"The only other way it could've happened is if someone was out there," I say. "And secured the latch so Olivia couldn't get out."

"Beth," Derek says, giving me a look to keep quiet. He doesn't want me panicking people, but if someone did this to Olivia, everyone needs to know. They could be next.

"From now on, I'll get the wood," Ryan says. "Nobody else go out there."

"Thanks, Ryan," Shelby says.

"You should go right now," Tyler says to Ryan. "The fire's almost out."

Ryan gets up and leaves while Derek and I bring Olivia to the table to sit down. She's shivering, even with the blanket around her.

"Do you want some coffee?" I ask.

She nods. "That would be nice. Thank you."

"No more trying to do stuff for us," Shelby says to Olivia.

"Yeah, we'll get the firewood," Tyler says. "Make the meals. Clean up the house."

"Thank you," she says. "You've all been so kind."

We really haven't. We've kind of ignored Olivia since we got here. But she really hasn't given us a chance to spend time with her. She's always in the kitchen making meals, or picking up after us, or cleaning the house.

"I think I'll go upstairs and take a bath," Olivia says. "Try to warm up."

"Here's your coffee." I hand it to her.

She takes it and makes her way upstairs.

"I feel so bad for her," Shelby says.

"Does anyone find it odd that she got locked outside?" I ask. "After the same thing happened to Amber?"

"She wasn't locked out," Derek says. "It was the wind. It could've easily blown the door shut and caused the wood to drop in the latch." He pauses, a look of concern crossing his face.

"What?" I ask. "What is it? What are you thinking?"

"Nothing. I'm probably remembering it wrong."

"Remembering what?" Tyler asks.

"The back door," Derek says. "When I went to go out of it, I think it was locked."

"The back door was locked?" I ask.

"Someone must've locked it," Shelby says.

Someone locked Olivia outside, hoping she'd freeze to death. Just like they did to Amber.

I don't believe Amber's death was an accident. The door wasn't jammed or frozen shut. Someone locked it. I'm sure of it.

CHAPTER 28

"It wasn't me," Shelby says. "I was upstairs when Olivia went out there."

"I didn't lock it," Tyler says.

"Me either," Derek says.

"That only leaves one person," I say, knowing it was Ryan. It had to be.

Shelby turns to Derek. "Are you sure it was locked?"

"I'm pretty sure, but I could be wrong. I was in a hurry to get out there. But I think I had to unlock the door first. I'm almost certain I did."

"Well, just because it was locked doesn't mean someone did it intentionally," Shelby says. "None of us knew Olivia was even out there."

"That we know of," I mutter.

Shelby shoots an angry look my way. "Beth, I swear, if you start accusing Ryan again—"

"Okay, stop," Tyler says. "Let's think about this. If Olivia had been locked out, she'd just bang on the door and we'd hear her and let her in. If someone was out to harm her, locking the door wouldn't have done anything. I think it was just an accident. Maybe Ryan saw the door was unlocked and locked it to keep us safe."

"Safe from what?" I say. "There's nobody out here."

191

"It was an accident," Shelby says through gritted teeth. "Let it go."

Ryan returns with the wood. "I almost got locked in the shed like Olivia."

"What do you mean?" Shelby asks, sounding alarmed.

"The wind," he says as he adds wood to the fire. "It blew the door shut. I shoved it open before the board fell on the latch, but I get how it could happen."

"Be careful when you go out there," Shelby says. "Make sure you tell someone so we know to check on you."

Tyler pushes away from the table. "You guys ready to get working on the truck?"

"In a minute," Derek says. "I need to add another layer of socks so my feet don't freeze."

"Good idea. I'll do the same."

Tyler follows Derek upstairs.

"I'll help clean up," Shelby says. "I just need to run to my room and get a sweater."

She takes off, leaving me alone with Ryan, but at least he's not near me. He's at the fireplace, using the poker to stoke the embers.

I gather up the plates from the table and bring them to the kitchen. I'm not hungry, but I could use some coffee after not sleeping last night. I haven't slept a full night since we got here.

As I'm pouring myself some coffee, I hear Ryan. "Where do you want these?"

Looking back, I see him holding the platter of eggs. He's right behind me, standing far too close.

"Just set it anywhere," I say, wishing he'd go away.

He places the platter on the counter beside me, then puts his hands on my shoulders and leans down to my ear. "You're so tense, Beth." He massages my shoulders. "You need to relax."

I swallow, my heart going faster. "Get away from me, Ryan. I mean it."

"I know it was you," he whispers. "The person responsible for locking me up in the psych ward? I know it was you."

"I . . . I don't know what you're talking about," I say, trying to remain calm. He can't hurt me. Not when everyone's in the house. Derek and Tyler will be coming down any minute.

"You took the journals," Ryan says. "And the sketches. You brought them to my counselor. You told him I was dangerous. You got him to start the process to have me committed. You got Derek, Tyler, and James to go along with it. To support your case."

How does he know that? How does he know we were involved? The judge who made the order to have Ryan put in a mental hospital promised us we'd be protected. He assured us Ryan would never find out that we were the ones who provided the evidence needed to have him locked away. We didn't want to do it, but we didn't have a choice. We knew it was just a matter of time before Ryan did something that would end someone's life. His journals were filled with morbid stories and poems about death and killing people, and he had all these sketches of people being stabbed. I showed Shelby and she blew it off, saying the journals and sketches were just Ryan's way of expressing the anger he felt over all the horrible things he'd gone through during his childhood. I didn't buy it. I knew Ryan was dangerous.

I whip around to face him. "You're wrong. It was your counselor who did it. I wasn't involved. I don't know why you're saying this."

"I went to see him. Last summer." Ryan plants his hands on the counter on either side of me. "He told me what you did. He told me everything."

"No." I shake my head. "That doesn't make sense. Why would he do that?"

Ryan smiles. "I have ways of getting people to tell the truth. But here's the thing. They weren't mine."

"What . . . what do you mean?"

193

"The journals. The sketches. They weren't mine. They were Shelby's." He laughs a little. "The girl you spent all your time with back then? The one you told all your secrets to? She's the one with the dark, twisted mind. But she's my sister. And I love her. So I took the blame. I let myself get locked up so she could have a life. Finish college." He leans down to my face. "I didn't tell her what you did. If I had, she would've killed you."

Does he really believe that Shelby's the crazy one and not him? If so, he's even more disturbed than I thought.

"So that's what this is about?" I ask. "This is why you've been trying to scare me all week? You're trying to get revenge because of something you think happened ten years ago?"

"There you go again. Assuming I'm the bad guy, just like you did back then." His lips rise to a slight smile. "I'm not threatening you, Beth. I'm letting you know I'm on to you. I know what you did. What *all* of you did. You had me locked away, and the whole time, it was Shelby you should've been worried about."

He's lying, or delusional, or both. Shelby's one of my closest friends, or she was back then. We've grown apart over the years with her living in the city and me living upstate, but we still talk on the phone or connect on social media. She struggles with bouts of depression, but she's not crazy like Ryan. She's never talked about killing people like Ryan used to do.

"Get away from me," I say. "Get away or I'll scream."

He takes a step back. "Seriously, Beth, you need to relax." His slight smile turns into a full-on grin. "It'll all be over soon."

"What do you mean? What are you going to do?"

"Ryan, you ready?" Tyler asks, coming down the stairs.

"Yeah, I was just helping Beth clean up breakfast." Ryan walks over to Tyler. "My coat's in the laundry room. I'll grab it, then get the shovels and meet you outside."

"Sounds good."

194

I wait for Ryan to go out to the garage, then race over to Tyler as Derek comes down the stairs.

"He knows," I say to both of them. "Ryan knows what we did."

"What are you talking about?" Tyler asks.

"He knows we had him committed," I whisper. "He just told me. He said he talked to his old counselor and found out it was us that gave him Ryan's journals and sketchbooks."

"He's lying," Derek says. "There's no way he talked to his counselor. The guy has to be dead by now. He was ancient ten years ago."

"So maybe Ryan lied about that, but he somehow found out what we did. And he claims the journals and sketches weren't his. He said they were—"

"What are you guys whispering about?" Shelby asks, coming down the stairs.

"We were just talking," Tyler says. "We were trying to be quiet in case Olivia is sleeping."

"She's not. I just talked to her. She said she might go take a walk." Shelby looks at me. "She wants to know if we want to go too."

"I'll pass. It's cold, and I don't really like going on walks."

"What are you talking about?" Derek says to me. "You go on a walk almost every day."

After ten years of marriage, you'd think Derek would be able to sense when I don't want to do something. But no, he's completely clueless.

"I walk on the sidewalk," I say. "In our neighborhood. Not in the woods when it's freezing cold outside."

"Then I'll go with her," Shelby says. "I don't want her going alone."

I look at Shelby, wondering if anything Ryan said about her is true. He had to have been lying. Shelby didn't write those journals. I'd be able to prove it if I still had them. They had Ryan's handwriting, which is strangely similar to Shelby's, but I'm sure it was Ryan who wrote them.

"Before you go," I say to Derek. "Can I talk to you a minute?"

"Beth, we need to get out there. We need all the time we can get to work on the truck."

"It'll just take a minute."

"I'll see you out there," Tyler says, taking off.

"Let's go upstairs," I say to Derek.

He sighs, sounding annoyed and frustrated with me. I don't know why he's being this way. He's been dismissing my concerns all week, acting like I'm crazy for even suggesting something might be going on.

We go up to our room and I shut the door.

"Beth, I get that you're worried about Ryan, but the only way we're getting out of here is if I go work on the truck. So can we just—"

"He knows." I grip Derek's arm. "Don't you get what's going on here? Ryan knows we had him locked away and now he's getting revenge."

"How?" Derek folds his arms over his chest. "How is he getting revenge? He didn't cause James to fall on the ice auger. And he didn't even know Amber. Why would he kill her? Same for Olivia. You think Ryan locked her in the shed? Why would he do that? She wasn't involved in what we did to him. If he was really here to get revenge, we'd be dead by now. Tyler would be too."

He's right. This doesn't make sense. Everyone involved in getting Ryan committed is still alive except for James, and what happened to him does seem like an accident. We were all here at the house when it happened, unless Ryan somehow snuck out. Even if he did, there's no way he'd be able to attack James, a former linebacker who's still as big and strong as he was when he played football.

"Let it go," Derek says. "Even if Ryan knows it was us, it doesn't matter. He's not going to do anything. There's still more of us than him. We'd overpower him."

"Unless someone was helping him."

"So now someone else is trying to kill us?" Derek rolls his eyes, which infuriates me.

"Would you stop dismissing me? I'm your wife. You should at least listen to me even if you don't believe me."

"I *am* listening. I'm just tired of this. I'm tired of being here. And I'm angry. I lost one of my best friends, and my other best friend lost his girlfriend. I don't want to keep standing around, waiting for the next bad thing to happen. I want to do whatever it takes to get us out of here."

"Fine." I walk to the door and open it. "Go. Go work on the truck."

Derek walks over to me. "I'm not dismissing you. I just don't have time for this. We'll talk later, okay?"

I nod.

He leans down and gives me a kiss. "Try to relax. Maybe take a bath."

A bath? Does he really think a bath is going to make me feel better with everything that's going on? I'm so on edge, I can't even make myself eat. And now he's leaving me alone here with Shelby, who could be crazy. I don't think she is, but who knows? At this point, anything could be true. I don't know what to believe, or who to trust.

CHAPTER 29

Derek's been gone for over an hour. I hate that Ryan is with him. I keep imagining him doing something horrible, like hitting Derek over the head with the shovel. The only thing making me feel better is knowing Tyler is there. He's a big guy. Not as big as James, but Tyler is muscular. He has a trainer and works out all the time. He could take down Ryan if he needed to, unless Ryan came up behind him and hit him before he knew what was happening.

Now I'm worried again. What if they don't come back? Or what if Ryan does, and tells us Derek and Tyler are dead?

There's a knock on the bedroom door, the sudden sound making me almost jump out of my skin.

"Who is it?" I yell.

"Olivia. Can I come in?"

I get up and open the door. "How are you feeling?"

"Not great." She tries to smile, but her lips barely rise before falling again.

"Come sit down." I take her arm and lead her to the bed.

"I'm sorry to bother you," she says. "I just didn't want to be alone."

"Where's Shelby?"

"I think she went for a walk. I was going to go with her, but I just don't have the energy for it." She stares down at the floor. "I don't know what I'm going to do. How I'm going to get through this."

"You will." I gently rub her arm, attempting to comfort her. "It'll just take time."

"That's what Shelby said. But what does that mean? How long will it take for me to accept that James is gone?"

"Everyone's different. You should take as long as you need."

She nods, sniffling. "Shelby said that too. You two are a lot alike. I see why you're such good friends."

"We're actually really different, but sometimes that's a good thing."

"Yes, James told me what she was like back in college. I am a little surprised you two became so close."

"What do you mean?"

"Those drawings she used to do. And the paintings." Olivia shudders. "I can't imagine how her mind could come up with such things. But then again, I'm not an artist. I've heard their minds can be quite dark."

Her comment brings me back to the conversation James and I had before he died, when he told me he wouldn't be interested in Shelby even if he was single. He said something about all the dark stuff she was into, but I didn't know what he meant. I didn't get a chance to ask.

"What drawings?" I ask. "I'm not sure what you mean."

"James said she drew sketches of people being stabbed, and killed in other ways. I don't remember all that he told me, but it was very disturbing."

"I never saw her draw anything like that."

What Olivia just described sounds like the sketches I gave Ryan's counselor. I was sure he was the one who drew them, but what if I was wrong? What if it was Shelby who did the sketches? What if Ryan was right?

But if James knew those sketches were Shelby's, why didn't he tell us that? Why did he let us all think Ryan was the one who drew them? Was it because he wanted Ryan to be locked away? He hated him back then. He was always saying how he wished we could find a way to get rid of Ryan so he'd stop bothering us.

What if that's what happened? What if I helped James get Ryan committed to a mental hospital when it should've been Shelby?

That can't be true. I couldn't have gone all these years being her friend and not known that she's the disturbed one instead of her brother.

"You said something about her paintings," I say to Olivia. "What did James tell you about them?"

"He said she used blood for some of them instead of paint. I thought he was joking but—"

"Wait, where did she get blood?"

"From a man who had a farm outside of town. James said Shelby went on a few dates with the man's son and asked him to get her some pig's blood, which she used for her paintings."

"How did I not know about this? I was her best friend."

"Do you think Derek knew?"

"If he did, he didn't tell me." I pause, thinking back to those years, wondering what else I overlooked.

"I didn't mean to upset you. I honestly thought you knew."

"Why did James know? Did Shelby show him the paintings?"

"No, he found one of them when he was at her apartment." Olivia looks down. "I'm sure you know James and Shelby were involved back then."

"Yes, but it was just the one time. And they were both drunk."

She looks at me. "It wasn't one time. It went on for over a year."

"What? No. That can't be right. Shelby said it was just one time."

"She must not have wanted you to know the truth. I only know because I demanded James be honest with me about his relationship with Shelby when I discovered they'd been involved back when James and I were dating."

"Yes, he told me about that."

"When?" she asks, sounding surprised. "When did he tell you?"

"Just the other day. Olivia, I'm sorry he hurt you like that. James was a great guy, but he wasn't without his faults."

"He claims it only happened once when we were together, but who knows?" Her shoulders slump.

"Olivia, no. James loved you. I'm sure it was only one time."

"I didn't find out until after we were married. I was devastated. I demanded he tell me his history with her or I wouldn't agree to stay with him."

"And that's when he told you the relationship they had in college went on for a year?"

"Yes. He said he dated other women while he was with her and that she went out with other men. Maybe that's why you believed they weren't seeing each other."

"That was part of it. The other part was I just didn't see them together. James was the typical jock. Obsessed with sports. Working out. Partying. He had no interest in art, or anything else Shelby liked. And she hated sports."

"Well, I don't like sports either. That didn't seem to matter to James."

"Yes, but you have, or had, other things in common. Sorry. I don't mean to keep talking about James. I'm sure it's upsetting to you."

She nods. "Actually, yes. It's getting to be too much."

"Why don't we go downstairs? We could sit by the fire. I could make some tea."

"That sounds nice." She puts her hand over mine. "Thank you, Beth."

"Of course. Whatever you need, just ask."

We go downstairs and I tell Olivia to relax by the fire while I make the tea. When it's ready, I bring it to her, then get some for myself.

"Are the men out working on the truck?" she asks.

"Yes." I check the time. "I was hoping they'd come back to warm up. The wind is really picking up out there."

"I feel like such an idiot for causing all this trouble." She sips her tea. "I'm still not used to driving the truck. I was going too fast. I overestimated its capabilities on the ice. Before I knew it, it was spinning sideways and then it just stopped. The tires were jammed in the snow. I panicked and pushed on the gas to get it moving again, which only made it worse. The tires just dug deeper into the snow. I can't believe I was so stupid."

"It was just a mistake. There's no use beating yourself up about it."

She sighs. "I should've had James take me into town that day. He's better at driving on icy roads. If I'd just let him drive me, the truck wouldn't be blocking the road and we wouldn't be in this mess." Her lips quiver. "James would still be alive." A tear slips down her cheek.

I go over to her on the couch and sit beside her. "Olivia, don't blame yourself for what happened. It isn't your fault. It was an accident."

"An accident that could've been prevented. He never would've gone to the lake to get the auger if I hadn't caused this mess with the truck."

I don't know what to say to make her feel better. She clearly blames herself for the situation we're in, and honestly, I kind of agree. If she'd kept the truck on the road, we would've been able to get out of here after our phones went missing. Amber and James would still be alive. I'd be safe at home instead of trapped here.

"I should add another log to the fire," Olivia says, setting her tea down.

"I'll do it." I get up and take a log from the stack and add it to the fire. "What time did Shelby leave?"

"I'm not sure. After I told her I was staying here, I heard her go downstairs, but I don't know if she left then or later."

I turn back to Olivia. "When did she ask you to go on a walk? How long ago?"

"Maybe an hour? I'm sorry, I wasn't paying attention to the time."

"If she left an hour ago, she should've been back by now. She wouldn't be out that long in this weather." I glance outside at the swirling snow in the air. "Maybe I should go look for her."

"I don't know, Beth. It seems dangerous."

"I won't be out there long. And I'll make sure to bundle up."

Olivia clears her throat. "When I said it could be dangerous, I wasn't referring to the weather."

"I don't understand. What did you mean?"

"Shelby." She looks down.

"What about her?"

"I know she's your friend but . . ." Olivia's eyes rise to mine. "I think she's dangerous."

"Dangerous?" I laugh. "Shelby? She's the opposite of dangerous. She won't even hurt a bug. In college, she got mad at me for almost killing a spider. She insisted we catch him and take him outside."

"Perhaps I'm wrong, but . . ." Olivia pauses.

"But what?"

"I think she's the one who locked Amber out in the cold. I think Shelby killed her."

CHAPTER 30

My thoughts are racing, trying to figure out if it's even possible that Shelby killed Amber. I can't imagine her doing that. The Shelby I know would never intentionally hurt someone. Her brother would, but not Shelby.

"Why would you say that?" I ask Olivia. "Did you see something?"

"I heard Shelby leaving her room that night. The night Amber died."

"I think what you heard was Amber. She was fighting with Tyler and left their room to go downstairs."

"No, the noise I heard was definitely coming from the room next to mine. The one where Shelby and Ryan are staying."

"Are you sure it wasn't Ryan who left the room?"

"No, it was Shelby. I tried to go back to sleep but heard some commotion downstairs, like two people arguing. I wasn't sure what was going on. I was going to wake up James to have him check, but then decided to just go down there myself. I only made it halfway down the hall when I ran into Shelby. She was holding a glass of water, heading back to her room."

"Maybe that's all she was doing. Getting a glass of water."

"It's possible, but I could've sworn I heard someone else that night. And I think it was Amber. I think Shelby was arguing with her, Amber went out to smoke, and Shelby locked her out there."

"How do you know Amber smoked?"

204

"I caught her smoking her first night here." Olivia picks up her tea and takes a sip. "She asked me not to tell Tyler. I told her I wouldn't, but asked her to please be careful. One of the houses up here went up in flames last year from a cigarette that wasn't properly disposed of. Anyway, I can't say for sure that's what happened, but I find it disturbing that Shelby was down here that night and didn't mention it after we found Amber."

"Why didn't you tell anyone this?"

"I did. I told James. He assured me Shelby would never hurt anyone and told me to keep this to myself. But I don't feel it's right to keep this a secret if she is, indeed, dangerous."

"I can't imagine her doing anything to harm someone. I think she really was just getting a glass of water that night."

"Or maybe you just don't want to let yourself believe she's capable of something like that." Olivia sets her tea down on the table. "I hate to speak poorly of her, given that she's your friend, but when I think about what James said about her having a dark side, I can't help but wonder if she truly is disturbed in some way. Disturbed enough to cause harm to others."

I think back to what Ryan said about Shelby being the crazy one and not him. What if it's true? What if she really is crazy?

"But why would Shelby want to harm Amber? She had no reason to."

Olivia pauses to think. "Perhaps she didn't like Amber's relationship with Tyler. Did you notice how Amber reacted when Tyler mentioned having lunch with Shelby? Even after he explained that he met with her to get Amber a gift, she still seemed upset that the two of them got together without her knowledge."

"Yes, I noticed that, but it was Amber who was upset, not Shelby."

"As far as we know, but maybe there was more going on that we weren't aware of."

"Like what?"

"Perhaps Amber was jealous of Tyler's friendship with Shelby, or thought there was something going on with the two of them. Maybe she demanded that Tyler stop seeing her."

"I suppose it's possible," I say, knowing how angry Amber was at me for sleeping with her boyfriend years ago. If she thought Shelby had something going on with Tyler, it's possible Amber demanded that Tyler stop seeing her. If Shelby found out about that, she'd be furious. But would she be angry enough to kill Amber?

"I could be completely wrong about this," Olivia says. "You know Shelby far better than I do. I just can't ignore the bad feeling I get when I'm around her."

"Maybe that's because of . . ." I pause, not sure I should bring it up.

"Her history with James? Yes, I considered that, and it's quite possible that's all it is. I thought I'd made peace with it, but perhaps there's still a part of me that hasn't."

"It's understandable. Actually, I'm surprised you were okay with her being here."

"James and I did a lot of work to get past what happened. We went to therapy. Had several difficult conversations. I truly felt like we were in a good place. I felt like James was finally committed to us, and to our future." She sighs. "Maybe I'm just being paranoid. After everything that's happened this week, I'm looking for answers, trying to explain why things turned out this way."

"It's not just you. I feel the same way. I've been trying to explain it. Looking for someone to blame. I was sure Ryan was involved, but maybe . . . maybe Shelby was too."

"Beth, I'm sorry I put that thought in your head. I can't prove she did anything, so I really should've kept quiet about it."

"No, I'm glad you said something. I admit I'm concerned Shelby didn't tell anyone she was down here the night Amber died. I'm surprised she didn't say something to you after you saw her in the hall that night. Like tell you to not mention that you'd seen her."

"I was surprised by that too. Honestly, I was worried she might come after me. When I found myself locked in the shed, I thought—" She shakes her head. "I'm not going to say it. I'm sure she didn't do it. I'm sure it was just the wind."

But what if it wasn't? Would Shelby try to kill Olivia to keep her quiet?

I don't even want to think that way. Shelby is my friend. She's a good person. She's not a killer.

"She shouldn't still be out there," I say, noticing the time. "I'm going to go look for her."

"I'll go too," Olivia says, getting up.

"You don't have to. I don't plan to be out there long."

"If you don't mind, I'd like to go. I don't like the idea of being here by myself."

"Okay. I'm just going to run upstairs and make sure she's not in her room."

"Oh, yes, good idea."

I'm really starting to connect with Olivia. She seemed so aloof earlier in the week, but she's been opening up to me the past few days, letting me get to know her, and I'm finding that I really like her. I could even see us being friends, assuming we ever get out of here. I'm glad she let her guard down with me and admitted she's just as worried as I am about our situation. I'm not sure I believe her theory about Shelby, but part of me is starting to wonder if I don't know Shelby as well as I thought I did.

I go up to her room and knock on her door. "Shelby? Are you in there?"

There's no answer. I open the door and peek inside. The room is a mess, with clothes all over the floor and dirty dishes on the nightstand. Shelby has never been someone who cleans up after herself. She used to tell me the artist in her didn't like a clean space, and that the mess was an expression of her creative spirit.

"Shelby?" I call out. I check the bathroom, but it's empty.

I leave her room and go back downstairs.

"Olivia?" I call out, noticing she's not there.

"I'm back here," she says. "Getting my coat on."

I find her in the mudroom, getting bundled up to go outside. I do the same, making sure to wrap my scarf around my face so it doesn't freeze in the bitterly cold wind.

"Do you have a key?" I ask Olivia as she opens the door.

"A key for what?"

"The door. Just in case we get locked out."

What I mean is, in case someone purposely locks us out. We're the only ones here, but I'm not taking any chances.

"Good idea," Olivia says. "I'll go grab it." She runs off, returning moments later. "Okay, I got it. Let's go."

We walk outside, past the shed to the woods. There's a trail of footprints in the snow that I'm guessing belong to Shelby.

"Shelby?" I yell as Olivia and I walk down the trail. "Shelby, are you out here?"

There's no answer.

"How far do you think she'd go?" Olivia asks.

"Not far enough that she couldn't hear us." I cup my hands around my mouth and yell, "Shelby! Where are you?"

There's still no answer. We keep walking.

"I'm getting worried," Olivia says. "Why isn't she answering?"

"I don't know."

I'm trying to remain hopeful, but I'm becoming more concerned the farther into the woods we go. We should've found her by now.

"What do we do?" I ask, noticing the path breaking off in two directions. There are footprints going both ways.

"I guess I'll go one way and you go the other."

"Are you sure? I don't know if it's a good idea for us to split up."

Olivia nods. "Yes, you're right. We should stick together. Which way should we start?"

"Let's go to the right."

We head down the snowy path, stopping abruptly when we come to a steep drop-off.

"Watch out," I say, grabbing Olivia's arm. "The ground is slick. You shouldn't get too close to the edge."

"Shelby!" Olivia yells, her voice echoing.

We wait to hear something, but don't.

I look back to where we just came from. "Maybe we should try going the other way. If she came to this spot, she'd turn around. She doesn't like heights. She wouldn't walk along a steep cliff."

"Then let's turn around."

I go first, making my way down the path.

"Beth!" Olivia screams.

"What?" I ask, turning back.

Olivia's standing at the edge of the cliff, looking down. She's shaking, and I get the feeling it's not because of the cold.

"What is it?" I say. "Why'd you stop?"

"Shelby," Olivia says, her voice trembling. "I think . . . I think she's down there."

Please let her be wrong. If Shelby fell off the cliff, there's no way she'd be alive.

I walk up to Olivia. "Move back. Get away from the edge."

She takes a few steps back while I look down over the cliff.

"Oh God," I gasp, covering my mouth.

"It's her, isn't it?" Olivia says.

"Yes," I whisper, staring down at Shelby's body. She's lying face up in the snow, as if she didn't realize the cliff was behind her, took a step back, and fell to her death.

She's dead. Shelby is dead.

CHAPTER 31

"Why did she go out there alone?" I ask when we're back in the house. "She had to have known it'd be dangerous."

"I should've gone with her. I know these woods better than she does. I could've warned her."

Olivia's pacing the floor behind the couch while I stand in the kitchen, trying to figure out what to do next.

"The guys should've been back by now," I say, checking the time. "They shouldn't be out there this long."

Olivia stops pacing and looks at me. "Let's go down there. We have to tell them what happened."

"Ryan," I mutter, imagining his reaction when he finds out his sister is gone. "He's going to be devastated. Shelby was everything to him. She took care of him. Looked out for him. I don't know how he'll survive without her."

It sounds dramatic, but it's really not. Ryan depends on Shelby for everything. I truly believe she's the reason he has a somewhat normal life. Shelby practically raised him. She protected Ryan when they were growing up, and continued to do so after he left home. I've never seen siblings have such a close relationship. Without Shelby, Ryan will be completely lost.

"What do you want to do?" Olivia asks. "We can't just do nothing."

"We'll go down there. We'll go find the guys."

I'm about to get my coat when the front door opens. Derek walks in, followed by Tyler and Ryan. Their faces are red from the cold and they look exhausted.

"We've got good news and bad," Derek says, taking off his coat.

"Start with the good," I say, desperate for some good news.

"We dug out the tires and got the engine running."

"And the bad news?" I ask.

"We couldn't get the truck back on the road," Tyler says. "It's still sideways."

Ryan takes his hat off and shakes the snow from his hair. "We need a tow truck to move it."

"So now what do we do?" Olivia asks as Derek and Tyler join me in the kitchen, searching for something to eat.

"We're going to try to walk to the main road," Tyler says. "But we needed to come in and warm up first. And eat something."

"I'll heat up the leftovers from last night," Olivia says, hurrying to the kitchen.

"Here." I hand Derek one of the muffins Olivia made for breakfast a few days ago.

"I'll take one too," Tyler says.

"Ryan?" I call out to him. "You want something to eat?"

"In a minute," he says, taking off his boots.

As much as I don't like Ryan, I feel bad for him, knowing his world is about to collapse. I don't know if I can tell him. Maybe Derek could do it, although he's not the best person to deliver bad news. He gets nervous and stumbles over his words.

Ryan walks over to us. "Is Shelby upstairs?"

I look at Olivia. She was putting a plate in the microwave, but stops and looks back at me.

"Beth," Derek says, chomping on his muffin. "Is Shelby upstairs?"

"No," Olivia blurts out.

"Where is she?" Ryan asks.

Olivia gives me a look to tell him.

"She, um, went for a walk," I say.

"A walk?" Ryan laughs. "She wouldn't walk in this weather. She doesn't even like walking when it's nice out."

He's right. Shelby isn't someone who'd go on a walk, especially by herself, and she doesn't like being outside when it's cold out. So why was she out there?

"When did she leave?" Tyler asks, opening the fridge.

"I'm not sure," I say. "Ryan, can I talk to you?"

"Go ahead."

"In private."

"Just tell me here." He walks up to me. "What's going on?"

The room goes silent.

Tyler closes the fridge, sensing something's up.

"Beth?" Derek says, concern in his voice. "What is it? What's going on?"

"It's Shelby." I swallow past the lump in my throat. "She went on a walk. In the woods. She'd been gone for a while, so Olivia and I went out to look for her and . . ."

I pause and see Ryan slowly shaking his head. He knows.

"She must've slipped," I say. "Off the side of the cliff."

"No!" Ryan grips my shoulders, shaking me. "You're lying! She's not dead! You're lying!"

"Hey!" Derek pulls Ryan off me. "Let's go sit down, okay?"

Ryan sinks to the floor. "She can't be gone. She can't. She can't be gone."

He repeats the words over and over, sobbing into his hands, his body crumpled on the floor.

"We have to do something," Olivia whispers, looking at me.

Tyler walks up behind Ryan. "Give us a minute," he says, shooing us away.

I nod, realizing it makes sense for Tyler to be the one to comfort Ryan. Living in the city, he sees Ryan more than the rest of us do. It sounds like they've even hung out together a few times.

Olivia, Derek, and I go upstairs. Olivia goes to her room, while Derek and I go to ours.

"What the hell happened?" he asks, closing the door.

"I don't know. She must not have noticed the cliff was behind her, and took a step back and fell." I shudder as I think about that.

"Why was she even out there?"

"She told Olivia she was going to take a walk."

"Shelby doesn't go on walks."

"Maybe she wanted to get out of the house. Or maybe she was doing that forest-bathing thing that Ryan does."

"Forest bathing? What the hell is that?"

"You walk around the trees. Take in nature. It's like a meditative thing."

"That sounds like something Shelby would do, but it's odd she'd do it in this weather. That wind is brutal. So when did you find her?"

"Ten . . . twenty minutes ago? I wasn't watching the time. Olivia and I didn't know what to do. We were about to walk down to the truck and find you guys, but then you showed up."

"How long was Shelby out there?"

"I don't know. Maybe an hour? Olivia said Shelby came to her room, asking if she wanted to walk with her. Olivia didn't feel up to it, so Shelby went by herself, but Olivia wasn't sure when she left. We got worried when she didn't come back so we went looking for her." I pause, my thoughts going to Ryan. "Ryan's never going to survive this. Shelby was his whole world. I don't think he even has any friends. Except maybe Tyler, but they're not really friends. I'm sure he'll try to help out, but he can't replace Shelby. He can't keep an eye on Ryan the way Shelby did."

Derek goes to the bed to sit down. "Maybe he doesn't need that."

"What do you mean?"

Derek looks over at me. "I don't think Ryan's as helpless as we think. I think Shelby was treating him that way because she didn't want to lose him."

"Lose him? Derek, what are you talking about? Shelby didn't want to take care of Ryan. She did it because she had to. Because she didn't have a choice."

"Or is that just what she told us? Or what she made us believe?"

I walk over to the bed and sit beside him. "Are you just speculating, or do you know something you're not telling me?"

He turns to me. "Remember that weekend when I went to the city to see Tyler? He took me over to Shelby's place, and it kind of seemed like Ryan was the one taking care of things." Derek shrugs. "Maybe Shelby was just going through one of her depressive cycles that week, but Ryan was definitely the one taking care of her. It wasn't the other way around."

"Why didn't you tell me that?"

"I didn't see a need to. Honestly, I wasn't even thinking about it until now. But even on this trip, Ryan hasn't acted like he needs her. If I didn't know his history, I'd think he's just a normal guy."

"He's not. The things he's said to me are not at all normal."

"Okay, but aside from that, if we're just talking about him being able to live his life, I think he could do it without Shelby. I think all these years he could've lived on his own, but she wouldn't let him."

"Part of that is because they couldn't afford it. You know how expensive it is to live in the city. It'd be tough for even *us* to afford it."

"They could've gotten roommates. They didn't have to live with each other. I'm just saying I think Ryan could've had his own life, maybe even had a girlfriend, if Shelby hadn't held on to him so tightly."

"She's always been that way. She helped raise him. She was almost like a mother to him."

"And I think that made him feel like he owed it to her to stay with her. To not go out and get his own life. Shelby needed Ryan, and Ryan knew that. It's why he's never even considered moving out and getting his own place."

"Is that just your theory, or did Ryan tell you that?"

"He kind of implied it."

"How? What did he say?"

"That she's been really depressed. Like not able to get out of bed. Missing work. He was worried she might get fired. He said she's been like this before, but never this bad. He's had to take over and do everything because Shelby hasn't been able to. He was hoping coming here, being with all of us, would make her feel better."

"When did Ryan tell you this?"

"Today. When we were digging out the truck."

"Did Tyler know about this?"

"No, but other than having lunch with Shelby last week, he said he hadn't seen her much. He said she stopped texting and calling him. He just thought it was because she was busy."

"How long has Shelby been like this? Did Ryan say?"

"He said it's been going on for a while, but got worse last summer, after Shelby brought her paintings to an art fair and none of them sold. She told Ryan she was going to give up being an artist."

"That doesn't sound like Shelby. All she's ever wanted is to be an artist. She wouldn't just give that up."

"Exactly, so the fact that she was even considering it proves she wasn't doing well."

I shake my head. "I think Ryan's lying. Shelby seemed fine when she got here. She didn't seem depressed."

"You don't think it was odd that she kept going upstairs to be alone? And according to Ryan, she wasn't sleeping. She kept getting up in the night and going downstairs."

His comment reminds me of what Olivia told me, about Shelby being downstairs the night Amber died.

"So what are you saying?" I ask. "Are you implying that what happened to Shelby wasn't an accident?"

"I don't want that to be the case, but . . ." He sighs. "What if it wasn't? What if she couldn't take feeling this way anymore and . . . wanted it to end?"

"No. I don't believe it. If she was that depressed, she would've talked to me. She would've told me she needed help."

"Not if she didn't want you to know. Beth, I'm not saying that's what happened. I just think it's possible if what Ryan said about her is true. And really, if you think back to how she was in college, it's clear she had issues."

"Meaning what?"

"Like those drawings she did. Of people dying and being stabbed. You have to admit those were creepy."

"Those weren't Shelby's. Those were Ryan's drawings."

"No, they were Shelby's."

My mind goes back to what Ryan said, about the sketchbook belonging to Shelby, not him. But it wasn't true. It couldn't be.

"I think we're talking about two separate things," I say. "I'm talking about the drawings Ryan did. The ones we found in his sketchbook."

"That was Shelby's sketchbook. She made those drawings."

"I don't understand. We gave that sketchbook to Ryan's counselor. Those drawings were part of the reason we were able to get him committed. Because they were so disturbing. And now you're saying the drawings weren't his?"

"No, but why does it matter? We needed something the courts could use to commit him. That sketchbook did a lot to help our case. It helped us get rid of Ryan so he'd stop bothering us." Derek rubs my arm. "It's what you wanted. We all did."

I yank away from him and get up. "You're saying we lied? Derek, how could you not tell me this?"

"I thought you knew. You and Shelby were best friends. How could you not know she had this dark side?"

"I know she had a dark side, but not like that. Not like she fantasized about killing people."

"They were just drawings. She didn't actually want to kill anyone."

I pace the floor. "This doesn't make sense. Why would Shelby let the court believe those drawings were done by Ryan, knowing they'd be used to show he was dangerous and needed to be committed?"

"Because she didn't want it to be her. Or that's what I'm guessing. She either didn't want to be the one in the mental hospital or she wanted Ryan to go there so she could get a break from him."

"She wouldn't do that. You saw how upset she was when they took him away."

"Maybe she was pretending to be upset when she really wasn't. Put yourself in her place. You're young, trying to have a normal college life, and you're stuck taking care of your little brother. Wouldn't you want a break?"

"Yes, but not enough that I'd have my brother put in a mental hospital."

"It's not like he didn't belong there. Everyone knew Ryan had issues, even if he didn't make those drawings."

"How do you know he didn't? How do you know they were done by Shelby? Did she tell you?"

"No, James did. He caught her drawing in that sketchbook. The one we gave Ryan's counselor."

"Did he ask her about it? Did he ask why she was drawing that stuff?"

"No. She didn't know James saw her. He was going to talk to her about it later, but then got the idea to use the sketchbook to get Ryan locked up."

"So you're saying we had Ryan committed using false evidence. And you don't have a problem with this?"

"I get it wasn't the most ethical thing to do, but I was a kid back then. I didn't make the best choices. And thinking back on it now, I don't regret it. Ryan needed to get help, and having him committed was the only way to do it. He wasn't going to do it on his own."

"What if we sent the wrong person there? What if it was Shelby who needed to be there and not Ryan?"

"Are you serious?" Derek stands up. "Beth, you've spent every moment since Ryan arrived telling me how deranged he is, and how you think he's responsible for everything that's been going on. You even accused him of killing Amber."

"I still believe he's disturbed. What I'm saying is that maybe Shelby was too. Maybe she needed help just as much as Ryan did and none of us noticed or did anything about it. What if you're right and what happened today wasn't an accident? How could I call myself her friend and not even notice she was suffering?"

Derek pulls me into his arms. "Honey, don't blame yourself for this. We were all her friends, and none of us knew she would do something like this. And maybe she didn't. Maybe it really was just an accident."

CHAPTER 32

Ryan

"This wasn't supposed to happen," I say, staring at the top of the dresser. Shelby's things are still there. The beaded bracelet she made. Her star-and-moon necklace. The bottle of lavender essential oil she'd dab on her wrists every night. Her hairbrush. It's all there, like she's still alive.

"I'm sorry," Olivia says, running her hand up and down my arm. "I'm so sorry she's gone."

"Why would she do this? Why would she leave me?"

"I know you're upset, but please, quiet down," Olivia says. "You don't want them to hear us."

"Why? We both lost someone. It makes sense that we'd want to talk."

"I suppose." She glances at the door. "It's just that it's late, and I'm in your room. I don't want them making assumptions."

"Why does it matter? They won't be around much longer."

"Honestly, Ryan," Olivia scolds. "Keep your voice down."

I grab Shelby's pillow, hugging it to my chest as I lie down. "I want her back. She can't be gone. I need her. I need my sister."

Olivia lies down beside me. "You'll get through this, Ryan. You're stronger than you think." She runs her hand along the side of my face. "And you have me." She smiles. "We're a team. We can get through anything. Look how far we've come. What we've been able to do."

I gaze at Olivia, at her pale porcelain skin and light blue eyes. "I didn't think we'd be able to do it. I really didn't. I thought—"

"I know. But we did it. James is gone, and I'm yours." She leans over and presses her lips to mine. "All yours."

My body reacts to her, wanting more, but I can't do it. Not now. It wouldn't be right. Not after what happened to Shelby.

"I can't," I mutter. "It's too soon."

"I understand," she whispers, running her fingers down my chest. "It's just that we've waited so long for this."

"I know. I just . . . I can't right now."

"You know, it's entirely possible that she fell. That it wasn't intentional."

"Either way, she's still gone."

My mind recalls the past few months, trying to find any signs that Shelby would want to end her life. She'd been going through a dark time, questioning if she wanted to keep trying to make it as an artist, but then she got better. She knew this trip was coming up and it lifted her spirits. She was looking forward to seeing everyone. She wouldn't admit it, but I knew she was most looking forward to seeing James.

I never understood her obsession with him. The guy was a selfish bastard who used my sister, pretending to be her friend when all he really wanted was her body. And she gave it to him, over and over again, thinking he loved her. I thought when James got married, it would end, but it didn't. Every time he came to the city, she'd hook up with him, even when I begged her not to.

James deserved to die. He'd been stringing Shelby along for years — making her think they had a future while he cheated on her, then married someone else. He played with her emotions, not caring how much he hurt her. He treated me even worse. Back in college, he bullied me, made fun of me, and told people I was crazy. One time he punched me, then told everyone I got into a fight. I told Shelby he was lying, but she didn't believe me. She took his side over mine.

That's when I knew I'd lost her. She'd fallen in love with a guy who would never love her back. She loved him so much that she was willing to go along with the court's decision to have me put in a mental hospital. I know James was the one who put Shelby's sketchbook in my backpack and made sure that Beth found it. Beth is such a tattletale, and James had already convinced her, and all his friends, that I was insane. He knew she'd take that sketchbook and give it to my counselor, who would then build a case against me that would end with a judge deciding I needed to be locked away.

James was the mastermind behind it all, but he sat back and let Beth, Derek, and Tyler do all the work. They were the ones who told the judge I was dangerous, especially Beth. She was convinced I was going to hurt someone, just because of things I said when I was joking around. I decided to keep it up when I saw her again. I like scaring her, and she deserves it after what she did to me, believing James and all his lies.

James was determined to get rid of me back then so he could have Shelby all to himself, and so that I wouldn't be there to tell her that he was using her. Manipulating her. Turning her against me.

I don't blame Shelby for what happened. I know why she did it. She thought James loved her, which is all she ever wanted. She wanted to feel loved. We both did. All our lives, we'd never had anyone love us, other than the love we had for each other. Our parents hated us. If they could've killed us and gotten away with it, they would've done it. I'm convinced they were trying to get us to do it ourselves. When we were kids, they'd leave us alone for weeks at a time, hoping they'd come back and find we'd electrocuted ourselves or drowned in the tub. They'd even leave knives out, hoping we'd play with them.

When Shelby got an art scholarship for college, it was our ticket to freedom. We finally got away from our psychotic parents, but the memories remained. I had terrible nightmares. I still do. Shelby dealt with her trauma by writing in her journal or drawing. She'd put her dark thoughts on paper, either through words or through sketches of our parents being tortured and killed. When those sketches were used against me, and everyone thought they were mine, I decided not to speak up and tell the truth. I was protecting my sister. She had a brighter future than me. She was in college and had friends. I had nothing. I didn't want her being with James, but I knew I couldn't stop her. I also knew she was seeing other guys. I held out hope she'd get serious with one of them and end it with James.

That never happened, but at least she moved on after she graduated. James got a job in Boston, and Shelby and I moved to New York City. The distance was enough to keep them apart for long stretches of time. But then James would plan these stupid reunions every year and Shelby would fall for him all over again.

It had to end. Shelby would never find someone who truly loved her if James was still around. So I killed him. With Olivia's help. We followed James to the lake that day, knocked him out with a shovel, got the auger running, set it down on the ice, and shoved James on top of it. We watched his body get chewed up by the blades, then we shut off the auger, and left him there. When we returned to the house, everyone was still upstairs in their rooms, unaware that anything had happened. But if one of them had been downstairs and seen us, we had a story ready to tell them. We have a story for everything. Olivia insisted we be prepared for every possible scenario.

"What if we're responsible?" I say.

"Responsible for what?" Olivia asks.

"For what Shelby did. What if losing James was too much for her? What if that's what made her do this?"

"Ryan, stop it. You're torturing yourself with stories that aren't true. First of all, I truly believe she just backed up and fell. And as for James, she knew she didn't have a future with him. He told her we were going to start a family this year."

"He told her a lot of things. None of them ever stopped her from wanting to be with him. Even when you and James got married, she still held out hope that he'd be with her. And he was. It never would've ended, even if you and him had kids."

"Yes, well, that was never going to happen. I would've gotten rid of him long before that."

"The bastard is finally gone. And it all worked out. Just like we planned. The cops will think what happened to James was just an accident."

"Just like Amber. It's a shame she was so careless." Olivia's lips rise to a slight smile. "Tell me the story again," she says, putting her leg over mine and moving closer.

"I don't feel like talking about it."

"Come on, baby. Please?" Olivia puts her mouth by my ear and whispers, "It gets me all tingly."

Olivia has a dark side. It's why I fell for her. We understand each other. We accept our darkness and choose to celebrate it, not shame ourselves for it. It's our darkness that allows us to get rid of evil in the world, like James. It gives us the strength to get back at those who have wronged us, like Derek and Tyler, who picked on me years ago just because James did. Because they're followers who don't have minds of their own. And Beth, the tattletale who feels the need to get involved in things when she shouldn't. They all deserve what they're about to get. It's time they pay for what they did.

As for Amber, I had nothing against her. I didn't even know her until just a few days ago. But Olivia said she had to die. We couldn't have her leaving here when this was over and telling people what happened. But I still felt bad punishing someone who didn't deserve it. I considered finding a way to get her out of here before people started dying, but then she caught me kissing Olivia and the decision was made. Amber had to die.

When she came downstairs that night and saw us, Olivia and I went into acting mode. Olivia yanked away from me, told Amber she'd made a horrible mistake, then started crying and ran upstairs. I remained with Amber. She seemed upset, but not about Olivia and me. She didn't seem to care that she'd caught us. She was upset about something else. I asked her what was wrong, and she told me she'd been fighting with Tyler. She said she needed a cigarette to calm down. She went out to the garage where she'd hidden her cigarettes, then came back inside to get her coat. I told her I'd get it for her while she went out back to smoke. As soon as she was out the door, I shut it and locked her out. She banged on the door, but luckily, no one heard her. I watched out the window as her face froze, her lips turned blue, and ice crystals formed on her eyelashes. She eventually quieted down and fell to the ground.

When I went back to my room, Shelby woke up and asked where I'd been. I told her I went to the kitchen to get a drink. She knew I was down there the night Amber died, but she never told anyone. She was looking out for me. Like she always did.

Shelby was more than my sister. She was everything to me. I don't know how I'll go on without her. This week was supposed to end with just Olivia, Shelby, and me. We'd go on with our lives as one big happy family. I'd be with Olivia, and Shelby would find a man who actually loved her.

It's what I always wanted. For Shelby and me to find love. To be happy.

And now she's gone.

CHAPTER 33

Olivia

It breaks my heart to see Ryan suffering. But I had no choice. It had to be done.

Shelby was in the way of our future. Ryan and I could never truly be together if she were alive. She would never let him go. Never let him have a life separate from hers. She'd guilt him into letting her live with us, which I couldn't let happen.

After waiting years to be with Ryan, and enduring a horrible marriage to James, it's time for me to finally be happy. But that wouldn't have happened with Ryan's sister making herself a permanent part of our lives.

I've been dreaming of Shelby's death for quite some time, since the moment I found out what she'd done to Ryan. I'd already fallen in love with him by then. My love for Ryan developed soon after I met him. It was one of those rare moments in life when you meet someone and instantly know they're your soulmate.

When Ryan arrived at the psych hospital, I'd been there for over a month. He walked by me, then turned back, as though he felt something between us. I felt it too. A magnetic pull that neither of us could deny.

We began our relationship that night when I snuck into his room. It was a bold move, but I had to act fast. I didn't know how much longer I'd be there, and I didn't want to miss the chance to be with the man who had already stolen my heart.

The first time we kissed was magical. A euphoric ride for the senses that made me feel like I was flying high on some kind of hallucinogenic drug. It was something I'd never experienced, despite having been with numerous men in the past. Ryan and I had such intense chemistry that we found it hard to be around each other without acting on our urges. We were constantly sneaking away to indulge our desires.

When we weren't doing that, we were talking, getting to know each other. It was during one of our talks that I found out how Ryan ended up there. He told me the story of how some football player his sister was fooling around with wanted to get rid of him. He said the guy bullied him and even punched him in the face, hoping it'd make Ryan go away. But he had nowhere to go. He was just a teenager, with no family other than his sister. The football player got his friends to turn against Ryan and convince a judge that Ryan was mentally unstable, to the point of being dangerous. What's even worse is that his own sister went along with it. She allowed people to think Ryan needed to be locked up, when the truth was, she was the one who should've been in the psych ward. Ryan doesn't believe that, but he could never see Shelby for who she really was. In his eyes, she could do no wrong.

Knowing what he'd been through, my love for Ryan grew and became deeper. He felt the same way about me. We couldn't stand to be apart, so we'd find ways to be together. I'd ask to sit with him at meals. I'd participate in group activities, which I despised, but I'd do it if it meant I could be with Ryan. And when I was about to be discharged, I pretended to have a relapse just so I could have more time with him.

Nobody knew about our love. We kept it a secret, knowing if anyone at the hospital found out, they'd try to keep us apart. When

I was finally released, it was my parents who kept me from Ryan. I told them I'd met someone, that I'd fallen in love. I assumed they'd be happy. But when they found out the man was someone from the psych hospital, they refused to let me see him. They said he'd only make my condition worse, that he wasn't good for me.

I hated them for it. How dare they tell me I couldn't be with the man I loved!

I shouldn't have been surprised. My parents never cared about my happiness. They only cared about how I made them look. Growing up, I was expected to be a daughter they could brag about to their wealthy friends. Someone who was refined and polite and well-educated. I played that role for as long as I could, until one day, I snapped. Ironically, my actions that day are what led me to meeting Ryan. My parents put me in the psych hospital hoping to 'fix' me and make me obedient, and instead I fell in love with a boy they despised.

I still remember that day — the one that led me to the psych ward. It was October, and I was home from college for a long weekend. I didn't want to go home, but my mother insisted I attend a charity event with her and my father. So I did as I was told, secretly seething with anger — at them for making me do it and me for going along with it. It was Friday, at three in the afternoon, when my father called me downstairs. When I got down there, I found him in the foyer with Asher, a boy I knew from prep school. My father informed me that Asher would be my date for the charity event. I refused to go with him, but my father ignored me and politely told Asher to pick me up at six the following night. As usual, my father didn't care what I wanted. I had to follow his orders, and he was ordering me to go with Asher.

But there was no way I was going. I despised Asher after what he'd done to me. Sophomore year, he'd forced himself on me at a party. I went home and told my parents what he'd done, thinking they'd go to the police and press charges. But they didn't seem the least bit concerned. They said I was overreacting and that Asher was being a typical boy. They wouldn't have said that if he'd been poor. The only reason they took his side was because his family was wealthy and well-connected. They were using me to get closer to Asher's parents and their connections.

After Asher left, my father found me in the kitchen. I was cutting an apple, not because I was hungry, but because I needed to feel the blade of the knife slicing through the apple's flesh. I needed to feel the weight of it in my hand. I continued to cut the apple as my father yelled at me, calling me ungrateful and a selfish brat. At some point, his words began to fade, my mind shut off, and I felt this urge, an undeniable need from deep within me. I raised the knife above my head, walked up to my father, and plunged the knife deep into his shoulder.

He screamed, causing my mother to race in. I don't remember that exact moment, but according to my mother, my eyes were glazed over and I had a grin on my face as I gripped the knife, still lodged in my father's shoulder.

That's what landed me in the psych hospital — in a town five hours away so that no one my parents knew would find out where I was or what I'd done. I was twenty-one, but given my violent act, my parents convinced a judge that I needed to be admitted without my consent. They took away my rights, just like Shelby did with Ryan. My parents betrayed me, like Shelby betrayed Ryan. It's no wonder Ryan and I were drawn to each other. We'd both been abandoned by the people who claimed to love us.

After I left the hospital, my parents forced me to finish college, threatening to take away my trust fund if I didn't. I needed that money to pay for the life I would soon have with Ryan, so I agreed to finish school. I'd keep in contact with Ryan until I graduated, then go to wherever he ended up and we'd get an apartment together.

That was the plan. But it never happened. Because of Shelby. When Ryan was released from the psych hospital, Shelby had one of her breakdowns. That's what Ryan called it. I didn't know exactly what he meant, but he said he couldn't leave her side. When Shelby graduated from college, she moved to New York City and insisted Ryan go with her.

She took him from me. And Ryan went along with it. He chose his sister over me. He didn't even tell her about me, and when I demanded to know why, he said he didn't think he should. He didn't want her to feel bad that he had someone when she didn't. But what about me? Did he not even consider how *I* felt? Apparently not, because he refused to leave her.

I decided I had to let him go. My dream of being with Ryan ended when he chose his sister over me. I went back to the life I hated — the only life I knew — playing the role of the obedient daughter. My parents bought me a condo a few miles from their house and my father gave me a job at his company. I didn't do any actual work, but got paid a generous salary to show up at the office a few times a week. That's when I met James.

He was selling office equipment at the time, but had sold all sorts of things over the years. He'd get restless at a job and move on to another. The moment I saw him, I knew he was a player, the type of guy who went from one woman to the next. I saw him as a challenge, which I desperately needed because I was bored out of my mind. I decided to get James to marry me. I had no intention of the marriage lasting, or even feeling the slightest bit of love for him. It was all about the challenge of being the one woman who could make a man like James settle down.

It turned out to be easier than I thought. A month after we met, I got James to commit to being in a relationship with me. After three months, we were talking about moving in together. A month later, he moved into my condo. A month after that, he proposed. I'd like to say it was all me that got him to that place, but I'm sure my parents' money played a role as well. James grew up poor and never wanted to be that way again. With me, he'd always be wealthy.

I'd accomplished my goal. I'd gotten James to agree to marry me, and even better, my father approved of him, which meant I could get rid of my parents soon after the wedding and collect my inheritance. I was beyond pleased with myself and what I'd done . . . until I learned the truth about James. Even now, I could kick myself for being so stupid. But I've rectified my mistake, and looking back at it, I realize it had to happen. I needed James in order to get where I am now. He unknowingly brought me back to Ryan, and our brief marriage made me a very wealthy woman.

"I'm going to try to get some sleep," Ryan says, his eyes falling shut.

"I'll go back to my room." I kiss his cheek, then turn to leave.

"Wait." He grabs my arm.

I turn back and see his sad eyes looking back at me. "What is it?"

"I love you."

I smile. "I love you too."

"It's just you and me now."

"Yes. Just you and me." My heart leaps with excitement as I say those words. I've waited so long for this moment, and now it's finally here.

"You won't leave me, will you?" Ryan says.

"No, my love." I kiss him. "I'm yours forever."

He closes his eyes and I get up from the bed.

There's just one more thing we need to take care of, or three, actually. Tomorrow, we'll get rid of Beth, Derek, and Tyler, and then, finally, justice will be served and Ryan and I can be together.

CHAPTER 34

Olivia

My alarm goes off at six, but I didn't need it. I've been up for most of the night, too excited to sleep. We're so close to being done with this. I honestly can't believe it worked. When Ryan and I discussed it, we knew there was a good chance it wouldn't happen. Everything would have to align perfectly for us to pull it off. And somehow, it did.

First, there was the weather. It's common to have snowstorms here this time of year, but I couldn't count on it. I just had to hope the timing would work out and the snow would be heavy enough that our guests wouldn't be able to leave. I became concerned when I overheard Beth telling Derek she wanted to leave before they were snowed in, so I made an excuse that I needed to go into town. I must say, I did an excellent job turning the truck sideways on the road, blocking it so that no one could get past. I made sure the front and back tires were lodged in the snow, then revved the engine, digging them even deeper. The heat from the engine melted the snow around the truck, which then froze and secured the vehicle in a layer of ice. Then I drained the battery until it was nearly dead, before finally going back to the house and playing the role of the pathetic wife who doesn't know how to drive and somehow managed to block the road.

After that, the rest of my plan fell into place. With everyone stranded here and no phones to call for help, Ryan and I could begin getting rid of them. I wasn't sure what to do with Amber. She was never part of the plan, an unexpected guest Tyler didn't tell James about until they were on their way here. Amber hadn't wronged Ryan or me, so it seemed a shame to have to kill her, but it had to be done. She caught me with Ryan, and I couldn't have her telling the others and ruining our plan.

Leaving her outside was brilliant. Everyone assumed it was an accident, except maybe Beth. That woman is convinced Ryan is out to kill everyone, which is so unfair. This was all my idea, not his. It took me months to convince Ryan to go along with it. He's not nearly as sinister as Beth thinks. He may have thoughts of harming people, but he doesn't have the guts to go through with it. Or he doesn't without me. He was reluctant to kill Amber, since she'd done nothing wrong, but I reminded him it was for the greater good. She had to die to allow us to continue what we'd started. He agreed, but I knew he felt some regret.

With James, Ryan was fully committed. When he shoved James on top of that auger, he had a grin on his face and a sparkle in his eyes. He finally felt what it's like to make his darkest thoughts come alive. He felt the thrill of revenge, the satisfaction that comes with getting back at someone who wronged you. No court could ever do that. Knowing someone's locked up in prison is nothing compared to the feeling you get knowing their life has ended, and that you're the one who did it. I know because I've done it before.

My first kill was Asher, the boy who assaulted me in high school. Having him show up at my house that dark October day, assuming I'd be his date for the charity event, proved that he felt no remorse for what he'd done to me. It meant he'd do it again — if not to me, then to some other woman. I couldn't allow that, so I killed him. I lured him to a lookout point that was known as a place couples make out, and let him think that's what we were about to do. He parked and I got out of the car. He followed me, asking me what I was doing. I stopped at the edge of the lookout point, waited for him to get close, then pushed him. I laughed when I saw the terror on his face as his body fell hundreds of feet before finally smashing against the rocky ground.

It was a wonderful feeling, and one I felt again when I got rid of my parents. Their death was easy. I simply spiked my father's drink with a powerful sedative right before he went out for a drive with my mother. He veered off the road, the car went rolling down the hill, and he and my mother were killed. The accident got a lot of local press, given my parents' status in the community, and I, as their only daughter, received a great deal of sympathy.

With my parents gone, I could finally end my marriage to James. I was only in it to ensure I'd receive my inheritance. My father's will clearly stated that I would only receive an inheritance if, at the time of his death, I was married to a man he approved of. I never thought he'd approve of James, since James didn't have the proper upbringing or come from wealth, but my father admired James' ambition and skills as a salesman. My father began his career as a salesman, and although he never admitted it, I think he saw a bit of himself in James. He immediately liked him, which surprised me at first, but James was one of those people most everyone liked. He had a magnetic personality that drew people to him, even people like my father, who would typically ignore someone like James who lacked status and good breeding. My mother also fell under James' spell, telling me he was the perfect complement to my dismal personality. She said he'd add light to my darkness, which wasn't at all true. In fact, being with James just made my view of the world darker. He promised to love and cherish me, but then lied to me and cheated on me.

There's a knock on my door. I hurry over to it and open it enough for Ryan to sneak through.

"You shouldn't be here," I tell him, my lips pressing against his as he holds me in his arms.

"I had to see you one last time," he says, pulling me closer.

"Last time?" I ask, not sure what he means.

"Before it's over." He kisses me. "Before we can finally be together."

He backs me up to the bed so fast I stumble and nearly fall. "Ryan, stop."

"I can't," he says, lowering me to the bed. "You're all I can think about. All I want." He yanks down my pajama pants and gets on top of me.

Where is this coming from? Last night, he was so distraught about Shelby that he'd barely kiss me. Is this part of his grief? Is he using me to get over his loss? I'm sure that's what it is. I'm all he has left now. The only person to bring him comfort.

I smile, pleased that I have this power over him. Shelby is no longer the person he'll go to for comfort. She's no longer the person he'll confide in. With her gone, I'll be his everything. He's mine and I'm his, just like we planned years ago in the hospital. Before Shelby took him away. Before my parents coerced me into marrying a man I didn't love.

As Ryan uses my body, I gaze up at the ceiling, remembering the day we reunited. It was my wedding day, a day when I should've been happy. And I was, or I told myself I was . . . until I saw Ryan there and my whole world collapsed. He never told me the name of that football player who bullied him and wanted him locked away so he could have Shelby all to himself. I didn't know it was James. I never put it together. I couldn't imagine James being with someone like Shelby, so the thought never even occurred to me that he was the guy Ryan had told me about.

When I figured it out, it was too late. I'd married James. We'd said our vows. He was officially my husband. I panicked, knowing I'd made a huge mistake and feeling like I'd betrayed Ryan. When our eyes met across the room, he looked destroyed, like I'd taken what we had together and spit on it. Like I'd taken the pain from his past and thrown it in his face, laughing at him, mocking him. It wasn't at all true, but he didn't know that. He thought I'd intentionally married James to hurt him.

When I realized what I'd done, I felt like I might pass out. My head was spinning and my breaths became shallow. I ran into the bathroom at the ballroom where the reception was being held and got sick in one of the stalls. My bridesmaids rushed in and asked what was wrong. One of them asked if I might be pregnant. The thought of that horrified me. I couldn't imagine being pregnant with James' child. I'd be tied to him forever. It'd be my worst nightmare.

Weeks later, I found out my bridesmaid was right. I was pregnant, but that wasn't why I got sick on my wedding day. I just let people believe that. I couldn't tell anyone the truth, which is that I still loved Ryan, and wanted to kill the man that I'd married after I realized who he was and what he'd done.

The night of my wedding, I played along with my new role as James' wife, letting him do with me as he pleased while I planned his death. I knew it would take time. I'd have to get rid of my parents first, then claim my inheritance. It was excruciating to know I'd have to wait to be with Ryan, but I was determined to make it happen.

The only issue I didn't know how to deal with was my child. The baby growing inside me. How did it even happen? I was so careful about taking the pill. I didn't want to tell James about the baby, so I waited. I kept putting it off. But he noticed when I stopped drinking, and commented on the slight bump forming on my usually flat stomach, forcing me to fess up.

James wasn't excited about the baby. He said he wasn't ready. He accused me of not taking my pills in order to trick him into fatherhood. Hearing him say that made me hate him even more. I wanted him dead. I didn't want to wait, especially when I found out he'd slept with one of my friends. It was a woman I'd gone to prep school with who was at our wedding. James had his eyes on her the whole night. I later found out he'd slipped her his business card and met her for lunch the following week. I don't know exactly when the affair began or ended, but I knew it wouldn't be the last. James had already admitted to being with Shelby during our courtship and I was sure he'd be with her again, along with other women. He promised me he'd stop being unfaithful, but I knew it was a lie.

"I don't want to leave you," Ryan says, breathing hard from what we just did. I usually enjoy it more, but today my mind was elsewhere.

"You need to leave," I tell him. "They'll be awake soon."

He gets off me and stands by the bed, putting his pants back in place. "I've been thinking about this, and I think we have to change the plan."

"What?" I hurry up from the bed. "No. Ryan, the plan is final. We're not changing it."

"Just listen." He grips my shoulders and leans down to me. "Beth is panicking and she's got Derek panicked too. He's determined to get out of here today, even if he has to walk all the way to town."

"That'll never happen. He'd never make it that far."

"He's still going to try. And Tyler's going with him. If we don't change the plan, there's a good chance they'll make it to the main road and flag someone down."

"Then you're going with them. Make sure one of them gets injured so that all three of you have to come back to the house."

"Yeah, I guess that would work."

"It has to look like an accident. You can't make them think it was your fault."

"Yeah, I know. I'll figure it out." He holds my face in his hands and kisses me. "It's almost over. We're so close I can taste it."

Ryan's more committed than ever, not just to the plan, but to me. I can feel a change in him. Any doubt he had is gone. His loyalty is no longer torn between Shelby and me. She was holding him prisoner, convincing him she needed him and that he needed her. She wouldn't even let him look for his own apartment. She told him he wouldn't be able to live on his own, that he wasn't capable of it. But the truth was that Shelby was the one who wasn't capable. She had Ryan make her meals, clean their apartment, do their laundry. She was using him and it needed to end.

He'll never know what I did to her. It'll be the one and only secret I'll keep from him. But I'll replay it in my mind for many years to come. Shelby had no idea what was coming when I went on that walk with her, the one I told Beth I didn't go on. Shelby followed behind as I led the way. I knew exactly where I was going to take her. I'll never forget the terror on her face when I shoved her off the cliff and she fell to her death. It reminded me of when I killed Asher, but this time was even more exhilarating because getting rid of Shelby meant I would finally have Ryan all to myself.

I look into his eyes. "Go get ready, my love. Let's finish this."

CHAPTER 35

Olivia

Ryan checks to make sure the hall is empty before leaving my room. When he's gone, I take a quick shower and get dressed, preparing once again to play the role of the grieving widow.

When I get downstairs, my pulse races when I see Beth by the table, clearing what appears to be the remains of breakfast.

"Beth," I say, forcing a smile on my face as I hurry over to her. "What's going on?"

"We just finished breakfast. Would you like some? I could make more eggs."

"No, thank you." I look around. "Where's Derek?"

"He went upstairs to put on another layer of socks. He's heading outside with Tyler in a few minutes. They want to get out there early."

No! They can't leave yet! They have to wait for Ryan.

"Are they planning to walk to the road?" I ask.

"They're going to try." Beth glances outside. "I'm just worried about the weather. It looks like it's going to snow again." She brings the plates to the sink. "I made coffee if you want some."

"Maybe later. I need to get something from my room."

Racing upstairs, I hurry down to Ryan's room and lightly knock on the door. He opens it wearing a towel around his waist, his hair wet.

"What are you doing?" he whispers.

"They're leaving!" I whisper back. "Derek and Tyler are leaving any minute now. Throw on some clothes and get down there!"

"Did you tell them I'm going along too?"

"No, but I will. Hurry up!"

A door down the hall opens and Derek appears. "Hey, Olivia."

"Good morning." I walk down to Derek as Ryan quietly closes his door. "Beth said you're going to try to walk down to the main road."

"Yeah, I'm just waiting for Tyler, then we're heading out. It's probably going to take all day to get there in the snow."

"What about Ryan? I believe he was planning to go with you."

"I don't want to wait for him. Tell him Tyler and I wanted to get an early start."

As he says it, the door to Tyler's room opens. "Ready to go?" he says to Derek.

"Yeah, let's get out there."

"Hey!" I hear Ryan say. "You guys leaving?"

I turn back and see Ryan dressed in jeans and a thick sweater, a baseball hat covering his wet hair.

"Yeah," Tyler says. "We're going right now."

"I'm coming with," Ryan says, shutting his door.

"Your hair's wet," Tyler says as Ryan walks down to us. "You can't go out there like that. Your head will freeze."

"Go dry it," Derek says. "But hurry up."

"It's fine," Ryan says. "I don't need to dry it." He goes past us and down the stairs.

"Ryan," I hear Beth say, sounding startled. She's so jumpy around him. I find her fear of him rather humorous. Ryan does too. He loves scaring her. He's been making little comments to her when they're alone together to make her think he's dangerous. I suppose he is, but only to people who deserve to be punished. Like Beth, who's partly responsible for him being labeled crazy.

Sometimes I think I should be grateful that James and his friends orchestrated a plan to get Ryan committed. If they hadn't, Ryan and I never would've met. But then I think about how they treated Ryan and I'm back to wanting to kill them.

Derek, Tyler, and I go downstairs. Ryan is in the kitchen, stuffing a piece of bread in his mouth. I wish I could make him a proper breakfast, but there isn't time. Derek and Tyler are determined to get going.

"I'll see you later," Derek says to Beth. He goes to give her a kiss, but she turns so he gets her cheek.

That's interesting. Are the two lovebirds not getting along? I've noticed they've been bickering the past few days, and whenever Derek puts his arm around her, her shoulders stiffen like she wants to pull away.

"When do you think you'll be back?" she asks.

"I really don't know." Derek heads to the door. "I don't know what's going to happen out there."

Ryan gulps down some water, then meets up with Derek and Tyler at the door. Tyler opens it and goes outside.

"Wait!" Beth yells, running up to Derek as he's leaving. She wraps her arms around him. "I love you."

"I love you too," he says, giving her a kiss.

She lets him go, looking like she's worried she'll never see him again. She will. He has to come back here so we can continue the plan. It was designed to make everyone's death look like an accident, so that Ryan and I wouldn't be accused of any wrongdoing and would be free to go on with our lives.

When the men are gone, I go to the kitchen to get a cup of coffee. I need to be alert and awake for what's to come. I really should've tried to sleep last night, but my mind wouldn't let me. I just need to get through today and then I'll finally be able to rest, with Ryan beside me. I can hardly wait. It seemed like this day would never come.

"What is it?" Beth asks.

I look at her next to me as she rinses dishes in the sink. "I'm sorry, what did you say?"

"I just wondered what you're thinking about. The way you were smiling, I thought maybe . . . well, I shouldn't say it."

"No. Go ahead."

"I thought maybe you were thinking about James. Remembering something about him that made you smile."

A memory of James is the last thing that would make me smile, unless it's the memory of me killing him. But I can't tell Beth that, so I decide to play along.

"You're right." I grip my coffee mug between my hands and look longingly out the window. "I was remembering the first time I brought James here. It was winter and a fresh layer of snow had just fallen. James and I went on a walk in the woods. It was so quiet and peaceful. It's just what we needed after—" I gaze down at the floor, deciding to really pull on her heartstrings.

"After what?" she asks.

I look at her. "After losing the baby. We came up here to get away. We wanted some time alone, just the two of us."

Beth turns to me, drying her hands on a towel. "That must've been such a difficult time. I'm surprised James never told us about it, but I'm sure it was too painful for him to talk about."

Is she kidding? Did she even know James? Because if she knew him like I did, she'd know that he was thrilled when we lost the baby. He didn't even want children, despite knowing that I did. But I didn't want them with him. So I was relieved when the pregnancy ended, but I did grieve after it happened. I'd become attached to the idea of being a mother. I wondered if I ever would be, knowing I'd first have to get rid of my parents and James before I could be with the man I truly loved. What if by then I was too old to have children?

"It was difficult for us both," I say. "Just talking about it upset me. When James and I came up here that weekend, we agreed not to discuss it after that. We decided we would grieve our loss and move on."

"James told us you were trying again."

Why would James tell his friends that? After my miscarriage, we agreed we weren't going to have children.

"Do you think maybe—" Beth shakes her head. "Never mind. I shouldn't be talking about this."

"Please, finish what you were saying."

Beth sets the towel down. "I saw a story on the news where this woman's husband died and a month later, she found out she was pregnant. It brought her comfort to know he was still with her. I mean, not with her, but you know what I mean."

"I do." I put my hand over my stomach and look down at it. "But I'm afraid that's not the case with me. James wasn't ready to start trying again so we were taking precautions."

"Oh. I must've misunderstood." She goes back to cleaning the dishes.

"So James told you we were trying to have a baby?"

"He told Derek that, not me, but maybe he meant later this year. I assumed he meant now because he said this would probably be our last trip together. Our last reunion. Because he thought you'd have a baby by next year." She sighs. "I really need to stop talking about this. I'm just making you feel worse."

James told them this was the last time they'd have one of these reunions? Why would it be the last? He loved these reunions. He's the one who started them and kept them going all these years. So why would he want them to end? The baby excuse wasn't true, so what was the real reason? Was he planning to leave me for Shelby and the two of them would go off somewhere and start a new life? His friends would've loved that. They could go back to these reunions being just their little college group, instead of having an outsider like me intruding on their fun.

I don't know what James was up to, but it just proves how dishonest he was, giving me yet another reason to be glad that he's gone.

CHAPTER 36

Olivia

"What about you?" I ask Beth. "Are you and Derek planning to start a family soon?"

"I don't think so," she says, drying one of the plates.

"You know we have a dishwasher."

"Oh, I know. I just need something to do so I don't worry about Derek. Well, I'm still worried, but you know what I mean."

"I'm sure he'll be fine. He has Tyler and Ryan to watch over him."

I hold back my smile, knowing Ryan will make sure one of them returns injured. I'm guessing he'll choose Derek over Tyler, given that he likes Tyler more. This past year, Tyler's been taking Ryan to ball games or out to eat, which was concerning because it could've interfered with my plan. If Ryan became close with Tyler, he wouldn't be able to kill him. I'd have to do it myself and not tell Ryan, like I did with Shelby. But Ryan assured me he didn't have a problem getting rid of Tyler, explaining he was only spending time with him for Shelby's sake, because she wanted Ryan to have a friend.

"So you're going to wait for children?" I ask, before sipping my coffee.

"I didn't want to, but with everything that's happened this week, I'm not sure now is the right time."

"Why is that?"

Beth sets down the plate she was drying and turns to me. "I'm sure you've noticed Derek and I haven't really been getting along."

"Yes, but I didn't think anything of it. It's normal for couples to argue. James and I certainly had our share of disagreements."

"It's more than that. It's the fact that Derek keeps dismissing my concerns."

"Concerns about what?"

"It's not what. It's who."

I nod. "Ryan."

"Yes," she says with a sigh. "I keep telling Derek all the creepy things Ryan has said to me and he acts like it's not a big deal. He won't even consider that I'm right about Ryan being dangerous."

"Do you really think he's dangerous?" I ask, feigning concern.

"Yes. But Derek refuses to believe me, even after I told him how Ryan's been acting." Beth glances at the door. "I'm more worried about Derek being out there with Ryan than I am about him being out in the freezing cold for hours."

"Is that why Derek and Tyler were up so early? So that Ryan wouldn't go with them?"

"No, Derek just wanted to leave early to take advantage of what few hours of daylight they have. He actually thought it'd be better to have Ryan go with them instead of having him here with you and me."

I almost laugh, but force myself not to as I take another sip of my coffee.

"How long do you think it'll take them to get to the main road?" Beth asks.

"Probably all day. With the snow this deep, they'll have to go slow."

Beth picks up another plate, almost dropping it as she tries to dry it.

I take the plate from her. "Why don't we go sit down? I don't think doing chores is helping take your mind off things."

She nods and we go over to the couch.

"Do you really think the wind is the reason you were trapped in the shed?" Beth asks, gazing at the fire. "Or do you think someone did it? So you'd freeze to death like Amber?"

I almost laugh again. Beth is one of the most paranoid people I've ever met. She's so easy to fool. Ryan told me she was, but I didn't believe him until this week. The incident in the shed was completely made up. Ryan shut me in there so that it would look like someone had done it on purpose. We were trying to throw everyone off so they'd think I was in just as much danger as the rest of them.

"I'd like to believe it was just the wind that blew the latch closed," I say. "But I really can't say for sure."

"It just doesn't seem possible. I could see how the door could be blown shut, but it seems like someone would've had to put the board in the latch."

I make sure Beth is watching me, then shudder, letting her see my fear. "If that's true, then you're saying someone was trying to kill me."

"I didn't mean that. I just—"

"Then what did you mean?" I turn to her on the couch. "You just said someone locked me in the shed, hoping I'd freeze to death."

"You're right." She shakes her head. "Sorry. I shouldn't have said that. I'm sure it was just an accident."

"It's fine. We're all on edge after everything that's happened. It's hard to think straight when we're under so much stress."

"I wish we could find our phones. Maybe we should search the house again. They have to be here somewhere."

"Or maybe they're outside."

Beth cocks her head. "Why would they be outside?"

"Why wouldn't they be? If someone didn't want us to have them, they wouldn't hide them here in the house. They'd put them outside where we'd never find them. Maybe even bury them in the snow to make sure they wouldn't work if we *did* find them."

Beth's brows draw together, like she's wondering if that's what happened. Or maybe my comment has made her suspicious of me. At this point, it doesn't matter. Even if she suspects I'm involved, it's too late for her to do anything.

"I need to go put on a sweater," I say. "I can't seem to warm up today."

"Yes, go ahead."

When I'm back in my room, I reach under the bed and run my hand over the floorboards until I feel the one that's loose. I lift it up and out of the way, then reach into the hidden compartment where I put the router and the phones. I find James' phone and see the battery is almost dead. There's a message on the screen from Tony, the man who plows our road. Earlier in the week, I'd sent him a text from James' phone saying we were staying put this week and not to worry about clearing our road. He'd responded with a message saying he'd put us last on the list. His latest message says he could come out on Saturday, which is tomorrow. Everyone will be gone by then so it really doesn't matter if he shows up.

I put James' phone back and take out the burner phone I'll be using later today. I check that it's fully charged, then put the floorboard back in place and hide the burner phone in my dresser.

Just a few more hours and this will all be over.

I'm not cold, but I put on a sweater, since I told Beth that's why I came up here. I go downstairs and see her still sitting on the couch.

"Are you feeling any better?" I ask.

"No. I'm still worried about Derek. It's starting to snow and the wind's picking up."

"Yes, they said a storm was on its way." I realize what I said and silently scold myself.

"You saw the weather forecast?" Beth asks.

"Last week." I sit down on the chair. "I remember them saying we might get a storm today. Their forecasts are ten days out."

She eyes me with suspicion. Poor little Beth. Perhaps she should've pursued a career in detective work rather than nursing.

It's fine if she doesn't trust me. She'll be dead before she has a chance to share whatever suspicions she may have about me. I'm almost tempted to play on her fears and make her final hours even more terrifying, but then decide against it.

"What you said earlier," Beth says. "About the first time you came here with James."

"What about it?"

"James told us it was during the summer, not the winter."

"You know James. He could never keep his facts straight. When did he tell you this?"

"At the wedding. He was telling us how great this place was, and how he couldn't wait to spend more time here."

"You must've misunderstood him. Perhaps he was talking about some other place we'd gone."

"No, it was here. And it was summer, like a month before your wedding. You said you brought him here after you lost the baby. That was after you were married, not before."

"Yes, well, I misspoke. Losing James has been so difficult on me that I really don't know what I'm saying. But now that you've pointed it out, you're right. The first time he came here was during the summer."

"So it wasn't after your miscarriage."

"I suppose it wasn't."

"You suppose? That seems like something you'd remember."

"Beth, what is the point of this?" I ask, with anger in my voice. "Are you trying to make me relive painful memories from the past?"

"No, of course not. I was just confused by the timing."

"Why so many questions?" I smile at her. "Is there something on your mind? Something you'd like to share?"

Before she can answer, the front door opens, bringing a rush of cold air into the house.

"Derek!" Beth jumps up from the couch and runs over to him. He's hobbling on one leg, held up by Tyler and Ryan.

"Relax, honey," Derek says. "It's nothing serious. Just a sprain."

"Oh, how awful," I say, trying to sound sincere as I go over to him. "I hope it's nothing too serious."

"Let me take a look at it," Beth says, going over to the table and pulling out a chair. "Come sit down."

"How did it happen?" I ask.

"He twisted it when we were walking," Tyler says as he and Ryan help Derek to the chair.

"It's my fault," Ryan says. "I slipped on the ice and fell in front of him. Derek was just trying to get out of the way."

I've trained Ryan well. He's so believable that even Beth doesn't seem to suspect Ryan purposely caused Derek's injury. She takes a seat in front of Derek and rests his leg on her lap.

"Does that hurt?" she asks, gently tugging off his boot.

"Yes." He cringes in pain. What a baby. It's just a sprained ankle. "Let me do it," he says, cringing again as he takes off his boot.

"I'll get you some ice," Tyler says, dropping his coat on the floor and heading to the kitchen.

"I can't do ice yet," Derek says. "My legs are still frozen. I need to let them warm up first."

"It looks like just a sprain," Beth says, inspecting his ankle. "But when we get into town, I'd feel better if we went to urgent care and had it X-rayed."

She still believes they'll be leaving here. How could she be that stupid? Did she forget about the three dead bodies outside? Even if she truly believed they were accidents, did she not consider that the next accident might involve her?

"What do you want to do?" Tyler asks Ryan, who's standing by the door, shaking the snow from his hair. "Should we head out again?"

"No. We're done." He points to the window, at the heavy snow coming down. "We can't be out in this."

"He's right," Derek says. "It's too dangerous, and you're going to run out of light. You'll have to try again in the morning."

Tyler sighs as he yanks off his stocking cap. "I really thought we'd make it."

"We will," Ryan says. "We'll go first thing tomorrow."

Ryan glances at me as he says it. I can tell he wants to smile, but he holds back. So do I. But it's not easy. We're both giddy that it's almost done. That we're almost rid of these people and will soon have the life together we always wanted.

CHAPTER 37

Beth

"How does it feel?" I ask, checking Derek's ankle as he gets settled on the bed.

"It feels okay. The pain meds helped."

"Is it wrapped too tight?"

"No, it's fine."

Good thing I keep a first aid kit in the car because there was nothing in the house. Not even a box of bandages. Olivia should really keep some medical supplies on hand, although I doubt she'll come up here again after what happened to James. If I were her, I'd put this house on the market as soon as I got home.

"Do you want something to eat?" I ask.

"I already ate."

"That was hours ago. I could get you a snack."

"Beth, I'm fine. You don't have to keep waiting on me." He reaches for my hand. "You look exhausted. Why don't we go to bed?"

"It's only nine o'clock."

"Yes, but we were up early. Tyler's already in bed and Ryan went to his room an hour ago. Olivia will probably go to bed too after she puts out the fire."

I sit beside him. "Can I say something? Without you telling me I'm crazy?"

"Honey, I never said you were crazy."

"It was implied."

"Is this about Ryan?"

"No. Olivia. We were talking while you were gone and she was saying that the first time she brought James here was during the winter, after her miscarriage."

"Yeah? What about it?"

"James told us the first time she brought him here was during the summer. Before they were married. The miscarriage happened *after* they were married, in the fall."

"Yeah? So what are you trying to say?"

"It just didn't sit right with me. I felt like she was lying."

"Why would she lie about that?"

"I don't know. That's why it's bothering me."

"Beth, she just lost her husband. In a horrible way. I doubt she's thinking straight right now."

"I just don't understand how she could mix that up. Her timeline was way off, and when I asked her about it, she almost seemed angry at me."

"I think you should forget about it. We need to focus on getting out of here tomorrow. Tyler thinks he can make it to the road before dark."

"It's dark by late afternoon. He really thinks he can make it there that fast? Walking through deep snow?"

"He's in better shape than me. And he can go faster if he's alone. If Ryan wants to tag along, he can, but Tyler's not going to wait for him. The earlier he gets to the main road, the better chance he has of flagging someone down. He's hoping he doesn't have to fight against the wind like we did today. I wish we knew what the weather was going to do."

"That's the other thing. Olivia seemed to know we were getting a storm today. Like she'd heard the forecast."

"All she had to do was look at the sky. You could tell from the clouds that a storm was coming."

"But she didn't look at the sky. She said it like she'd just checked the weather." I turn to Derek. "What if Olivia is the one who took our phones?"

"If she had the phones, she would've given them back by now."

"Not if she didn't want us to have them. Think about it. She's the one who suggested we give them up. And she was here when they went missing. Oh, and she made some comment about them being buried in the snow."

"She told you they were in the snow?"

"She said they *might* be there. I suggested we search the house again and she said if someone didn't want us having our phones, they wouldn't hide them in the house. They'd hide them outside."

Derek rubs his chin. "That *is* kind of an odd thing to say."

"Right? It's almost like she was telling me that's where they are."

"But that doesn't make sense. Olivia wouldn't hide the phones. She wants to get out of here as much as we do."

"I know it doesn't make sense. It's just the way she said it. I got this weird feeling, like she knew where the phones were."

Derek yawns. "Honey, I'm exhausted. I need to get some sleep."

I help him up so I can move the covers back. As he gets into bed, I go to the dresser to get my pajamas. I take them from the drawer, then decide to just sleep in what I'm wearing. It's not something I'd normally do, but for some reason I feel like I should. I don't know why. It's one of those feelings I can't explain, like the feeling I got when I was talking to Olivia earlier. I felt like she was trying to tell me something.

An hour later, Derek is sound asleep, while I'm tossing and turning and trying to get comfortable. Even when I find a good position and have my pillow just where I want it, I still can't sleep. My mind is racing, wondering if and when we'll get out of here. I'm trying to stay positive and believe Tyler will make it to the road tomorrow and flag someone down. He has to. I can't take being here another day.

Two hours later, I'm still awake, counting down from a hundred in the hopes that it'll make me fall asleep. I get to forty-six when I feel my eyes falling shut.

"Just leave it," I hear someone say.

"Derek?" I feel for him in the bed. He's beside me, his back to me. "Did you say something?"

I hear him snoring, then hear someone talking again.

"That's good enough. We have to go."

It sounds like Ryan's voice.

"Did you lock it?"

That sounded like Olivia.

"Yeah, I already told you," Ryan says.

Why are Ryan and Olivia in the hallway? Talking? In the middle of the night?

I hear footsteps going down the hall.

"Derek." I jostle him awake.

"What?" he mumbles.

"Someone's in the hall. I think it's Ryan and Olivia."

"It's just a dream. Go back to sleep."

"It's not a dream. I heard them."

Derek sighs and rolls onto his back. "I don't hear anything."

"Because they left. But I swear, they were out in the hall."

"Yeah? So?"

"Why would they be talking to each other in the middle of the night?"

"I don't know. Who cares? Beth, I really need to sleep." He turns on his side and puts his arm around me. "Stop worrying about it. We both need to get some rest. I have a feeling it's going to be a long day tomorrow."

I listen for the voices again, but don't hear anything. Maybe it *was* just a dream, but it didn't feel like it.

Within minutes, Derek's snoring while I'm wide awake. I try counting down from a hundred again, but make it all the way to zero without feeling even a little drowsy. I gently move Derek's arm off me and get out of bed. I'm tempted to go downstairs and make a cup of tea, thinking it might help me sleep, but I'm worried I'll run into Ryan. I swear I heard him in the hall.

I walk to the door and press my ear to it, listening for the sound of voices, but all I hear is a crackling noise, like the fire's still going.

How could I hear the fire from upstairs? It's not possible.

I sniff the air. Is that smoke? I take another whiff. It's definitely smoke. It shouldn't smell smoky up here.

I open the door, then rear back as a wave of smoke hits my face. I step out into the hall and feel the smoke engulfing me. I cough as it hits my lungs.

"Derek!" I yell, running back to the bed. "Derek, wake up!"

He mumbles something and turns away from me.

"Derek!" I yank the covers off him. "Derek, get up! There's a fire!"

"Fire?" He sits up a little. "What are you talking about?"

"The hallway! It's filled with smoke! We have to get out of here!"

He finally wakes up as he realizes what I said.

"Turn on a light!" he says, getting out of bed.

I run over to the switch on the wall. "It doesn't work. The power's out."

"Shit," he mutters as I run back over to him.

"The fire must've started downstairs. How are we going to get out?"

"Maybe it hasn't reached the front door. We have to go check."

"I'll do it."

"Beth, no. Wait here. I'll do it."

"You can't even walk. Just let me go. I'll be faster."

"Okay, but be careful. And don't go down there. Just look from the top of the stairs."

I run out of the room, pulling my shirt up to cover my nose and mouth. Smoke stings my eyes as I feel my way down the dark hallway. I reach the stairs and gasp when I see the flames. The whole downstairs is on fire. The flames are everywhere, reaching all the way to the front door.

"We're never getting out," I say to myself.

"Beth!" I hear Tyler yell. "Is that you? Are you out here?"

"Right here!" I turn and bump into him.

"Holy shit," he mutters, seeing the flames behind me.

"We have to get out of here!" I yell.

"How? The fire's blocking the door."

"Then we'll go out the window. We'll go out the one in my room. I need your help with Derek." I grab Tyler's arm and we make our way down the hall.

"We're on the second floor," Tyler says. "We can't jump out the window."

"We have to! We don't have a choice!"

My throat is burning and I'm having a hard time breathing as the smoke fills my lungs.

"Derek!" I yell when I get to our room, not seeing him through the darkness and the smoke.

"I'm by the window!"

Tyler and I race over there and find Derek yanking the window open.

"Shit," he says, looking outside. "We can't get out this way."

"Why?" Tyler pushes past me to the window. "Shit."

"What?" I say. "What is it?"

"There are boulders along the house and then a big drop-off," Tyler says. "It's too dangerous to jump."

"Let's try a different room," Derek says.

"Mine's the same," Tyler says. "The boulders go all along the side of the house."

"We'll try Olivia's room," I say. "It faces the back. There aren't any boulders along the back."

"Where is she?" Tyler asks. "How could she still be asleep?"

"Maybe she passed out from the smoke," I say, coughing. "Come on. We have to hurry."

"Put your arm around me," Tyler says to Derek. "Beth, let me go first. Hold on to my shirt and stay right behind me."

"Yeah, got it." I wait for Tyler and Derek to move in front of me, then I grab Tyler's shirt and we make our way back to the hall.

"Ryan!" Tyler yells, banging on his door. Tyler tries to open it, but it's locked. "Ryan, get up!"

I feel the heat in the hallway becoming more intense. I look back and see the flames are now at the top of the stairs.

"Ryan, get up!" Tyler yells, banging on his door.

"We have to hurry!" I scream. "The fire's right behind us!"

Tyler glances back at it. "Shit."

"Go!" Derek yells. "We can't wait for Ryan!"

We go to Olivia's room and find her door is locked too.

"Olivia!" Tyler bangs on her door.

Derek and I bang on it too. She must've passed out from the smoke. There's no way she'd sleep through this.

"Take Derek," Tyler says to me. "I'm gonna try to break the door open."

"Just do it!" Derek yells, using the wall for support as he moves out of the way.

I take a step back as Tyler rams himself against the door. He does it over and over until it finally gives way and opens.

257

"Shit." Tyler grabs his shoulder and bends over. "I think I broke it."

"I'll look at it when we're out of here," I tell him, trying to remain hopeful that we'll actually make it out. "Come on. We can't wait."

I help Derek, and the three of us go into Olivia's room.

"Olivia!" I stop at her bed and feel around for her. "She's not here."

"Are you sure?" Tyler yells.

"Check the bathroom," Derek says.

Tyler runs over there. "Olivia!"

"Head to the window," Derek says to me.

We make our way there and Derek moves aside as I open it.

"I think we can make it," I say, looking down at the ground. "There aren't any rocks. Just a lot of snow."

Tyler returns. "She's not here. Maybe she's downstairs."

"If she is, we can't save her," Derek says. "It's too late."

"Who wants to go first?" I shove the window up as far as it'll go.

"I will," Tyler says. "Beth, you go next and I'll try to catch you. Then we'll both try to catch Derek."

"Be careful," I say as Tyler climbs out the window. He falls to the ground and I hear him swear.

"Tyler!" I look out the window and see him getting up from the snow. "Are you okay?"

"Yeah, but I landed on my shoulder. It hurts like hell."

"Then don't try to catch me. The snow will cushion my fall."

"Beth, hurry up!" Derek yells.

I go out the window, landing with a hard thud on the frozen snow. It hurts, but I don't think I broke anything.

"You okay?" Tyler asks, helping me up.

"I think so." I look at the first floor of the house, seeing the flames and knowing the upstairs could collapse at any moment. "Derek, hurry up!"

He's already halfway out the window. He drops down, cursing when he hits the snow. He cringes and reaches for his ankle. "I think it's broken."

"Beth, help me get him up!" Tyler says, going behind Derek. "We have to get away from the house!"

We help Derek up and make our way to the path that goes through the trees. We take a moment to catch our breath, gazing back at the house as it goes up in flames.

"How the hell did this happen?" Tyler asks, coughing from the smoke.

"Olivia," I mutter.

Tyler looks at me. "There's no way we could've saved her. If we'd gone downstairs, we never would've made it out of there."

"That's not what I mean."

He waits for me to explain.

"She wasn't there," I say. "She left."

"What are you talking about?" Derek asks. "How do you know she left?"

"I heard her in the hallway. Before the fire started." I look at Derek. "I don't think she's dead. I don't think Ryan is either."

CHAPTER 38

Olivia

I gaze at the smoke billowing from the house. "It's beautiful, isn't it?"

"It's just like we imagined." Ryan comes up behind me and puts his arms around me.

"I would've loved to see their faces when they realized what was happening."

Ryan chuckles. "Beth was probably crying and yelling at Derek for not letting them leave when she wanted to."

"She couldn't have yelled at him for long. They probably passed out from the smoke soon after we left."

"You think they tried to save us?"

"I do." I smile. "Your idea to lock our doors was brilliant. I wonder how much time they wasted trying to get them open."

"Long enough that they didn't have time to save themselves."

"They had no chance of saving themselves. The flames engulfed the entire first floor of the house."

"They could've tried to jump out the window."

"Falling from that height and landing on the boulders would've killed them. Either way, they're dead." I turn to face Ryan. "We did it. We're finally rid of them."

Ryan smiles, then leans down to kiss me. His kiss is rough, almost painful, his teeth grazing my lower lip.

"I want you," he growls.

"Not now." I pull away. "Later. When we're done."

He yanks me against his body. "I don't want to wait."

I grip the back of his neck, my nails digging into his skin as I look into his eyes. "You'll wait until I'm ready. Do you understand?"

His shoulders relax. "Yes," he mutters.

I smile, loving the control I have over him. I used to have to share that control with Shelby. But now Ryan is all mine. In many ways, he's still a little boy, looking for direction and someone to tell him what to do. It's one of the reasons I was drawn to him when we met. I liked that I could easily persuade him and that he'd listen to me. I liked that he needed to be taken care of, because it meant he'd never leave me. He'd always be dependent on me.

Despite his childlike nature, Ryan is all man. He's a skilled lover and a powerful fighter. He'd kill anyone who tried to harm me. He has no fear when it comes to protecting me. That side of him is both frightening and arousing. I like a dangerous man, especially when I'm the one controlling him.

I reach up and kiss Ryan's cheek. "It's time, my love."

He takes my hand and we tromp through the woods, following a path that leads directly to the cabin. I know it well after years of exploring these woods as a child. It's dark out, but the light from the moon is enough for me to see where I'm going.

I've never taken James this way, or even told him about this path. He assumes the only way to the neighbors' cabin is off the main road, which is why he wouldn't have even thought of going there. That, and because he knows the owners aren't there this time of year.

The Greenwalds usually only use their cabin in the summer, but tonight they're there. I know because their porch lights are on, and because I summoned them here. They received a text earlier today from an anonymous number saying someone was trying to break into their cabin. I sent the text from the burner phone, knowing it would prompt the Greenwalds to immediately drive up here to check on their cabin. They're a very nice couple. I've known them since I was a child. They're retired now and live about an hour away. I'm sure my text alarmed them, especially since crime is rare in this area.

"Mr. Greenwald!" I yell, banging on their door. I ring the bell several times to make sure they hear me, and to alert them that this is an emergency. "Mr. Greenwald!"

I hear movement inside the cabin, the slow, heavy footsteps of the old man as he makes his way to the door.

It swings open and I see Mr. Greenwald, dressed in baggy sweatpants and a faded sweatshirt, his thin white hair sticking up. "Olivia. What are you doing here?"

I point to my house, my eyes wide, my hand shaking. "There's a fire! We need to get to town!"

"Fire?" He steps outside, his expression turning grim when he sees the smoke. "When did it start?"

"I don't know. I was asleep and woke up to find the house on fire. Ryan and I barely made it out." I point at Ryan, who's standing a few feet back. "Ryan's been staying with us this week. He smelled the smoke before I did and woke me up." I'm talking fast and gesturing with my hands, making sure I appear distraught and panicked. "The road to my house is blocked and we didn't know where to go! I saw your light on and ran over here!" I pause to catch my breath.

Mrs. Greenwald appears, pulling her housecoat closed. "What's going on?"

262

"Mrs. Greenwald!" I race up to her. "We have to go! It's not safe!"

She peers out the door and sees the smoke. "Oh my."

"Call the fire department," Mr. Greenwald says, shooing her back in the house. "I'll get my keys. We gotta leave before it spreads."

As soon as Mrs. Greenwald gets off the phone, the four of us get into Mr. Greenwald's truck. The road to their cabin is long and winding, but someone has plowed it, probably Mr. Greenwald. He has a plow attached to his truck. Most everyone who lives around here does, but I convinced James we could wait and get one later.

"I'm so sorry this happened," Mrs. Greenwald says to me as her husband turns onto the main road into town. "I know how much you loved that house. It's such a shame it's gone after all the work you and your husband did to fix it up."

"Yes," I say in a somber tone. "It's a huge loss."

"Why isn't your husband with you?" Mrs. Greenwald asks. "Is he going for help?"

"No, he . . ." I break down crying.

"He had an accident," Ryan says to Mrs. Greenwald. "We tried to get help, but like Olivia said, the road was blocked and James . . . he didn't make it."

Mrs. Greenwald gasps. "Oh, how horrible!" She reaches back and puts her hand on my arm. "You poor thing! Why didn't you call someone?"

"We didn't have our phones," Ryan says. "It's a long story." He glances at me. "Talking about it will just upset her more."

"Of course," Mrs. Greenwald says, patting my arm. "It's okay, dear. I understand."

"Where do you want us to take you?" Mr. Greenwald asks.

I wipe my eyes and look at Ryan. "The police station. We have to tell them what happened."

Mr. Greenwald glances at his wife, but doesn't say anything.

"Thank God you two were home," I say. "I don't know what we would've done if you hadn't been there."

"We didn't plan to be," Mrs. Greenwald says. "We drove up here after getting a message saying someone was trying to break in. But then we arrived and everything seemed fine. There weren't any signs of a break-in."

"We figure they gave up and moved on," Mr. Greenwald says. "I doubt they were robbers. There's nothing in that cabin that's worth anything. All I can think is that they were hikers wanting to crash somewhere for the night." He shakes his head. "I don't understand these people that go hiking in the winter."

A half hour later, we arrive at the police station and the Greenwalds go in with us. They know one of the officers on duty and tell him about the fire, which he already knows about because of the call Mrs. Greenwald made before we left the house.

"We've already got a fire crew there," the officer says. "Or almost there. The road wasn't plowed and there was a truck in the way. They're working on clearing the road so they can get the fire truck up there."

"We've been stranded there for days," I say to the officer, continuing to play the role of the distraught wife. "It was horrible! People were dying and we couldn't get help!"

"Dying?" The officer's brows draw together. "You're saying someone died at your house?"

"My husband. At the lake." I'm shaking, tears running down my face. My performance reminds me of the one I did when my parents died and I had to pretend to be devastated when I heard the news. "It was a horrible accident. Please don't make me talk about it."

"You poor girl," Mrs. Greenwald says, coming over to comfort me.

"We were all there for a reunion," Ryan explains. "We knew Olivia's husband from college. We were spending the week together and then . . ." He shakes his head. "Shit started happening. First Amber, then James." He rubs his eyes. "Then my sister." His voice cracks and I know he's not pretending. Ryan loved Shelby more than anything, even more than he loves me.

"You're saying all these people are dead?" the officer asks.

I nod, sobbing. "Yes."

He gets out his phone and makes a call. "Hey, Dan, sorry to wake you, but we've got a situation. I need you to get down here." He nods. "Yeah, see you soon." He looks at Ryan and me. "I'm going to need to question both of you about what happened."

"Of course." I sniffle. "We'll tell you everything."

Ryan and I could've taken a different approach. We could've run off, fled the country, and hidden out somewhere. But that would be a lot of work and would imply we did something wrong. So we decided to go to the police and tell them the story we wanted them to hear. Nobody could dispute our story because everyone else who was there is dead. And whatever evidence might point back to us was burned up in the fire.

"That's quite a story," the officer says after Ryan and I tell them our version of what happened. "I'm very sorry for your loss."

"Thank you," I say, wiping my eyes.

The officer looks at his notes. "And you have no idea who might've taken your phones?"

"Like I said, I think it was Amber," I say. "But I can't prove it."

"Tyler, her boyfriend, said she did stupid pranks like that all the time," Ryan says.

"And that's what you think it was? A prank?"

"I don't know why else she'd do it," Ryan says. "I think she hid the phones somewhere, but then she died and none of us could find them."

The officer shakes his head. "It's hard to believe all this happened. It was one thing after another."

"It was a nightmare." I sniffle, and dab my eyes with the tissue the officer gave me. "I don't know how I'll go on without James."

"I truly am sorry for your loss," the officer says. "Is there anything I can do? I assume you two need a place to stay tonight?"

"Yes," I say, "although I doubt I'll get any sleep."

"I'll take you over to the motel. I'm sure they have rooms. Nobody stays there this time of year." As he gets up, his phone rings. He answers it. "Hey, you got an update?"

I nudge Ryan's leg under the table. He glances at me, holding back a smile.

We did it. We got away with it. We're free to live our lives, be together, and go wherever we want.

"And you're sure it's them?" the officer says to whoever he's talking to. "That's great. Yeah, I'll tell them. Thanks." He ends the call and looks at us. "I've got some good news."

"What is it?" I ask.

"Your friends made it out of the fire."

"What?" I bolt up from the chair. "But that's not possible. The entire house was in flames."

"Apparently, they jumped out the window. The two men had minor injuries, but it sounds like the woman's okay."

I look at Ryan, forcing myself to smile. "They made it. Isn't that wonderful? It's a miracle."

"It really is," the officer says. "The fire crew is there now and said if your friends hadn't left when they did, they'd all be dead."

"Where are they now?" I ask.

"At the hospital," the officer says. "I can take you there. I'm sure you want to see them."

"Thank you, but it's far too late," I say. "They need their rest. We can see them tomorrow. We'll just go to the motel for now."

"If that's what you want. Let's head over there."

We leave the room and follow the officer out to his squad car. They're alive. Tyler, Derek, and Beth are alive.

How did this happen? They're supposed to be dead.

It doesn't matter. They can't prove I did anything. They have no evidence. Anything they tell the police would simply be speculation, their own personal theories of what happened. And if they were going to blame someone, it'd be Ryan, not me. They all think Ryan is crazy. Beth thinks he's dangerous.

If anyone's going down for this, it's him. And although I love Ryan, if it's him or me, I choose me. I'll always choose me.

CHAPTER 39

A Week Later
Ryan

"And you're willing to say all this in court?" the detective asks.

"Yeah, of course," I tell him. "I just feel bad that it came to this. I really didn't think she'd go through with it."

"Yes, well, she's clearly a very disturbed woman." He shuts the folder containing the evidence I gave him. "I'm sorry about what happened to your sister, but what you're doing will help get justice for her. I hope that brings you at least a little peace."

"I hope so too."

The detective stands up. "I'll walk you out."

We leave the police station, the same one I was at a week ago, the night of the fire. After the cop took us to the motel that night, Olivia was celebrating and talking about our future, but all I could think about was that my future wouldn't include Shelby. I hadn't fully comprehended that she was gone until that moment.

Olivia could tell I was feeling down, and when I told her why, she seemed annoyed. She told me I needed to move on and focus on her, and our future together. I was surprised she wasn't more understanding of what I was going through. Shelby was more than a sister. She was like a mom. She practically raised me. So how did Olivia expect me to just move on?

She wanted to make love, but I couldn't. I was too upset. Too sad. Olivia got angry and started shouting at me, telling me Shelby had been holding me back and keeping me from having my own life. She said we wouldn't have had a future together if Shelby were still alive. That she would've tried to keep us apart.

That's when I realized it wasn't an accident. Shelby didn't fall. She was pushed off that cliff. By Olivia.

I didn't want to believe it. When Olivia and I talked about our future, it always included Shelby. She's all the family I had. I made it clear to Olivia that I'd never leave my sister behind. That she'd always be part of our lives. Olivia agreed, but I know now that she never meant it. Her plan for us never included Shelby.

That night at the motel, I confronted her. I asked Olivia if she killed my sister. She denied it, which I knew she would, but I've known her long enough to know when she's lying. The left side of her lip ticks up just the slightest bit. Most people wouldn't notice, but I did, because I've seen her do it so many times.

I knew at that moment that I would take Olivia down. She'd spend the rest of her life locked in prison, or more likely, she'd convince the court she was crazy so they'd put her in a mental hospital. I'd hated being there, but Olivia loved it. She loved the attention she got. She loved playing mind games with the staff, pretending to be perfectly sane one day and crazy the next. If she had to choose prison or the psych ward, she'd always choose the psych ward.

The morning after the fire, I told Olivia I was going to walk to the store and get us some food. She gave me some cash from the wad of bills she'd stuffed in her pocket when we left the house. She went back to sleep while I took off and went to the police station.

The same cop we'd talked to the night before was there. We went into a room and I told him everything, or everything that would lead to Olivia being locked away. I didn't tell him my part in what happened. I know I did bad things at that house, but what Olivia did was a million times worse. She killed my sister, and I wasn't going to let her get away with it.

When I was done talking to the cop, I asked to use one of their computers. I needed to show him the evidence, all the screenshots I'd taken of texts Olivia had sent me, detailing what she wanted to do to James and his friends. I'd put the screenshots in a folder and saved them to a cloud account. I was careful to make sure I never agreed to her plan over text. I'd only do it verbally, so there'd be no evidence I was involved. I was being cautious. After being set up by James and his friends and put in a mental hospital, I wasn't going to take any chances. I loved Olivia, but I didn't trust her. I learned long ago not to trust anyone, even someone who claims to love you. I knew if our plan didn't go right and we got arrested for it, Olivia would put the blame on me. So I protected myself.

Whenever Olivia wanted to discuss details about the plan, I'd stop texting and call her. Or sometimes I'd respond back to her in a way that made it sound like I thought she was joking, that she wasn't seriously going to do something.

I said the same thing to the cop. I told him I'd met Olivia years ago and that she'd always had a dark sense of humor. So when she talked about killing her husband and his friends, I assumed she was joking. The cop asked why I didn't try to stop her when people kept turning up dead at the house, and I explained that, for one, I couldn't prove that she did it, and two, I was afraid of her. I told him if I confronted her, there was a good chance I'd end up dead like the others.

He seemed skeptical of my story until I got on a computer, logged into my account, and showed him the texts. I thought they'd prove my innocence, but instead they got me in trouble. The cop said I could be charged as an accomplice, because I knew what Olivia was planning and went along with it. I explained that I didn't go along with it, that I never killed anyone. It's a lie, of course. I helped her kill James, and locked Amber out of the house, but the cop didn't need to know that.

He let me leave, but said I had to stay in town. When I got back to the motel, the cops were there to arrest Olivia. I smiled at her as they dragged her away in handcuffs. I'll never forget the look she gave me. It was a mix of shock and rage at my betrayal.

I felt no remorse for turning on her. She deserved it after what she did to Shelby.

The week went on and I wasn't sure if I was going to jail or would somehow get out of this. I knew tattletale Beth would tell the cops what I'd said to her at the house. If anyone could get me locked away, it'd be her. She'd make stuff up if she had to.

When I got called back to the police station today, I was expecting to be put in a jail cell, but instead they made me a deal. I give them all the evidence I have against Olivia and agree to testify against her in court in exchange for them not charging me as an accomplice. I took the deal, then a detective brought me into a room and I told him everything I'd already told the cop the day after the fire. Then I told him the other stuff Olivia had said to me over the years, like how she'd killed some guy she knew from high school. Again, I said I didn't believe her, that it was just her dark sense of humor. I could've told him even more, like how she killed her parents, but I didn't want to risk getting in trouble for not turning her in. The dark-sense-of-humor excuse only works so many times.

I'm not sure what happens next. For now, I'm going home, back to my apartment in New York. It's going to be hard being there without Shelby. I'll have to find a new place, or maybe I'll leave the city and go somewhere else.

I feel lost without Shelby. She never should've died. It was my fault she did. I got involved with the wrong girl. But I'll make sure Olivia's punished. I'll make sure she pays for what she did.

CHAPTER 40

A Month Later
Beth

"Lunch break?" Jan asks as I go into the break room.

"Yes." I smile at her. "How about you?"

"Just finished mine." She points to the brownies on the table. "Those are delicious. Helen brought them in. Make sure to try one."

"I will. Thanks!"

I've been at my new job for a month now. My start date was delayed a week because of what happened at James' house, or what I now call the 'house of horrors.' After we escaped the fire, Derek and Tyler spent a few days in the hospital. I was treated for smoke inhalation and released, but I requested to stay in Derek's room while he recovered. He had to have surgery on his ankle after breaking it when he jumped out the window. Tyler tore his shoulder, but it wasn't broken. They kept him in the hospital for a few days because he couldn't stop coughing from the effects of the smoke. They wanted to make sure his lungs were okay before releasing him.

While we were at the hospital, a detective came by to talk to us. He told us Ryan and Olivia had gone to the police station the night of the fire. It was just as I'd suspected. The two of them were behind everything that had happened that week. They trapped us in that house and were hoping to kill us all. The only problem is, I couldn't prove it. They'd crafted their plan so that everything looked like it could've been an accident.

The detective told us Olivia had been arrested, but not Ryan. Apparently, Ryan claimed he was innocent in the whole thing and that Olivia was the one responsible for the deaths, that she hid our phones and the router and intentionally blocked the road with the truck so we couldn't get out. The detective said Ryan even gave them proof of her plan in the form of old text messages Olivia had sent him.

I was furious that Ryan got away with it. I'm convinced he was just as involved as Olivia, but without proof, it was his word against mine. I tried to get Derek to support my claim that Ryan was involved, but he wouldn't do it. He said he refused to lie to the police, but it wasn't a lie. Ryan told me I wasn't getting out of that house alive, and I told Derek that. But since he didn't hear it himself, he wouldn't agree to tell the police. Or maybe he didn't believe me.

I haven't been able to get past how Derek treated me the week we were at the house. The way he dismissed me and kept telling me I was overreacting did serious damage to our already strained marriage. When we finally got home, I told him I needed some time away from him. I was going to move out, but he offered to leave instead. He's been living in an apartment across town, and just last night, we met for dinner and decided to officially separate. Neither one of us is ready to file for divorce, but if I'm being honest, I think that's where we're headed.

We've been growing apart for years. We thought having a baby would bring us closer, which is why we were planning to start a family this year. But a baby can't fix a broken marriage. I know that, but I didn't want to admit that our marriage was broken. Now I know that it is, and I don't think it can be saved.

My phone rings as I'm eating lunch. I see Derek's name on the screen and answer.

"Hey," I say. "What's going on?"

"Can you talk?"

"Yeah, I'm on my lunch break."

"I just saw online that Olivia got charged with murder."

"How? I thought they couldn't get the evidence they needed to charge her."

When the police found the bodies of Shelby, Amber, and James, and they were examined for evidence, nothing was found that would prove Olivia killed them. The only thing the police could use against her was the evidence that Ryan gave them. I still don't know what was going on there. I'm convinced Ryan was working with Olivia, but then why did he turn against her? Does he think she killed Shelby? The police said Shelby wasn't mentioned in the texts Olivia sent about her plan to kill us all, but I still think Olivia was involved in Shelby's death. Maybe Ryan does too. He'd definitely turn on Olivia if he thought she killed his sister.

"They didn't charge her for the deaths at the house," Derek says. "They charged her for killing some guy she went to high school with. It happened a long time ago. Apparently, she took the guy to some lookout point and he fell to his death. Well, they're saying she pushed him."

"And they have proof of this?"

"The article said Ryan told the police that Olivia confessed to him that she'd killed the guy. The police looked into it, interviewed some people who were there that night, and whatever they said matched with what Ryan told them. I'm guessing there's some kind of physical evidence too, but the article didn't mention it."

"So she's definitely going to prison. That's good news."

"It's not definite. She has to go through a trial. And it sounds like her lawyer is going for the insanity defense."

"I can see why. She was murdering people, then making us breakfast and cleaning up the house like nothing had happened. Someone who does that has to be crazy."

"Yeah, well, you suspected something wasn't right with her." He pauses. "Beth, I know I should've said this sooner, but I'm sorry I didn't believe you. I just wanted us to have a nice trip. I didn't want to believe all that stuff you were saying was true. I should've listened to you and left when you told me you didn't want to be there. I was being selfish. Only thinking about myself."

"Thanks. I really needed to hear that."

"But it doesn't change anything." He pauses. "Or does it?"

"No," I say with a sigh. "I wish it was that easy to fix, but it's not. Derek, we both know things weren't working between us. We didn't even want to spend time with each other anymore."

"I know, but I'm not ready to let you go. I still love you, Beth."

I feel a lump in my throat and my eyes tearing up. "I love you too, but I'm not sure that's enough."

"Maybe it's not, but I don't want to give up on us yet."

I don't respond, not sure what to say. I'm not ready to end our marriage, but we can't go back to how things were, and I don't know how to fix us.

"Can I see you this weekend?" Derek asks. "We could meet for brunch. You love brunch."

"Yes, but you don't."

"Please, Beth. I just want to see you. It doesn't have to mean anything. And hey." He laughs a little. "Even if you hate the company, you know the brunch will be good."

"I don't hate you, Derek. As for brunch, I don't know. I need to think about it."

"That's fine. You know where to find me. Oh, before you go, the other reason I called was to tell you about Tyler."

"What about him?"

"He's writing a screenplay about what happened. He's going to pitch it to a guy he knows in the movie industry. He didn't want to do it until he'd talked to us first. I told him I'm okay with it. He said he was going to call you tonight and see what you thought."

"He's making a movie about what happened to us? I don't like the idea of that."

"It won't be exactly what happened. It'll be one of those based-on-a-true-story types of movies. It may not even happen. He said it's nearly impossible to get screenplays turned into movies, but he wants to try. Just hear him out. You might be okay with it once he explains it."

If Derek knew me the way he should, he'd know I would never be okay with it. Our friends died that week. And *we* almost died. I want to erase that horrible trip from my memory, not have it made into a movie. But Derek doesn't see a problem with it. It just proves how different we are, how we've changed and grown apart the past ten years. I still love Derek, but I don't see us ever getting back together.

"I should go," I say. "I need to finish my lunch."

"Yeah, okay. Let me know about this weekend. Bye, Beth."

"Bye." I end the call and go back to eating my sandwich. I'm scrolling through my phone when it rings again. I answer the call. "Hello?"

"Hey, Beth."

I drop my sandwich, instantly recognizing his voice. "What do you want, Ryan?"

"Just saying hi. It's been a while."

"How'd you get this number?"

"I found it when I was going through Shelby's stuff. I'm moving next week. I got a new apartment."

"That's good. Okay, well, I need to go, so—"

"Aren't you going to ask where?"

"It doesn't matter, Ryan. I'm not planning to visit."

"Maybe I'll visit *you*." He rattles off my address. "That's your house, right?"

"How . . . how do you know that?"

"I looked it up. All that stuff is online. It's not hard to find. Anyway, maybe I could stop by next week. You could invite me for dinner."

"Ryan, this isn't funny. Why are you doing this?"

"I just told you. I'd like to see you. Now that I'm moving back, I'd like to get in touch with old friends, starting with you."

"Moving back?" I say, hoping he doesn't mean here.

"To Syracuse. Back where we all met."

No. He can't move back. I'll never feel safe if he's here.

"We have so many good memories there, don't we, Beth? I'm really looking forward to us being friends again. I'm sure you have plenty of free time now that you and Derek have split."

How did he know that? Did Tyler tell him? Tyler wouldn't do that. I specifically told him not to tell Ryan anything about Derek and me. So how did Ryan know that Derek moved out?

"Ryan, I don't know what's going on here, but we're not friends. We never were. We never will be."

"You really should be nicer to me, Beth, especially now that we'll be living in the same town."

"I *am* being nice. I'm just telling you that I don't want to be friends."

"Well, I consider you a friend, even if you don't think of me the same way. And as your friend, I feel like you should know that living alone in that big, old house could be dangerous."

Is he threatening me, or was that just another one of his creepy comments meant to scare me?

Why is he doing this? Why can't he leave me alone?

"Ryan, I'm going to hang up now. Don't call me again."

"Just one more thing."

"What?" I ask.

"Make sure to lock your doors."

THE END

THE JOFFE BOOKS STORY

We began in 2014 when Jasper agreed to publish his mum's much-rejected romance novel and it became a bestseller.

Since then we've grown into the largest independent publisher in the UK. We're extremely proud to publish some of the very best writers in the world, including Joy Ellis, Faith Martin, Caro Ramsay, Helen Forrester, Simon Brett and Robert Goddard. Everyone at Joffe Books loves reading and we never forget that it all begins with the magic of an author telling a story.

We are proud to publish talented first-time authors, as well as established writers whose books we love introducing to a new generation of readers.

We won Trade Publisher of the Year at the Independent Publishing Awards in 2023 and Best Publisher Award in 2024 at the People's Book Prize. We have been shortlisted for Independent Publisher of the Year at the British Book Awards for the last five years, and were shortlisted for the Diversity and Inclusivity Award at the 2022 Independent Publishing Awards. In 2023 we were shortlisted for Publisher of the Year at the RNA Industry Awards, and in 2024 we were shortlisted at the CWA Daggers for the Best Crime and Mystery Publisher.

We built this company with your help, and we love to hear from you, so please email us about absolutely anything bookish at feedback@joffebooks.com.

If you want to receive free books every Friday and hear about all our new releases, join our mailing list here: www.joffebooks.com/freebooks.

And when you tell your friends about us, just remember: it's pronounced Joffe as in coffee or toffee!

www.ingramcontent.com/pod-product-compliance
Lightning Source LLC
Chambersburg PA
CBHW011453170626
46814CB00009B/3034

* 9 7 8 1 8 0 5 7 3 2 9 8 3 *